PAYAL MEHTA'S ROMANCE REVENGE PLOT

Payal Mehta's Romance Revenge Plot

Preeti Chhibber

Kokila

KOKILA
An imprint of Penguin Random House LLC, New York

First published in the United States of America by Kokila,
an imprint of Penguin Random House LLC, 2024

Copyright © 2024 by Preeti Chhibber

Visit us online at PenguinRandomHouse.com.
Library of Congress Cataloging-in-Publication Data is available.

ISBN 9780593461884

1st Printing
Printed in the United States of America
LSCH

This book was edited by Namrata Tripathi, proofread by Bethany Bryan and
Janet Rosenberg, and designed by Asiya Ahmed. The production was supervised
by Tabitha Dulla, Nicole Kiser, Ariela Rudy Zaltzman, and Vanessa Robles.

Text set in Milo Serif Pro

To me at seventeen—we're still laughing our way through it.

CHAPTER ONE

For twenty minutes I'd been holding this red SOLO cup of the *most* sickly sweet nail polish–smelling vodka-and-red-juice mixture. Holding ingestible paint thinner wasn't something I'd planned on doing with my evening, but . . . there were thick lines of black Sharpie spelling the name Jonathan Slate on its side. I mean . . . *Jonathan-freaking-Slate*! And so, I'd keep holding it while the party around me kept going. I'd been there for a few hours already and had been on the cusp of making a round to see what was happening poolside. Instead, the cup and I stayed, standing against the ugly brocade wallpaper for—oh, twenty-one minutes.

No worries. I could do this all day. I would stand here forever, if I was being honest. It was Jonathan-freaking-Slate.

Twenty-One Minutes Earlier

I'd been taking a minute to enjoy the general debauchery around me—picture almost any show on a premium cable network and you're halfway there already—when it happened.

"Hey, Pie, hold this for a sec. Thanks, I owe you." His words were slurred and rushed, so it took me a second to parse his meaning. But by then Jonathan Slate's fingers had brushed mine as he handed the cup off to me. And *obviously*, we fell in love . . . or, I fell a little more deeply into my three-year crush on a white boy who sometimes said nice things to me but by all accounts might not even know my real name. Which is Payal. PIE-yuhl. Not Pie[1].

Jon didn't wait for a response before he stumbled off, but that was okay. The world works differently when you're a six-foot-tall Adonis in a button-down shirt and fitted jeans. You don't generally have to conform to the same set of social rules as the rest of us mere mortals. Besides, maybe he did wait for a response and I was too busy trying not to drool to notice. (In case it wasn't immediately clear, people considered me to be a very cool person.)

Listen, Jon Slate was *it*. I'd had a crush on him *since freshman year*. He was in my very first high school class, and our Spanish teacher assigned us as partners on the very first day. I'd taken one look at his blue, blue eyes, sun-kissed cheeks, and surfer boy–blond hair and was gone. Then we didn't speak again for six weeks, but he smiled at me every day . . . or at least smiled in my direction. And one time, he gave me his pencil. Not lent, *gave*. It was *magical*. I still had it. I loved him.

Back to Now

I wasn't entirely sure how I ended up at this party. It was the kind of thing my parents might actually kill me for attending. It had all the elements of a grounded-for-the-rest-of-my-natural-life-and-whatever-lives-came-after-that event.

Alcohol? Besides the aforementioned vodka-and-red-juice drink, two kids I kind of recognized from school standing next to me were googling "How to shotgun a beer." I leaned over to peek at the search results and shook my head. They'd probably get distracted by a full

---

[1]My parents would *never* name me after a dessert pastry. Wait, no, one of my childhood nicknames was "Ladoo"—oh no. My whole life has been a lie.

Wiki on the history of shotgunning beers if they didn't move to YouTube.

Drugs? Janet Kwon was about to take her turn with the joint going around a circle of people, but—oh, there it is. I winced. She dropped it in her beer. *Yikes.*

Sex? . . . Probably? It hadn't gotten to a point where people were actually *doing it* in the open, but I was pretty sure it was happening somewhere. The house was one of those gigantic McMansions with a million rooms that littered South Florida thanks to the super-duper rich who moved here to build big, ugly houses. Which leads us to . . .

No chaperones. Rachel Finley's parents weren't even in town, and hadn't been for a while, as far as I could see. They were on a yacht somewhere (or in Paris or Prague or who knows? . . . I don't know how extremely wealthy people live).

So here we were, in a giant house filled with teenagers making bad decisions. Seriously, I'd just seen the rest of the pot smokers herd into the kitchen to microwave the beer-soaked joint. Bad choices all around! (Not me, though. My decision to hold on to this cup was going to lead to something big. I knew it.)

"*Finn!* Finn! Not here!"

Actually, you know what? I *did* know how I ended up here. The boy laughing and talking to Finn would be Neil Patel. Neil, who was currently trying to stop his boyfriend from taking his shirt off in a room full of people, had been my best friend for a million years[2].

Several hours earlier, he'd done his dirty work. We'd been lying

---

[2] This tracks as factually correct because of that whole reincarnation thing.

side by side on the grass in my backyard, trying to get some sun without Rajeshri Auntie noticing and immediately revealing her colonial roots by yelling at us for getting "too dark[3]." It was early enough in the Florida afternoon that the humidity level was actually acceptable. Instead of sweat and stickiness, there was a comfortable warmth on my skin.

"Neil, we are not going to Rachel's spring break party. She is awful. Are you forgetting that she called you 'Neila' for the entirety of freshman year?"

He turned to me, expression lazy and eyes half-lidded in the bright light of the sun. "Payal, you have to let things go. Rachel and I are certified besties now. The bullying is obviously over."

I gave him my best disbelieving side-eye. "Oh, are you? I take it she doesn't know you're the one who left her parents the anonymous tip about her I'm-grounded-but-I-need-to-go-to-Coachella crowd-fund?"

Neil sat up and looked completely aghast. "I was being a good friend. Who *knows* what goes on at those rowdy festivals? She could have gotten hurt."

"Oh, so it was in her best interest," I said, playing along with Neil's sarcastic response.

I was honestly surprised the American Dream Queen's parents stopped her from doing anything, because she did not act like someone who understood that her actions had consequences—but then I found out she was grounded because she'd wrecked her dad's car, and her only punishment was that she couldn't go to Coachella. Explanation finished, Neil lay back and threw an arm

---

[3] Colonialism, classism, *and* colorism persist in the twenty-first century; we do not love to see it.

over his eyes. I propped up on my elbows so that I could look down my nose at him.

"Besides," Neil added, "I can't help that now she thinks it's cool to have a gay best friend. Why shouldn't I take advantage?" I could see his lips quirk up. Typical.

"Take advantage of what? The party is going to be terrible and loud and awkward," I said.

"No way. It's going to be awesome. She has a pool and lots of expensive booze." Okay, fair point from Neil.

"Philip Kim won't be there, right?" I forced myself to ask, frowning at the thought of my school nemesis. Neil shot me a dry look.

"In what world does Philip Kim go to parties? He hates everyone except his nerdy holier-than-thou group of friends." Whew. Good. Anyway, the less said about Philip, the better.

"I'm just making sure!" I said, before pivoting back to what I knew to actually be true. "Whatever. You want to go because Finn is going." I collapsed back onto the ground, ignoring the way the blades of grass pricked at my neck.

"Lies!" He paused and then grinned. "I want to go because Finn is going and there is a pool, so Finn will be shirtless and that has *serious* potential."

What kind of friend would I be if I denied him that?

So here I was, standing against this ugly wallpaper, and there Neil was, enjoying the party he forced me to come to.

"Heyyyyyy, Pa-pa-pa-piiiiilel. You have my drink!" Jon-freaking-Slate had had a few more, if that slur was any indication. I squinted, trying to remember that old proverb. Oh, right: Internet gods say, *Four* y's *on a* hey *and they are totally into you.*

That *hey* had at *least* five *y*'s. He was stumbling toward me, one hand outstretched and the other braced against the wall for support. His floppy, curly blond hair was floppier, and his shirt was torn at the collar. Maybe it was the drink, but *maybe* he'd opened his heart to the possibilities of a Bollywood dance number with his true love: me.

Behind him, there was the blur of our fellow partygoers dancing and drinking, but none of it mattered. Just Jon stumbling toward me.

I pushed away from the wall and held his drink out to him. Maybe our hands would touch again.

"Uh, hey, yeah," I said, unsure of how to continue before finally settling on "I didn't drink it."

He smiled. Jon was smiling at *me*. His eyes were *crinkling*. Alert. *Alert.*

My brain was no longer connected to my mouth. I opened and closed it a few times, literally *floundering*[4].

He reached for the cup and took it from me, somehow managing to avoid touching my hand this time. I only had a split second to mourn the missed opportunity before he pulled away, slurring out a thanks before he turned to walk away. And then, *again* without my brain's approval, my mouth opened.

"Hey, Jon!"

Oh *no*. What was I doing? *What was I doing?*

Jon turned back to look at me, one eyebrow raised quizzically. I scrambled for something to say—anything. Why had I said his name?

---

[4] Even at my worst, I won't miss an opportunity for a pun.

6

"We should . . . hang out," I said falteringly. It took everything in me not to bite my own traitorous tongue. I resisted the urge to look around. It felt like time had stopped. Behind Jon, I was pretty sure a girl's cup was halfway between the table and the floor and was hanging in the air mid-spill because *time had literally stopped*.

Jon, for his part, was looking at me like he didn't know who I was. Like I was a complete weirdo. A very short, stick-figured Indian girl with deliberately messy hair, too-dark eyeliner, and burgundy lipstick she'd stolen from her mother . . . weirdo.

There was no way he knew about the lipstick thing. He still hadn't said anything. It was too quiet. This was the longest moment in history. Did the music stop? It couldn't have. Why did it feel like everyone was staring? Was someone filming? Someone was *always* filming. I needed to say something. *Anything.* But hadn't I already said enough? I should backtrack. I took a halting step toward him.

"I mean . . . since we both have Mr. Ansel's mock AP History exam coming up. I mean, we should study. I heard you needed a study partner, right?"

Good save, Payal. Killing it. Jon Slate narrowed his eyes, opened his mouth, and then—well, *then*, he threw up all over my Keds.

"Slate's lucky he's so attractive. Finn is by himself in the pool, and I'm here." Neil was helping me in one of Rachel's many guest bathrooms, sitting on the edge of the tub and scrubbing at my jeans with a spare loofah we found under the sink. My soiled shoes were lying on the ground, waiting to be wiped down next. Luckily, that was all Jon's vomit had hit. I was standing in front of the mirror, with a towel wrapped around my waist and avoiding my reflection, while Neil was busy being an actual best friend. I knew exactly what my face looked like; I didn't need to see the anxiety currently setting up shop in my own eyes. "I can't believe he threw up on you and then left without apologizing. Sorry, I know you like him, but that's a dick move."

I didn't answer him. Instead, I turned around and pretended to inspect a black-and-white print of Alfred Hitchcock's profile hanging on the wall. Maybe if I focused on the weird bathroom art, I would forget that I had put myself out there in the most awkward way possible.

"Payal, yes, we both agree the decor in here is weird as hell, but don't ignore me while I'm complaining about cleaning some dude's ulti off *your* jeans[5]."

I looked back at him; he was holding the loofah in one hand and my soiled jeans in the other but had stopped what he was doing—presumably until I deigned to answer him.

"You know, it's unfair that you still look cute cleaning up throw-up, Neil." I sighed.

"Nice try." He grinned wryly. "Complimenting me isn't going to stop me from asking what the hell happened. What did you say to him?"

I *was* trying to distract him, but I also wasn't wrong. He *did* look cute even while cleaning up vomit. Neil was that rare sort of teenager who never went through an awkward phase. He was an adorable child, and then he turned into an annoyingly good-looking teen. He was tall, with strong shoulders, and wore his hair long and curly on top and short on the sides in the way that boys—especially Finn—loved. He had huge brown eyes with long lashes, and brows

---

[5] Get you a friend, etc.

shaped by the most meticulous of aunties with a spool of thread. His one secret shame was how bad his eyesight was, which I always thought was ridiculous. Your eyes are your eyes! But he'd sworn me to secrecy about it, and as his best friend, I'd take it to the grave. Funeral pyre. Whatever. He was looking at me with those astigmatic eyes now, waiting.

"You didn't hear what I said?" I asked finally.

"No. Finn was about to . . . you know." He gestured vaguely between his face and an imaginary Finn in a way to imply *things*.

I waggled my eyebrows at him suggestively. "Oh, were you guys hooking up? Going on a trip to make-out town? I never would have guessed!" His cheeks went purple-red. I laughed. "I'm glad you were doing something worthwhile while I was throwing my reputation to the ground and setting fire to it."

Neil's admittedly appropriate reaction to my dramatics was to roll his eyes and tell me to shut up.

It was conjecture what hooking up actually felt like. The closest I'd ever come was at Janet Kwon's (yes, joint-in-the-microwave Janet Kwon) boy-girl party freshman year, when Joey Alvarez kissed me in a closet and I broke out in hives because apparently I'm allergic to Axe body spray. I'd never forgive my mom for raising me in an environment that made me develop *that* allergy.

"Here, these are clean." Neil's voice brought me back to the present. He was standing and had my damp and happily vomit-free jeans held out to me. "Now tell me what happened," he repeated while turning around and kneeling to grab the shoes to work on next, so I used the privacy to pull my pants on.

"Don't laugh." I stepped into the jeans and cringed when the wet fabric hit my feet. I hopped a little as I pulled them up over my hips, and then I zipped and buttoned them. "Okay, you can look now. I asked Jon if he wanted to hang out." Neil's response was to almost drop my shoes in the toilet. "Neil!!!"

"Sorry!" He sat back down on the edge of the tub and picked up the loofah again before continuing. "But . . . I mean. Wow. How much have you had to drink that *you* asked *him* out?"

"I have had like *a* sip of one drink! I've been abstaining because you begged me to be DD. Remember?" I clasped my hands against the back of my neck and then quietly wailed, "I don't know what I was thinking," before dropping against the door and sliding down until I was sitting on the cherry-colored bath rug. "Clearly, I *wasn't* thinking."

Neil shrugged. "I don't even know why you like him so much, honestly. He's good-looking, but that's basically it in terms of what he might have going for him. Other than that . . . a blank *slate.*"

I wished I'd grabbed the decorative soaps before sitting on the ground because then I could have launched one at him. I settled for scowling at his terrible one-liner.

"That was a *horrible* pun, and it's not true. He has a deep and meaningful side-life!" Neil threw one of my now-clean shoes at me and adopted his favorite Payal-what-are-you-doing-with-your-life look.

"It was a pretty good pun. And I'm *sure* he does," he placated. I groaned in response. "Listen, I know you know he is really, really, really good-looking. But you literally don't know anything else about him. Okay, here's your other shoe."

"I do too," I mumbled, taking the offered footwear from him.

"Does he have any siblings? Who taught him to drive? What color socks does he have on *right now*?" Neil said, peppering me with questions he knew I didn't have the answers to.

I wanted to ask Neil if it would be so terrible if I ended up lying on the floor of this bathroom at this spring break party I didn't even want to be at. Instead, I put on my shoes and said, "I guess I'll go find out."

Neil stared for a second and then laughed way too hard.

"Too much," I said, twisting my fingers together and frowning. "That's mean."

He wiped his eyes and apologized. "Sorry, yaar. But first of all, your dude is so wasted he probably doesn't even know his first name, let alone the answers to those questions. And second, you've literally had a crush on him for three years. Why now?"

"Because I *have* had a crush on him forever, and I feel like such a loser. It's ridiculous that I haven't said anything! It's not like I'm some invisible weirdo he never looks at. We've had conversations. Friendly ones! Besides, what the heck else am I doing? Nothing. And we're getting to the point where my mom is going to start inviting random Indian aunties and uncles over with their sons to make sure her daughter doesn't end up an old maid even though we're only seventeen. And ugh. I don't know."

Neil stepped back and put his hands behind his head. He was thinking. This was probably going to end poorly for me.

"Well, when you put it that way . . . I support your decision to talk to Jon, one hundred percent. Not that I haven't loved having you to myself as my actual-and-not-in-the-internet-ironic-way bestie[6]."

"WHAT THE FUCK ARE YOU DOING IN THERE?!" Someone chose

---

[6] According to my mom, Neil and I have been best friends since she and Seema Auntie had our ears pierced at the same time when were six months old. Formative.

that moment to bang out a concerto on the bathroom door. "I HAVE HAD TO PEE FOREVER. GET OUT OF THE BATHROOM. JESUS CHRIST."

"Aaaand that's our cue. Let's do this." I pulled the door open and headed out to get to know the boy I'd loved—okay, well, at least been seriously crushing on—for the last three years.

PAYAL MEHTA

I can't believe he was already gone.
It was only freakin midnight!

NEIL PATEL

Well, he did throw up on e-v-e-r-y-t-h-i-n-g.

PAYAL MEHTA

Ugh.

NEIL PATEL

I don't get it, why is HE your knight in
shining armor or whatever. I mean . . . other
than those shoulders. I get the shoulders.

PAYAL MEHTA

Because he's *My Guy*. Because I've liked him
for SO LONG. And he's a . . . good athlete
and stuff.

NEIL PATEL

A good athlete? Name one sports thing.

PAYAL MEHTA

A wrestling singlet.

NEIL PATEL

You can't use the picture of Finn in his wrestling uniform I texted you to prove that you like sports!!!

PAYAL MEHTA

idk!!! He's a good athlete, which means he knows how to commit to something. It makes sense in my brain. Shut up. And he is really nice to everyone. He stood up for Kiran the other day when Sam was being an asshole to her. Also, like you said. Shoulders. Shoulders are good. Great, even. Why is he so good looking. It's not fair.

NEIL PATEL

I gotta go, my dad's home and wants to talk about colleges.

PAYAL MEHTA

Ok. text me later if it goes south.

NEIL PATEL

thx <3

☞—♥—→

I closed my laptop and fell backward onto my pillows. It had been two days since the party. It had *also* been two days since I'd changed out of my pajama pants, but that didn't need to be discussed, really. Neil and I were rehashing the Jon situation . . . again, because I couldn't stop thinking about it. It was possible he didn't even actually have to leave; maybe he was tired of listening to me whine.

No, that wasn't true. Neil would have said something. *Dude, frea-kin' say something. Put up or shut up, because I cannot take you talking about it anymore.*

We'd known each other so long that sometimes Phantom Neil popped into my head. It's weird. He loved it. I loved and hated it.

Right now, Phantom Neil was telling me to stop moping. I was not moping—at least not entirely. I was lying in bed considering the possibilities of approaching Jon Slate. On the upside, no one seemed to have noticed my little outburst with him. I had checked the various apps over the past few days, and there wasn't anything online about it. So that meant it hadn't happened, right?

My phone was peeking out from under my pillow like it knew what I was thinking. Maybe I should check one more time. I picked it up and loaded HotGoss[7]. On the home screen I saw one notification. I clicked through—and then the blood drained from my face.

Oh *no.*

Jon Slate had sent a post out to everyone in the Brighton High School group. It was a picture of him making a sad face and I'M SORRY IF I PUKED ON YOU written across his mouth. *Oh my god.* My thumb and forefinger pressed against the sides of my phone to take a screenshot for the group chat. I looked at the picture again and frowned. Jon looked amazing, of course. I could see the reflection of a ring light in his blue irises.

---

[7] This was our high school's latest digital watercooler of choice—six months ago, the hot social app had been something called WereHere. People were *still* arguing over whether that one was supposed to be a funny rhyme or something existential and sad. It's the internet, so I was squarely in the existential-and-sad camp.

It was unfair that in normal circumstances, Jon would be the one who was totally mortified. I hadn't even *done* anything. I should have been collateral damage in his humiliation. *But no.* High school had these "rules." He was the hot, popular guy, and I was about to lose my relative comfortable anonymity the second people figured out who his post was about. Instead of "Oh, uh, that's Pie," I was going to become "Hey, isn't that Payal Mehta? The girl Jon Slate threw up on at Rachel's party?"

Forget saying *anything* to *anybody*, because I was going to go die with the words *Jon Slate threw up on my shoes* having never been said out loud. Ever. I pushed my phone away and pulled one of the pillows over my eyes like it would block out the cruel, cruel world. What was I going to do?

I turned over so I was face down, then lifted my head and banged it against the mattress a few times. Maybe that would knock some past-life-font-of-knowledge shit into my brain.

Maybe it needed some time to work.

Ten minutes later I could categorically say that it did not work. What was the point of having past lives if they didn't do anything for my boy problems today?!

School would be starting back up tomorrow and now my somewhat nervous anticipation had turned into feelings of pure dread. This was impossible.

A knock interrupted my spiraling, and my mom's voice came through the door. "Payal! Are you sleeping?" She was definitely checking in on me because she was sadly aware of my tendency to stay awake watching reality trash on Netflix. I lifted my head so I wouldn't be speaking into my mattress to answer.

"Nope. Come in!"

She pushed the door open and came into my room, already dressed for bed in her nighty.

My mom was not what you might call a "cool mom," but she could occasionally be an awesome one. If you took away her somewhat irrational fear of me being outside after midnight. Oh, and her response to boys. That could be better. Also, about drinking. She was not the kind of mom to confide in about drinking.

My mother took one look at me, face down on top of my covers, clearly angsting in the way that according to television only teenagers can angst, and asked, "Theekh hai, bete?"

"I could be better," I answered her honestly. "Something embarrassing happened a few days ago and I'm worried about going to school tomorrow." Unfortunately, my mom decided it was a good idea to smile at my pain. "Mom! It's not funny. This is going to be *the worst*." I punctuated that by groaning into my bed.

"Payal, don't worry about these silly things," she said. I glared at her.

"It's not *silly*. It's excruciating." I said, my voice sounded embarrassingly whiny. Which made me even more irritated. She sat down next to me and rubbed my back.

"In a few months, you won't be seeing these people every day. That is nothing. You can do a few months, na?" she said without stopping her movements. I turned my head and looked at her.

"That is . . . a good point, actually," I admitted. She smiled and pushed my hair back off my face.

"See? No silly things for you, meri bachi[8]. No silly people. Only schoolwork and going to a good college to become a good doctor,

---

[8] Sometimes my parents used this pretty standard term of endearment in a really sarcastic way that I definitely have never deserved.

okay?" She looked at me with such an earnest expression that I couldn't help but laugh.

"Keep dreaming, Mom. I told you I'm going to give up my spot at Penn so I can be a comedian." I grinned, some of the anxiety finally slipping away and out of my head.

"Payal!" She pretended she was going to hit me before leaning down to kiss my forehead. "Okay, now go to sleep." She got up and walked to the bedroom door, where she paused. "And none of these *kachra*[9] shows. Sleep! Tomorrow is an early morning!"

"Okay, okay. Night, Mom. Love you."

"Love you too." She smiled at me and shut the door.

Okay, just me and you, brain.

I turned off the lights, double-checked my alarm, and fell back into bed. My mom was right. I had two months left in school, and honestly, whatever happened tomorrow, happened. No sense in stressing out about it.

But what if Jon Slate had found a girlfriend in the two days since I'd seen him? Or what if his parents decided to move? Well, that wouldn't be so bad. Then I wouldn't have to worry about what I'd say to him. Or what if they *didn't* move—

Go to bed, Payal!

Ugh, fine, Phantom Neil. You've won this round.

The next morning, I decided to take the day as it came. Carpe diem, kal ho na ho[10], we knew the drill. It wasn't like there was anything I

---

[9] My mother, the critic.

[10] Today I will be guided by the great philosophers Horace and Shah Rukh Khan.

could do until I got to school anyway. After a quick shower, I pulled my hair back into a thick ponytail, threw on some jeans, a T-shirt, and a hoodie. At the front door, I shoved my feet into my sneakers.

"Payal! Nashta?" My mom's voice carried out from the kitchen.

"No, I'm not hungry! See you when I get home!" I called over my shoulder before letting the door slam behind me. I also didn't need my mom asking me why I looked like a garbage person. She was not a fan of my hipster-pajama-chic look. And she *hated* my NOT TODAY, SATAN T-shirt—I'd tried to explain why it was empowering when I bought it, but she'd shaken her head and muttered something about how Americans didn't know what good jokes were. But I *had* to wear it today of all days.

I stepped outside to find that my dad had already left, so my car was the only one in the driveway. A fine layer of dew dotted the black exterior. I loved my Little Black Honda of Death[11]. I curled my fingers under the handle and grimaced at the wetness before opening the door and slipping inside.

"Ugh." It might have been cool outside, but the inside of my car was *hot* in a way that only the Florida sun could manage. I wiped my hands clean against my jeans and then pushed up the sleeves of my hoodie. After I twisted the ignition on, I sat in the driver's seat for a second, took a deep breath of the warm air pumping out of the AC vents, and started the LBHoD.

It was a relatively short drive from my neighborhood to my high school—well, short for the long highways and massive roads of Palm Beach County anyway. Plus, morning traffic on Okeechobee wasn't ever *too bad*. And it was early enough that I didn't need to

---

[11] Affectionately! But this car was truly a disaster and had broken down more times than I could count.

blast the AC to combat the usual late-spring Florida heat, which was nice. I pulled into the school parking lot twenty-five minutes later, sunglasses on, and very nearly ready to face the day, if not my fellow students.

The morning air was refreshing as I made my way across the forty feet or so between my car and the school. The palm trees at the edges of the parking lot swayed slightly in the breeze, and I pulled the sleeves of my hoodie back down over my arms. Despite the cool air, the sky was blue, the weather was nice, the ground was solid beneath my feet, and it was quiet around me. There were only, like, three other people around, and no one I knew by name. I was starting to feel pretty okay about the day.

I'll admit I let my guard down. That was on me.

"Hey, Pie!" Jon Slate's voice rang out from somewhere behind me.

Oh no. No, no. It couldn't be. My shoulders came up behind my ears, and I hunched over. Jon—for what had to be the *first* time in his life—decided to get to school early. Because *why not*? I'd known the kid for four years and had his schedule memorized within days of every semester starting, and he had *never* gotten to school before the first bell.

I didn't want him to think I'd heard, so I couldn't turn around to see what the hell he was thinking. It was too early for an interaction. I was not ready. I resolved to walk faster. He couldn't talk to me if he couldn't catch me.

"Pie?"

Why *was* it so annoyingly sunny outside anyway? Give me darkness, give me an overcast sky with plenty of shadowy spaces. Give me a patented Florida thunderstorm! I could hear his footsteps getting closer. It felt like this was a horror movie and I was the token minority character about to get murdered.

The doors weren't *that* far away. Just a few more steps over the lawn and up the stairs. I put my hood up and tucked my hands into my pockets to walk a little faster. I had the briefest mental image of myself speed-walking-but-make-it-goth-lite and had to bite back a hysterical laugh. Slowing slightly, I took a deep breath. I needed to think about this. What was worse, stopping and talking to Jon—Jon, who was now kind of hilariously chasing me toward the school entrance—like a normal person, or leaving all pretense and straight-up sprinting to the closest girls' bathroom?

Then Jon's voice rang out as he shouted, "Look, I'm sorry I vommed on your shoes!"

His words made my decision for me. I would love to say that I stopped, turned around, saw Jon bent over with his hands on his knees, breathless. I'd love to say that I walked back to him and we laughed about his faux pas. And then I put my hand on his chest, looked up into those blue, blue eyes, and made him realize what he'd been missing. The kind of person that I knew I could be: confident, beautiful, alluring. Right? Wrong.

What actually happened was this:

He yelled his apology. I panicked and ran. My hood flew backward off my head and I might have dropped my car keys, but there was no stopping because I was going to get the *hell* out of there. Sadly, instead of using my survival instincts to become more sure-footed and have quicker reflexes, my feet just worked faster than my brain. As I skipped stairs two at a time, somehow one foot got tangled up in the other and I totally and 100 percent ate it on the sixth step leading up to the school doors. My right knee landed on the corner of the step, and I yelped loudly. I think I heard an "OH MY GOD" from someone nearby.

Then I rolled over and lay on the stairs. My knee was pulsing with pain, and my palms were scraped as hell. So I leaned my head back and looked at that beautiful blue sky and waited for my ears to stop ringing. Maybe this was fate's way of telling me to deal with it and stop running from my problems.

I sensed movement on the stairs as Jon ran up to me.

"Jeez, Pie. Are you okay?! That looked like it hurt, dude. Like, *real* bad. Like, you tripped and *BAM*, and . . . can you move? Should I get the nurse? Wait, let me *help* you to the nurse. Oh god, you're bleeding." I turned my head to look at the boy who was currently living in the center of a Venn diagram; one circle was ruining my life and the other was making my heart sing. He looked panicked and worried about *me*. His mouth was moving, but I didn't register a word he was saying. His hair was distracting. It looked so soft and blond and perfectly tousled, falling over his forehead. I gave it a half smile before dragging my eyes back down to meet his. He still looked concerned. And maybe a little green.

"I don't do well with blood. And your knee is really—" Jon was hunched over, and his shoulders convulsed a little.

"No, wait, Jon—" I managed to utter.

But then, no joke, Jonathan-fucking-Slate threw up on me. Again.

Alright, that was a slight exaggeration. This time he was nice enough to throw up *next* to me.

This better be how our freakin' love story starts, I swear to god[12].

***

[12] All of them. I swear to all the gods.

CHAPTER THREE

I was sitting in the front of the school nurse's office, alone. Two sophomores had seen the entire thing go down and ran to help *after* Jon spilled out his breakfast onto the stairs. One of them had walked me to the nurse's office. I think he even grabbed my car keys. After a brief attempt at apologizing and quite literally turning green the moment he opened his mouth, Jon had followed a few steps behind. His arm was wrapped around his middle, and his mouth was decidedly closed. I was glad for the quiet—I wouldn't even know what to say.

Ms. Bunting, the nurse, looked at my knee for exactly fifteen seconds after I rolled my jeans up and decided that I'd be fine with some peroxide, a Band-Aid, and some help to get to calculus. Jon, on the other hand, was allowed to lie down in the back because of his nausea. Seemed fair. I'd be on display for anyone who walked into the office, and he'd get to stay mysterious and invisible in the back.

I groaned, closed my eyes, and leaned my head back against the wall as I waited for the student aide to come walk me to my class.

A few months. My mom's words were echoing in my mind. That seemed easier to imagine in the comfort of my bedroom. I took a deep breath and tried to ignore the pain radiating from my knee. Sitting here under the awful fluorescent lighting in the same building as my peers made me realize how foolish I'd been. A few months in high school was a *long time.* I needed to make up my mind about how I was going to spend them.

I resisted the urge to put my face in my hands.

"Payal?" A voice I recognized floated over from the doorway. I looked up to see Divya Bhatt standing and looking at me questioningly.

"Hey, Divya."

I had known Divya, like Neil, *forever.* She was cool. Really cool, actually. Maybe *too* cool for me. Sometimes when we hung out, I couldn't help but feel like a little baby who knew nothing of the outside world. But not because of anything she said or did. She was smart and beautiful and well-dressed and well-read and clever and—okay, I could keep going, but I'll stop. But, for example, she walked in with her long hair pulled back into an elegantly disheveled bun, wearing a tank top and drop-crotch pants that on anyone else would look like diaper pants, holding what looked like a collection of essays. And she did all this without looking like a parody of herself. She looked authentic. How was that fair? No one should look good in drop-crotch pants! And her eyeliner was *always perfect.* Like Aishwarya-Rai-in-*Devdas*-style perfect[13].

"How are you feeling? Do you need to put your arm around my shoulders?" She was also the nicest person I knew.

"Nah, I think I can walk, but company is probably a good idea in case I'm wrong." I stood up from the painfully uncomfortable orange office chair and gingerly tested putting weight on my offended knee. It would hold okay.

"Alright." She hovered near me while I picked up my backpack. I took one last look back to where Jon was still lying down. No movement that I could see. Good.

---

[13] I love my friend *so* much and am only mildly jealous sometimes.

"Ready?" Divya asked. I shouldered my bag and nodded.

"I can hold your bag for you, you know." She grinned and held out her hand.

"Eh. It's already on."

She gave me an *acha* head nod in response. "Whatever you want, di[14]," and she followed my limping butt out the door.

Our school was set up like *the* most generic of TV-show high schools. Long, locker-lined hallways, tiled floors, and the least flattering lighting you could possibly imagine. I cursed my boring high school under my breath—if I went to one of the open-air schools in any other part of South Florida, with their fresh air and beautiful green quads, I wouldn't be in this mess. If I went to one of *those* schools, I wouldn't have tripped on the stairs, because there would be no stairs. At least school was twenty minutes into first period, and so our long hallways were blessedly empty.

"So, Jon Slate threw up on you, huh?" Divya asked, voice echoing slightly in the otherwise silent space around us.

Scratch that. The hallways were hatefully empty and quiet.

"Divya, can we talk about literally anything else?"

"Sorry, when I saw that post come through last night, I already felt bad, but twice in the span of three days . . . *yikes*."

"Try experiencing it firsthand," I said drily.

Divya grimaced before changing the subject and sparing me further thoughts of Jon's weak stomach. "Okay, okay, I can tell you about how much Bharatanatyam practice is totally kicking my butt."

I looked down at my bum knee. "I am so glad my mom made me take tap. And then let me quit." I paused, taking in her outfit

---

[14] *Di* as in *didi*, not *di* as in *Divya*, since technically she's three months older than me.

again. "Oh, those drop-crotch pants make more sense in the Bharatanatyam[15] context."

"You're lucky you're hurt, or I'd push you down for that one. I look amazing in these." She'd stopped and posed against the wall like only a classically trained dancer can, her strong arms raised above her head in mirrored arches while her hands formed into a mudra I didn't understand. I sighed and kept limping along.

"I know. I hate you."

"Like you could ever hate me." She laughed. "You and your family are still coming to my performance this weekend, right?" It was the city's South Asian Society social event of the month, so there was no way we'd miss it. Divya's mom would never let my mom live it down if we didn't show. Also, these things were usually super fun.

I flashed Divya an excessively goofy smile before opening the door to my class. "Obvio[16]!"

Her laughter followed me into Ms. Díaz's calculus class.

"Payal, Neil told me you were with the nurse, but you look fine." Ms. Díaz narrowed her eyes. "Do you have a pass?" I reached into my pocket and grabbed the paper Ms. Bunting had scribbled on earlier.

"Here you go." Díaz glanced at the note in disdain. Puzzled, I waited to see if she'd say anything. It was unclear what the note had done to piss her off.

---

[15] Google it. You'll see. I'm right.

[16] When you grow up in an immigrant household, you get two whole worlds' worth of pop culture references.

"Please take a seat," she finally said.

I hobbled—exaggerating my lumbering movements to prove a point—over to my desk in between Neil and our friend Caitlin Martin. Ms. Díaz turned back to the board and started talking about derivatives. Instead of paying attention, I sat down and wondered how many people knew I was Jon Slate's partner in the Vomit Olympics.

"*Pst.*"

I looked to my left. Caitlin was looking at me and holding a folded-up piece of paper. She was usually very attentive during calculus—which I appreciated, considering she was my math tutor—but it seemed like there were other things on her mind today. She tossed the folded-up note onto my desk. I opened the note, careful not to tear Caitlin's intricate origami-level work, and read over her wide block letters.

> **Did Slate really tackle you on the stairs this morning? Joey is telling everyone that he saw Slate try to kill you.**

Sighing, I turned the paper over to reply. I needed Neil to handle this. I turned to look at him, but he was actually taking notes on what Díaz was teaching.

Payal, laugh it off. Literally no one is going to care.

Phantom Neil was probably right, but he could have been nicer about it. I threw real Neil a glare in his stead. It took a second, but like he could feel my death rays, Neil's shoulders came up around his ears. Then he turned to see me glaring and mouthed, *What?!* like his phantom self had not been *super* rude to me a split second ago.

I continued to glower at him. He rolled his eyes and turned back to the front of the class. How did we live in the future, but I couldn't mentally connect to my best friend whenever I needed to?

As I considered what to say, I gnawed on my pen cap, my teeth finding the well-worn grooves on it. I needed to minimize.

No, I tripped and he tried to help. No big.

I passed the note back to Caitlin and then threw another glare at Neil because I was handling this. He looked over at me and caught the irritated look, but returned it with his best seriously-why-are-you-looking-at-me-like-I-hurt-your-favorite-pet-Payal look. Not that I was overly familiar with that one or anything.

Caitlin seemed to take my explanation at face value, because she read the note, shrugged, and shoved it into her calculus textbook. I hid a grin. Then Díaz's voice shook me out of my momentary relief.

"Payal! Can you tell me the answer?"

"Uh, can you repeat the question?"

"Sucks that Díaz busted you like that, Pie."

Caitlin and I both had a brutal ninety-minute block of calculus followed by a ninety-minute block of AP Psych. Our school wasn't set up for seven subjects a day, every day. We did four classes each day, with one class being shorter and repeated every day of the week, and then we alternated between odd days and even days. It was probably more complicated than it needed to be, but it meant that you got more of your favorite class on a given day and more of your least favorite class on another day. And AP Psych was definitely a favorite class.

"Eh, it's fine. Eventually, Díaz is going to have to accept the fact that math and I will probably never be friends."

Caitlin chuckled and tucked a strand of her dark brown hair behind her ear. "Oh, come on. It's not that hard."

I clenched my jaw in annoyance once or twice before replying. "Not all of us are cut out to be mathletes, you nerd," I joked, and then added, "Also, thank you for holding my bag even though you didn't have to." Caitlin had graciously offered to be my human support.

The loud sound of flip-flops slapping against tiles hit me just before Jeremy Owens almost followed suit as he dashed past us on his way to class. Despite the near miss, Caitlin and I both ignored him, since this was standard Jeremy Owens behavior.

"You're welcome, friend!" She hoisted both our bags onto her shoulder. "I don't know how you're so terrible at math, Pie. I mean, it's like you're not even Indian!" I'm not sure there's anything better than when someone says that particular sentiment out loud.

"Hilarious, Caitlin. Hilarious," I said sarcastically.

"Come on." She laughed. "Can you blame me for relishing the fact that this white girl"—she gestured to herself—"gets to tutor a person whose culture invented zero?[17]"

"Oh, look, we're here." Luckily, we'd made it to our psych classroom in time to cut the conversation short. Don't get me wrong, I liked Caitlin, and she really was doing me a solid by tutoring me in the god-awful experience that is calculus. But I hated feeling bad about something I supposedly should be great at. Or at least something every other Indian kid seemed to be good at. Comments like

---

[17] Caitlin Martin starring in the role of My Mom, ladies and gentlemen.

that always had a way of burrowing under my skin and sitting there just waiting to dart into my brain and make me feel gross.

"Let me get the door for you." Caitlin opened the door, and I limped to my desk. She dropped my bag next to me and moved back a couple rows to find her seat.

"Thanks for the assist!" I said with an enthusiasm I didn't feel. She waved a hand in response. Caitlin was generally cool, but I could have done without feeling dense on top of feeling awkward today.

Mr. Lutton breezed into the room with his characteristic lively energy. He was one of my favorite teachers. I didn't know if they realized it, but we could tell when teachers were excited about their subjects, and it helped. I swear. Like, I don't know if I *really* cared about what Carl Jung had to say about literally anything . . . but Mr. Lutton did, and his excitement was infectious.

"Alright, kids, today we're going to talk through psychological experiments. It's a short class thanks to the pep rally schedule, so let's get started!" No! I forgot about the pep rally. Mr. Lutton turned and started writing on the whiteboard, and somehow managed to keep speaking words while writing different words on the board. "As you know, everyone is expected to complete one experiment from start to finish." He spun around with the word *experiment* half-written on the board. "Can one of you tell me what the first step is?"

I raised my hand along with a few other kids. This was my *jam*.

"Yes, Ms. Mehta?"

"First we have to have a hypothesis about something."

"Yes!" Mr. Lutton exclaimed. I sat back, more than a little pleased with myself. Lutton looked out at the entire class. "We've been reading up on psychological experiments this semester. Over the next few days, spend some time thinking about what you could test using student surveys as well as primary and secondary sources. You have until next class to turn in your hypothesis." I heard a few groans around me, but I didn't care. This could be really fun if I could think of something good. He stopped writing due dates on the board and turned around. "I mentioned at the beginning of the year you'd have it a little easier on the final project since it'll be due during exam week . . . so you get to have partners!"

Now it was my turn to groan. I *hated* partner work. Someone always got stuck doing the majority of the work while the other person coasted.

"Now, after the Great Snake Disaster[18] two years ago"—there was another collective moan, which he wisely ignored—"you are not allowed to pick your own partners, and so, Katie, you're with"—he glanced down at a piece of paper on his desk—"Jamal. And, Oliver, you and Julio will be working together . . ." People got up as he called their names to move next to the kid they'd be working with. Mr. Lutton continued to slowly nix names from my mental list of potential partners. As he went on, I realized where this was going. I gripped the edges of my desk. *Please don't say it, please don't say it*—"Payal, you're going to be working with . . ." *PLEASE DON'T SAY IT*—"Philip Kim." *NOOOOOOOOOOOOOO.*

---

[18] Don't ask.

CHAPTER FOUR

Philip Kim was seriously sort of my . . . nemesis. That sounds dramatic, but it was also true. There was a reason I'd asked if Philip was going to be at Rachel's party. Actually, a lot of reasons. Our enmity started four years ago. We'd had a single class together every semester since freshman year, and from that very first day, we'd *known*. It was ninth grade and I was working on a terrible still life in art class when this short Korean kid with spiky hair, a thin scar under his right eye, and a bomber jacket at least two sizes too big came over to my canvas, sneered, and said, "I bet I finish my landscape before you finish your still life. And I'll get a better grade."

At the time I was more confused than anything—who *was* this guy? I asked him as much, and with—trust me—a *lot* of ego, he replied, "Philip Kim."

I did remember looking back at his canvas and being pretty sure of my success. It was supposed to be the beach near our school, I think? The fact that it was questionable gave me some confidence. So I took the bet. And I lost . . . but only because when I reached for my paints, they were gone. Philip had hidden them. And I learned a lesson. There was no playing fair with Philip Kim.

Then there was sophomore-year world history. We both did diorama projects on the French Revolution, but mine was so good it basically decapitated his. Okay, I built a mini fake guillotine and maybe I put his tiny marshmallow Robespierre in it and then ate the head. Anyway, it's gone on like that for the last three and a half years: sabotage, drama, and a semi-constant war. That *he* started.

This year, our single class together was psych. He was the only one who could ever beat my grades, and it was driving me bananas[19]. I narrowed my eyes at him as he loped to my desk, all arms and angles. Philip still had the bomber jacket, but he'd grown enough that it fit him now. The scar under his eye had faded to a light line, and his hair was longer and disheveled, hanging over his forehead and nearly hiding his ears. Unfortunately, his personality hadn't changed much. He caught my eye and smirked. He *actually* smirked. Could he be more annoying? But as I watched, he tripped a little, and I snickered. There was an awkwardness to his gait these days that I relished. Philip wasn't so short anymore. He was probably hitting near six feet, if I was being more generous than I needed to be—but he had one of those teenage-boy bodies that grew too fast . . . like he hadn't quite gotten the hang of using his limbs yet. He looked like a baby lamb walking through the aisle toward me. He sat down in the recently vacated desk in front of me and turned sideways.

"Mehta."

"Philip." I hoped I was emanating a sense of cool disinterest.

He looked at me strangely, his dark eyes assessing. "Are you constipated?"

I threw my pencil at him.

Meanwhile, Mr. Lutton was still talking. "We've only got twenty minutes until you have to head to the gym, so take some time right now to go through the experiments we've read over the last

---

[19] I wasn't good at math or physical sciences. Psychology is my thing, Philip Kim!

few weeks with your partner and see if it sparks anything. You can model an experiment we've studied, but you can also come up with something new. Use your own experiences to inform your hypothesis! I'll be at my desk if you have any questions." Lutton looked back at the board and chuckled. "After I finish writing the schedule for you, of course."

This might need some actual research. I looked around the class. Everyone else was either flipping through the pages of their psych textbook or pretending to flip through the pages of their psych textbook while surreptitiously looking at their phones.

"Okay." Philip's voice cut through my voyeurism. "We can use my notes; they're thorough."

"*So are mine*," I hissed while I pulled out my binder. "I am a *very* meticulous notetaker." This was mostly true. I'd at least been filing away the experiment printouts we'd gone over in class so far.

"Okay, calm down—"

"Don't tell me to calm down. You were implying that I'm bad at note-taking."

"I was not!" He looked down at me from his annoyingly high stature. Philip Kim, apparently, didn't believe in slouching.

"Why don't we look at our own notes and quietly think about what we might want to do, and then we can discuss it later?" If there was an award for the most words said through gritted teeth, I would win it. In response, Philip shrugged and turned his giant body away from me. I stuck my tongue out at his back. Immature? Yes. Satisfying? Also yes.

I looked down at the pages in my binder, but it was hard to concentrate while my knee was still throbbing and all I could think of was working out an experiment that didn't involve having to show my face to the rest of the school at all. As long as Lutton had been talking, I could concentrate on him and push the memory out of my brain, but now it was just me and my thoughts for—I looked up at the ancient clock affixed above the whiteboard—at least ten more minutes. Then I'd have to hide out in the library with Neil while everyone else went to the pep rally.

Pep rallies at our school were *notoriously* boring. Not that I didn't appreciate how hard the cheerleaders and the dance team worked on their routines, and not that I didn't want to support our sports ball teams, but . . .

But.

Look, you can only watch sixteen girls and ten boys dance to Ariana Grande so many times.

"Hey, Mehta." Philip Kim had turned back around to face me. "I think I have an idea."

Lips pursed and brow furrowed, I gestured for him to keep talking. Working with him was going to give me premature wrinkles. Fortunately for both of us, my scowl-stare was interrupted by the crackling of the PA system.

"All students please report to the gymnasium for the pep rally. Thank you."

Mr. Lutton stood up as we started gathering our things and heading toward the door. "Alright! Next class, please come prepared with your hypothesis and experiment idea!" The class collectively gave him what could have been categorized as an affirming sound.

"Okay, let's connect after school. I'll call you." Philip didn't wait for me to answer before he grabbed his messenger bag and slung it over his head mid-stride to get out the door. I stared at the empty space he'd been in. What was up with the universe lately? First the vomit, then the vomit, then Philip Kim? I raised my eyes to the sky in a silent plea for the gods to give it up already.

I was only slightly limping now, but I still waited for the majority of the class to get out before making my way to the door.

"Payal." Neil was waiting for me in the hallway, arms held out to take my bag. He looked mildly guilty. My guard went up. "Bad news."

"Of course there is. Me too, by the way," I said. Neil lifted my bag onto his shoulder and looked at me askance.

"How can you have *more* bad news? Mine's that I have to go to the pep rally. So you have to go to the pep rally." He'd slowed his pace to match mine, but I stopped short at that, and he ended up a few steps ahead anyway. He turned back when he realized I wasn't beside him anymore.

"*Whyyyyy?*" I knew I sounded whiny, but also, *whyyyyy?* "This is not my day. Mr. Lutton assigned us partners for the psych final." Neil looked at me expectantly.

"And?" Then he got it. "Not Philip!" he said, aghast. I nodded as sadly as I could. "I'm sorry," he said with a frown. "And now I'm extra sorry that I forgot today's pep rally was for the wrestling team."

"Ugh. Yeah. Philip. And now, ugh. You and your irritatingly cute relationship. Fine." I needed to shake this funk out of my system . . . Lovingly mocking my best friend should help. "Though I can't believe you didn't dress up more for Finn's big moment."

Neil ran a hand through his hair and grinned, gesturing at the light-to-dark-maroon ombré linen button-down he had on. "Please, I bought this shirt in Mumbai over winter break, and it looks good.

You already told me it looked good the last time I wore it. Be better at talking trash."

I laughed because he wasn't wrong. We'd almost made it to the gym doors. In a rush, I realized what I'd be walking into. "Wait, is everyone going to stare when I go in there?"

Neil barely kept from rolling his eyes. "Payal, stop acting so weird about this—you are not this person and you have never *been* this person." He wasn't wrong. I was *usually* way less anxious—granted, I *usually* didn't have a bunch of teenage witnesses to my humiliating experiences. "I am putting a moratorium on the topic of Jon Slate until you either talk to him or quit freaking out over something so ridiculous. Now, come on and let's go support my very kind and attractive boyfriend."

"Fine. Though that was almost too harsh, FYI."

He quirked a lip up and threaded his arm through mine. "Yaar, sometimes you need it." Best friends. There for the real truths. He shoved the door open and walked through. I followed him to a spot a few rows up on the bleachers. He was right, though. No one paid any particular attention to me. There were no knowing glances or whispers. Hope rose inside of me. Maybe it would be fine.

The pep rally was pretty much the exact same thing it always was. Neil was predictably grossed out by the lack of interesting choreography. "And now I bet they're going to do another cartwheel. Oh, look. It's *another* cartwheel."

His commentary did make the whole thing more fun. Eventually, the thrum of the bass died down and it was time for the wrestlers to come out and for us to cheer on their existence as a not-so-great team. They filed out as their names were called. Neil screamed extra loud when Coach Watanabe called out, "Finn Jacobs," and it was very sweet. Finn shuffled out with red cheeks. He was cute, though sometimes people didn't notice him until he smiled. He was on the short and stocky side, with hazel eyes and close-cropped mousey brown hair. Very quiet. He was unobtrusive and sort of a perfect balance to Neil's . . . louder tendencies.

"You know, you are *very* lucky." I bounced my good knee against Neil's as the coach continued to call out names.

"Huh?" He turned his head a little my way without taking his eyes off the court.

"You get that look on your face like you're watching the end of a perfectly sappy drama when Finn's around sometimes." I reached up and ruffled his hair. "He's your Ranveer."

"No, I don't! Shut up. Don't be such a dork," he protested.

"Whatever you say, Deepika." I smiled wider. That was too far, I guess, because then he pinched me. "Ow!" I rubbed my arm and knocked my uninjured knee against his again, but with a little more force than I'd normally use.

The pep rally took another fifteen minutes to wrap up. The student body president had to say some words about something . . . parking spots, maybe? I don't know. By then, Neil and I had moved on to a very intense game of digital Scrabble.

"Uh, excuse me?" someone said. My head snapped up from my phone.

"He's not." Neil's voice was full of shock. *"He is."*

Jon Slate was standing next to my seat, and my first instinct was to bolt. But that was ridiculous! I should just talk to him. Maybe this could be the beginning our love story!

I wanted to see Jon's face to catch his eye, but he was looking at his feet, sort of shuffling in place awkwardly. Because of me. I could feel Neil's stare boring into the side of my head.

. . . Along with the *entire* gymnasium. Pretty sure Julia Wong-Ramos was recording this on her phone. No, wait, scratch that. She was definitely recording this on her phone. She'd left her flash on. I hoped it wasn't a live stream so she could at least put on a good filter.

"Payal, I am so sorry I threw up on you." Jon paused and offered me a hand to help me up. Oh my god. He flinched and added, "Twice."

"Look, it's fine." I started to wave him off, but he interrupted me and grabbed my hand. My heart hammered so intensely, I briefly considered nicknaming it Mjolnir.

"No, no, you should let me buy you lunch as an apology." He pulled me up so I was standing in the aisle with him. I may have snatched my hand back because *Hello! Panic!* Then he looked down at me through his bangs, and how the hell was I supposed to say no to those unnervingly blue eyes? And that unbelievable jawline. And that frustratingly, rudely perfect face.

Wait.

Did he just ask me to go to lunch with him? Did he just—

"Payal, answer him," I heard Neil hiss at me through the haze that was my brain.

"Uh." I had to force myself not to stare at the steps where my own shoes were scuffing the floor to the point that the janitor might actually kill me. My gaze shifted to Jon's shoulder and focused on the clean black-and-white flannel of his well-fitted button-down, worried I'd lose my nerve. He had really asked me.

"*Payal,*" Neil whispered again.

"I—uh, yeah, okay. Yeah." My eyes drifted up to his face as I got through my answer, and Jon's expression lifted. I died a little when he broke into a toothsome smile.

"Great!" He reached a hand out as if to grab mine again, but I'd already shoved my hands into my hoodie pockets to keep them from doing something outrageous like touching his face. Because that was where we were now—I wasn't sure I had total control over my own limbs because of this boy. He withdrew his hand and hooked a piece of hair behind his ear instead, then repeated himself. "Great. Great, okay. Meet you outside at one?" I didn't trust my voice, so I nodded instead. Then I felt Neil's hand pulling my arm.

"Yes, one is great, Jon. She'll meet you at your car as soon as next period is over, cool? Great! Okay! Bye, man!" I had Neil on one side, and somehow Divya had materialized on the other, and together they frog-marched me down the aisle and out of the gym, past the faces of people who cared and people who didn't.

As soon as we were out of the doors, Neil looked up at the ceiling. "Please make a hot dude throw up on my shoes at the next party we go to, okay? Thanks." I elbowed him in the side.

"Shut up, Neil." Divya had moved away to lean against the wall. "Payal, you know that it's not because he threw up on your shoes, right? You're cute and funny. He only needed to notice it." I could have kissed her. Neil rolled his eyes.

"She knows that, Div." He turned to me with a more critical eye. "You know that, right?" I shrugged half-heartedly. I sort of knew it. Sometimes. Not all the time. Not in the last few days. "Alright, well, clearly we're going to skip next period to create a plan for this date."

CHAPTER FIVE

We spent the better part of the next forty minutes hunkered down in an empty classroom planning out a detailed strategy of potential topics for conversation and smooth transitions in case I had to use the restroom (or if I needed to go hide and text the group chat for help), and then Divya managed my hair and makeup. Finn was sitting quietly in the corner, mostly trying to stay out of the way, but he'd said he wasn't surprised that Jon had asked me to lunch when he'd joined us.

"Besides," he'd added with a mischievous grin, "we can finally go on a double date with people I actually like instead of random couples Neil keeps asking."

"Finn, you've never once said yes, and maybe those would be amazing," Neil interjected while typing up a list of topics for me. Then he stopped and looked in my direction. "But you would obviously be more fun, Payal."

"Thank you," I said sardonically. Finn laughed.

"Stop moving your mouth," Divya ordered as she swiped shimmer across my bottom lip. "Okay, finished." She took a step back and held up her phone in selfie mode so I could see.

"Divya, you are a miracle worker!" Whatever she'd added to my face made it seem like I was glowing. I did have large eyes, but the liner she used on them made them seem even bigger, and the brown of my irises looked so dark they were almost black. Luckily, Divya and I had more or less the same skin tone, so the blush she'd put on the apples of my cheeks made my round face seem more cheekbone-forward in a very supermodel kind of way. She'd even darkened the small beauty mark on the left side of my chin so it would stand out. Small steps, but miles of improvement from my perspective.

"The key is to look like you're not wearing makeup. Because *society*." She glanced at her phone. "It's time for you to go. The bell is going to ring in, like, two minutes. I'm so excited for you! Go get it."

"You're gonna be fine," Finn said.

"And don't be weird. Or argumentative," Neil added, because I had a tendency to play devil's advocate for the fun of it sometimes.

"I won't! Unless he says something really wrong."

"If it's about any pop culture, *let it go*," he pushed back, and I stuck my tongue out at him in irritation.

"Look, I'm going to be lucky if I can get a full sentence out, so don't worry, auntie-ji."

"You're going to be *fine*," Finn said again before biting his lip, and I think he was trying not to laugh a little bit. Neil had a doting look on his face; it was gross and cute.

"I feel like I need to forward him your biodata[20] before anything happens. Then he'll know that he's lucky to be taking you out," Divya said.

"Aw, stop it, you guys." I threw my arms around Neil and Divya in gratitude. Finn was not the group-hug type, but he smiled from behind them. Then I stepped away and nodded once. "Okay, I'm

---

[20] I'm guessing my mom reserved my profile name on ShaadiWaadi.com when I was an infant, but I can dream that she didn't.

doing this. I'M DOING THIS." We left the classroom and they turned left to head to the cafeteria, while I turned right toward the parking lot.

"Good luck!" Divya called out, immediately followed by Neil saying, "Even though you won't need it!"

"The bell hasn't rung *yet*," I heard Finn say drily. "So we may want to keep it down or we're going to get busted for skipping, and Payal won't get to have lunch." Neil and Divya started to protest.

Their voices got farther away from me, and a smile wide enough to split my cheeks stretched across my face as I walked purposefully through the hallways. This was going to be the best lunch of my life. I glanced at my watch—another minute and the bell would ring. I started walking a little faster, wanting to beat the crowds. Then out of nowhere, one of the classroom doors ahead of me swung open unexpectedly and I had to legitimately slide to a stop.

"Argh!!!" I couldn't help it; the noise erupted out of me. But in my defense, I almost got face-slammed by a door.

"Mehta?"

A sour pit formed in my stomach. Of all the people to see before the best lunch of my life. Philip Kim poked his head around the open door. His eyes were narrowed at me like I was the one who was opening doors willy-nilly and almost killing girls on their way to their very first extremely hot dates[21].

"What are you doing?" he asked, staring at my face like a weirdo. "Did you cut bio or something?"

"I don't have time for this, Philip!" I said instead of answering. "Stop trying to ruin my day!"

"Huh?" he said, sounding genuinely confused. But I wasn't going to

---

[21] I am *manifesting*, okay?

fall for it. I was already moving past him, leaving him and his annoying questions behind me. Then something occurred to me. How did he know what class I was cutting? Was he planning something?

Payal! Get to the parking lot!

Thoughts of Philip flew out of my head, and I speed-walked the rest of the way.

I made it to the lot with a few seconds to spare before the surge of kids heading to their cars to get off campus for lunch reached me, so I didn't have to deal with anyone openly staring. Jon was already leaning against his car. The Florida sun had really come into its own in the last few hours, and it was significantly hotter than it'd been that morning. I tied my hoodie around my waist and hoped the humidity wouldn't undo the work Divya had done on my hair in the short walk to his car.

"Pie! Over here!" Jon called. As if I hadn't locked in on him the moment I'd stepped into the lot. Like I hadn't learned where he parked his car the *minute* he'd gotten one for his birthday and started driving it to school. I raised a hand and waved and then immediately forgot what normal waving looked like. Oh god, what was I doing? Was my hand moving too fast? I brought my hand down and took a deep breath and forced myself to relax.

The concrete was rough and uneven under my sneakers. The pain in my knee had weakened to a slight ache, and thankful for that, I walked carefully, unwilling to repeat this morning's performance.

"Hey, Jon." *I can do this. I can do this. I can do this.* I mean, he'd smiled at me and my heart managed to keep beating. I took that as a good sign. As soon as I was close enough, he opened the passenger door for me. It was chivalrous and charming, and my heart fluttered in my chest. Then he ran around the car and hopped into the driver's seat.

"Where are we going?" I asked. He turned and cocked a grin that lit up his whole face. My cheeks started to heat up, and I bit the fleshy part inside so I wouldn't accidentally give him a terrifying clown smile.

"Oh, you'll see," he said.

Five minutes later, he pulled into the Taco Bell near school and I almost swooned.

"I hope this is cool." And somehow that was all it took to put me in my comfort zone. The promise of a suburban Taco Bell that looked exactly like the hundreds of other Taco Bells I had been inside of. Stable. Reliable. I shot him my most dazzling smile and hoped it didn't look creepy.

"This is perfect."

He shrugged and grinned. "Awesome, let's do this!" We got out of his car, and I half hoped he'd grab my hand on the walk to the building. I'm not sure how he could resist; I was exuding confidence. But he didn't. I followed him up to the glass doors, and he graciously pulled the door open and gestured for me to go in ahead of him. And as an added bonus, there was no barf in sight. I bit my lip as I stepped onto the brown ceramic tile inside, holding in a squeal.

Thanks to Taco Bell being Taco Bell, within fifteen minutes we were already seated and eating and . . . laughing. We were laughing and talking! I'd told a few jokes and he'd *laughed*.

"Yo, Payal, you are hilarious. How have we not hung out before?" Jon almost snorted his Coke through his nose at the last story, the one about my dad accidentally taking me to see an R-rated movie when I was seven. I was feeling pretty good.

"I don't know, Jon. It was so easy. All you had to do was throw up on me." The corner of my mouth turned up, and he snorted again. I needed something to do with my hands, though. They were lying on the table like dead fish or something. I played with the edge of my chalupa wrapper.

"Careful, Pie. I did just eat three burritos." I feigned shock, held a hand in front of my face, and scooted my chair back a few inches.

"You wouldn't!"

Jon grinned at me and I smiled back, but my smile quickly turned into a gasp as my chair was pulled back toward the table. I looked down and found Jon's ankle hooked around the leg as he worked to bring me close again. I swooned internally for the second time.

We were sitting in a table at the back. The conversation was easy. Our legs had sort of tangled under the table. I'm not sure we stopped laughing once. Is this what it felt like to get the guy? This was awesome. I could feel myself grinning like an idiot. But so what? I was sitting here with him, and it was perfect. Then I realized it'd probably been a minute since I'd said anything at all. I covered by taking a sip of my Coke. *Smooth, Payal.* I opened my mouth to say something—anything—but stalled at the sight of Jon's expression.

He was looking at me with his head cocked like he'd never seen me before. I cut my eyes away and took another sip.

"Do you have a boyfriend?" he asked, and I choked on my soda.

After a few minutes of coughing into my napkin and trying to apologize, I finally responded.

"What?"

Jon handed me another napkin so I could dab at my watering eyes. I hoped the liner Divya used was waterproof.

"I asked if you were dating anyone."

IT.

WAS.

HAPPENING.

Keep it together, Payal. I dropped my hands to my lap and gripped my fingers together tightly, channeling my nerves into my clasped hands.

"Uh, well, not really, no." Did I imagine a breeze inside of the Taco Bell? I was 90 percent sure that Jon-fucking-Slate's hair was actually ruffling in a breeze. It was actively tousling while I was looking at him.

"That's awesome! You're funny and cute and totally, like, normal. If I was Indian, I'd totally date you, but that's not happening anytime soon with, you know . . ." He gestured between us with some kind of meaning I clearly wasn't picking up. "Oh!" he continued. "You have to meet my friend Rohit."

Wait, what?

"Wait, what?" I asked.

Now he was talking really fast and motioning with his hands, and I was starting to have trouble understanding the words coming out of his mouth. Something about "No, really, a great Indian guy my cousin introduced me to" and "It's so great that I know two cool Indians who can get together. So awesome."

"You guys will love each other," he said. Oh. Now I understood the gesturing between us. Between my brown skin and his white skin. There was a buzzing sound coming from somewhere, right? Or was that static in my head trying to drown out what I was hearing? "He's super funny too!"

What the *hell* was going on?

"What?" Had I said that out loud? Jon was again looking at me like he had no idea who I was, only this time, he didn't look quite so romantic. He looked more like an awful boy who didn't know he was being awful. And I wasn't sure there was anything I could say that he'd understand. Or that wouldn't make me sound too sensitive. Ugh, my jeans felt too tight. Maybe I shouldn't have had the extra Fire Sauce on my chalupa. I needed to get out of here.

"Jon, you need to take me back to school."

"Uh, what's wrong?" His eyes went wide with worry, and he started to reach for my hand, but I clasped my fingers together and dropped my hands to my lap.

"No, nothing, nothing. It hit me that, uh, I have a quiz in calc and I totally forgot to study." *Yeah, that sounds real convincing, Payal. Good job.* I didn't even have calc in the afternoons. Not that Jon knew *my* schedule.

"Um, okay." A strange look settled on his features, and I knew I was weirding him out, but I didn't care.

Really, you know an Indian guy who would be great for me? Cool. So glad I'd skipped bio to get ready for this. "If I was Indian . . ." Great.

I stood up from my seat and walked toward the door without waiting for him to follow. I threw a half-hearted "Thanks" over my shoulder.

We spent the ride back to school in a heavy silence, during which I was really, really trying not to cry. Thankfully, the school was a few quick turns away from the restaurant. I spent those minutes watching the palm trees and strip malls go by until we finally made it back to the parking lot. A lone tear escaped my eye and rolled down my cheek, but I wiped it away, hating that a *boy* was bringing me to tears over something I shouldn't have to cry about. I don't think he noticed. I dug my nails into my palm, trying to distract myself. This was my life. Sitting in Jon's 2012 Kia, hoping that he couldn't see my quivering chin. I couldn't stop going over every minute of the lunch: When had he decided that I was good enough for his Indian friend but not good enough for him? Was it when he saw my brown face for the first time? Or was it when I got my food "minus meat"?

Oh my god, if he had ruined Taco Bell for me, I would kill him.

CHAPTER SIX

YAARON SUN LO ZARA

NEIL PATEL

> PAYAL HOW DID IT GO WHERE
> ARE YOU WE ARE WAITING

DIVYA BHATT

> Maybe she's still out with him?
> Did they cut class?

NEIL PATEL

> idk idk idk

DIVYA BHATT

> PAYAL WE ARE DYING

PAYAL MEHTA

NEIL PATEL

> Are you typing a novel???

DIVYA BHATT

> This is gonna be a gud story I think

PAYAL MEHTA

NEIL PATEL

I'm dying

DIVYA BHATT

(o.O)

PAYAL MEHTA

It was bad.

NEIL PATEL

???????

DIVYA BHATT

Oh no, I'm sorry! How can we help?????

PAYAL MEHTA

gonna process. ttyl tho

CHAPTER SEVEN

"And can you name one of the major themes in *The Sun Also Rises*, Mr. Djan?" Ms. Barnett was trying—and failing—to get any sort of response out of the seniors in her classroom. There were fifteen minutes left in the school day, and *what was the point of it all, anyway?*

My heart was breaking.

Really, Jon?! I should meet your Indian friend?! Thanks. Cool.

I looked down at the blank paper on my desk. There was no way I could pay attention in this class . . . Did I mention that my heart was breaking? Ms. Barnett should notice and let me leave early. She was compassionate. English teachers were supposed to be compassionate, right?

"Ms. Mehta!" My head snapped up. "Please pay attention. Daydreaming isn't going to help you write this essay." Compassion shmompassion.

After we'd driven back from lunch, I slunk out of Jon's car with a timid "Thanks for lunch, no hard feelings, see you later." And then I hightailed it to English, careful not to run into Neil or Divya.

Phantom Neil did not love that.

But I couldn't engage with real-life Neil or with Divya. My phone stayed deep in the pocket of my backpack because I could not relive the lunch with Jon yet. It had been so insulting. And infuriating.

How could he just make such a flawed call for both of us like that? Didn't I get a say?

Turns out, there were worse things than being thrown up on twice. I could wash my jeans off, but how did I scrub what I'd heard out of my brain? It was currently on overdrive, trying to figure out what impression I gave off that Jon Slate thought that it was cool to be like, *Hey, if I was Indian, you'd be a catch* . . . or whatever.

What made him say that? I rested my chin in my hands and stared out at nothing. Ms. Barnett's voice faded into the background again, a soft hum layered behind the anxiety filter currently running over my every thought. Was it . . . because of my social circle? Neil was my best friend and Divya was a close second, but we had a lot in common. We got each other. We'd grown up together. Was that a crime?

Wait, *this isn't my fault.* I frowned and glared at my empty notebook like it was a stand-in for Jon. He didn't know *anything* about me. What gave him the right?

The jarring sound of the bell interrupted my thoughts, but I was happy to hear it. *Finally.* I couldn't wait to go home and curl into my bed to forget about all of this.

"Don't forget! Papers on *The Sun Also Rises* are due in my inbox by end of day Friday!"

You have to meet my friend Rohit. If I was Indian, I'd totally date you . . .

The words were rattling over and over and over in head. They didn't stop when I drove home, or when I closed the garage door, or when I grabbed some matri to take up to my room to snack on, or when I waved vaguely in the direction of my mother on the way through our living room to my bedroom, or when I ignored the fifteen unread text messages on my phone, or when I threw myself onto my bed, Jon's words becoming an echo of an echo of an echo. I pressed my face into the soft fabric of my comforter and sighed into it before turning to the side to stare blankly at the wall.

You have to meet my friend Rohit. Like what does the word *meet* even mean? *Meet meet meet meet.*

"PAYAL!" How did my mom have the uncanny ability of knowing exactly when my butt hit my mattress to call for me to come back downstairs?

"WHAT?!"

"PAYAL!!! IDHAR AA!"

"MOM, WHAT IS IT?!"

"PAYAL." When the yells ended with a straight-up period instead of an exclamation point is when one should listen to the parental figure, because you did not want to find out what's on the other side of that tiny, terrifying punctuation mark.

"COMING! *God.*" Pushing myself up and off of my bed was much more difficult than it should have been. As if every ounce of energy had been sapped out of my muscles and into my brain in order to overthink the day. My body had, as they say, no chill. Dragging my feet down the stairs, I stepped into the living room to find my mother sitting on the couch gesturing to the ZeeTV entertainment news currently blasting from the television.

Normally, she'd be at my dad's practice, where she helped out weekday afternoons, but a friend's kid was taking a sabbatical from med school and his dad wanted him to continue to have medicine shoved in his face . . . so now he was working in my dad's office instead. This meant my mom had her days free for the

54

foreseeable future, which was both a blessing and a curse.

"Dekho! Did you know your Fawad Khan[22] is in a new movie?" My mom was sweet, and under normal circumstances I would have proceeded to freak the heck out because it'd been ages since Fawad Khan had been in a new movie. Instead, it was another thing Jon Slate's words took away from me. Because now instead of freaking the heck out, I was wondering if it was weird that I got excited about my favorite Pakistani actor getting a new gig. *Was* it weird that I had a favorite Pakistani actor?

I shoved my hands in my pocket and mumbled a response. "Oh, that's cool."

My mom shook her head, surprised at my lack of enthusiasm. Her kohl-lined eyes held mine for a second before patting the spot next to her in a clear invitation to sit down.

"What's wrong? School mein kuch hua?" I sighed deeply and flopped onto the couch.

"Nothing." Remember that thing about not being cool about boys? I couldn't tell her what had really happened because she'd be mad that I went (a) off campus for lunch without telling her and (b) with a boy she didn't know. Having protective Desi parents[23] meant that while I loved them dearly, there was a wall we couldn't get past.

Then my mom put her arm around me and pulled me close. She might not be a cool mom, but she was a good mom. I hugged her back. There was the blessing.

---

[22] It is a complete travesty that Fawad Khan's IMDb page is not a thousand movies long, because I deserve a thousand movies with his handsome face in them.

[23] Not all Desi parents were like mine, obviously. Divya's mom was the Cool Desi Mom™—the unicorn that fit into the very-Hollywood ideal of "Oh, my mom? She's my best friend." Who even???

"Thanks, Mom."

She squeezed my shoulder. But then shifted to pinching my cheeks, and I squirmed to get away.

"Mom!"

"Sorry, bete." She laughed. "But your cheeks are just so perfect and round, sometimes I have to pinch them." She shifted to push up from the couch. "Homework hai? Bring it to the table. I'll cook and you can do work." And there was the curse.

An hour later, I was sitting at the counter, books spread out, idly typing words into and then deleting words out of the document open on my computer. My mom bustled around the kitchen, preparing dinner. The smell of onions and garlic sizzling in hot oil had me feeling safe and sheltered. Although . . . would I be more appealing if we were eating . . . I don't know . . . green bean casserole?

I held in a snort. My mom would probably die first[24].

It had been about five hours since my disaster of a lunch and I was ready to talk to my friends. I opened the chat program on my laptop and opened the group message with Divya and Neil.

PAYAL MEHTA

Hiiiiii

NEIL PATEL

FINALLY

DO

YOU

---

[24] Followed by me dying for want of a good paratha.

KNOW
WHAT
TIME
IT
IS

DIVYA BHATT

srsly, payal, what happened??

PAYAL MEHTA

lol

NEIL PATEL

WELL????????

My hands hovered over the keyboard in indecision. How was I going to handle this? I started pressing keys until I had something. I sat back and reread it.

PAYAL MEHTA

This time he threw up on my heart.

That was probably not it. I pressed the backspace key and started over, typed away, and then hit send before I could second-guess myself again.

PAYAL MEHTA

He took me to lunch, we had a great time, I thought he was into it, and then he said I was cool and that if he was Indian he'd date me and that I should meet his Indian friend Rohit.

A few long minutes passed by. The ellipsis of someone typing kept popping up and disappearing. I tried focusing on the sounds of the daal and sabzi simmering behind my laptop screen—my mom had three pots on the stove and had moved on to creating the atta for the roti. She kneaded the dough, punching down into it, her hands shining with oil and water.

Finally, my computer dinged with a response.

NEIL PATEL
That's . . . really messed up.
DIVYA BHATT
I'm so mad for you, girl!!

The messages came nearly in tandem, and I had to wonder if they were texting about me separately.

Well, this is awkward. We have to plan how to talk to you so we don't mess it up. Phantom Neil was smart. If the situation were reversed and he or Divya had gone through the afternoon I had, I wouldn't know what to say either.

PAYAL MEHTA
Yeah. It sucked.
NEIL PATEL
Sry, dude. Gross, ignorant yt dudes.
DIVYA BHATT
Ugh! You're too good for him anyway.

I paused, considering what to say to change the subject, and then a separate chat window popped up on my screen.

PHILIP KIM

> Hey. I started working on the psych project already, so if you wanna put ur name on it, let me know. 😈

With a shock, I remembered Philip had been the last person to see me before I had lunch with Jon! Did he secretly jinx me??? It was that ridiculous thought that made me realize maybe I was losing it. Without answering Philip, I closed my laptop with a bang.

My phone dinged almost immediately, signaling a text from Neil asking if my internet went out, and then a second in quick succession asking if he could fill Finn in on what happened. I shot a text back letting him know I was going to go offline until tomorrow and that he could tell Finn whatever.

"AAAAH, kyaa banari hai, Deepa?" My dad's deep voice echoed in from the garage, beating him into the room by a few seconds. Before my mother could answer him, or even say hello, the landline rang as his house slipper tapped softly against the kitchen tile. He rushed to answer the phone.

"Hello? . . . Who? Why? Who are you? . . . It is dinnertime. Payal will have to call you back." He glanced at me as he said that last line. That couldn't be good. Who would be calling the house phone asking for *me*? I thought the landline was for spam and my dadi-ji in India, who adamantly refused to write down any other phone numbers.

My mom had paused rolling out the last roti and was looking at me. She subtly nodded at the phone. I made a face and shrugged.

"Payal. Who is this American boy calling for you?" I turned back to face my father.

My dad's not an imposing man at first glance. He's *maybe* five foot six, clean-shaven, and has finely coifed hair . . . always very well put together. When new friends meet him, they're always impressed with him. *"Payal, your dad is so cool. He looks so young,"* et cetera, et cetera, et cetera. It's annoying because usually when they're talking about how awesome he is, he's yelling at me in Hindi to clean my room. Now he was in one of the tailored suits that he wore to his practice every day, but with a look that could strike the fear of god(s) into you. Sometimes I thought my dad might have been a scary Halloween mask in his last life. Right now, he used that scary mask energy to glare at me.

"What? I have no idea. What was his name?" I frowned.

"Philip, no surname." His expression matched mine.

But at his words, I hung my head, because why did you call my *house*, Philip Kim? Why?

"Oh, that's Philip Kim." Out of the corner of my eye, I saw my mom go back to finishing up the roti for dinner. My dad was standing on the other side of the counter still holding his briefcase, staring at me as if he could figure out whether I was going on dates with an evil boy named Philip Kim just by seeing the truth of it on my face. I carefully settled my features into something neutral.

"Jaante hain? Yeh American?" My dad loved to talk about "Americans" like I wasn't one. Most of the time it was funny; right now it was annoying. The false neutrality broke, and I sighed.

"Yes, I know the *American*, Dad. We're partners on a psychology project." His mood immediately brightened.

"Oh, why didn't he say it was for school?! Stupid boy. Chalo, make sure you call him back." He started to head upstairs to get into more comfortable clothes before dinner.

"Dad, you know that I'm American, right?" I asked him, not for the first time.

"Payal, don't be silly. I know you're *very* American." It wasn't the first time he mocked me with that answer. After the day I'd had, I almost replied and asked if he'd consider calling Jon Slate and telling *him* that. But I bit my tongue. I was just sad, not trying to get murdered by my own father.

Besides, I knew some of my dad's annoyance came from the fact that his dad—my papa-ji—tried to immigrate here in the 1970s but hated it so much that he went back to India after, like, eleven months. Knowing that didn't make my dad's teasing any less irritating, though.

"Oi! Arun! Don't go upstairs and turn on the TV, okay, khana taiyar hai!" My mom knew my dad too well.

"Haan ji, haan ji." He called back to her from the stairs.

"Payal, table to set karo." I got up from my perch at the counter and pulled plates and glasses out of the cabinet. "Who is Philip?" Mom was moving food from the pots into serving dishes. Dinnertime was for real in my house. Mom did not mess around.

"He's no one—some jerk from class. Mr. Lutton made us be partners."

She paused her movement and caused some daal to drop onto the counter as a result. She rushed to grab a wet paper towel to stop the haldi from permanently staining the surface yellow. Once that near disaster was averted, she looked at me again.

"Payal, you don't need to say such mean things." I rolled my eyes at her obvious naivety.

"Mom, trust me when I say this"—I grabbed the rice and daal from her to place on the table—"Philip Kim can handle it."

And I knew it was true—Philip might be my nemesis, but we had an agreed-upon mutual respect for our disrespect! I nearly dropped the glass I was holding as I was hit with a sudden realization—was Jon Slate a new nemesis *worse* than Philip Kim?

CHAPTER EIGHT

In the parking lot, the cool morning air mixed with our state's famous humidity to make my skin feel extra clammy. I was *not* into it. I'd emailed Philip before going to bed to meet me before homeroom so we could go over whatever his idea was for the experiment. Our project deserved at least some of my focus, but I couldn't stop thinking about how I wasn't American[25] enough for Jon Slate or for my parents or for . . . maybe anyone at all.

I leaned against the side of my car and knocked my heel against the tire. Why was I letting this affect me so much? I didn't want to be the kind of girl who let a cute boy ruin her self-esteem. According to society, I was supposed to be strong and independent and not care about anyone else's opinion but my own. *But that's hard.* I scowled at the empty lot around me. Now I felt bad because of Jon's ignorance and how easily he'd implied that I was only an option for his Indian friend *and* because I cared about what he thought. I let my head fall back against the roof of the Honda and stared up at the sky. There was a huge, cartoonishly fluffy cloud passing by, and I wished on it to stop thinking about Jon Slate and his annoying opinions.

The sound of wheels turning into the gate broke through my

---

[25] Nothing like having a long history of your immigrant parents equating being American with being white. One might get some kind of complex or something.

thoughts. Philip pulled into the spot next to me. I watched him get his things together and wondered if he ever went through the same thing I was experiencing—people making assumptions about who he was based on his culture. Like me, he couldn't hide how different he was. He didn't only hang with other Korean kids, though; his friend group was a mixed bag. If there was one commonality within his friend group, it was that they were people who liked to talk about being smart.

I wasn't being mean; it was a fact. He opened his door and unfolded out of his tiny compact to join me in my leaning.

"How do you even fit in that car?" I asked, but I knew the question sounded more tired than biting.

"Very comfortably, Mehta. What's up your butt?" I shot him a stink eye. But he didn't even notice, choosing instead to survey the path to the school ahead of us. Like he was deliberately not looking at me. My stink eye shifted to a glare.

"Nothing, jerk. Tell me your idea that we probably won't even do because I'm sure it won't be good." Philip laughed at me, and I glowered. He scrubbed at the back of his head before shaking it.

"Okay, we will not go into Payal Mehta's weird psyche and instead I'll tell you about my excellent plan to get us both A's on this project." But before Philip could go into it, another car turned into the lot. We both turned toward the sound, and then I did a double take. It couldn't be. It was a Kia. A Kia containing a guy who'd thrown me into the depths of an identity crisis. *Shit*. I immediately dropped down to a crouch on the ground between my car and Philip's. "Mehta?" Philip looked down at me, his bangs hanging forward so I could see thin black brows drawn together in confusion.

"Shhh!" I reached up and yanked on his sleeve to get him to

duck down with me. He landed next to me with a thud.

"Ow—*hey*—what is happening right now?" He started to get back up, which could not happen.

"Just stay down, Philip. Please!" His eyes widened and he nodded, pulling his knees up and falling back against his car door.

"Okay, okay." He was talking to me like I was a scared puppy. I did not care for it.

"Don't patronize me! I just . . . don't want to see . . . someone." *Good job at explaining that one, Payal.* He gave me a deadpan stare and then crawled to peek around the hood of his car to see who I could possibly be talking about. "Philip! No!" I said as emphatically as I could while still being quiet enough to not be noticed by Jon Slate.

"Is that . . . Jon?" Jon was making his way to the school doors. Why did this keep happening? He never came to school early, and now two days in one week? "Oh, right. I heard about the vomit thing. Things." He looked back at me and how I was ducking my head extra deep into my hoodie. "This seems . . . excessive, though. Even for you, Mehta. Didn't I see him give you a very public apology?"

I covered my face with my hands.

"*Please* stop talking," I said into my palms before pulling my hands back down to see what was happening. Philip had turned back to watch Jon walk into the school. I fell onto my butt and sat on the cold, hard ground. Is this how it was going to be every time I saw him? Having to sit through the burn of inadequacy his words had manifested to run through my veins over something I couldn't. Even. Change. Something I didn't want to change!

"Okay . . . I'm standing up now if that's alright with you." Philip didn't wait for me to answer. He stood and dusted off the knees of his black jeans. I stayed seated. "Seriously, Mehta, what is with the drama? Who cares about that pill?" He softened his harsh words with a hand out to help me. I sighed and took it, surprised by how strong his grip was as he pulled me up. He let go as soon as I was standing, and I stretched my fingers out before running them through my hair, pushing it off my face.

"It's not the throwing-up thing. That was . . ." I paused, looking for the right words to finish the sentence, before finally deciding on "whatever." I pulled the sleeves of my hoodie over my hands. "He took me to lunch yesterday."

"Oh damn. Is that where you were running to with your face looking like that?" Philip gave me an appraising look, one eyebrow cocked.

"With my face looking like *what*?" I challenged. That was one thing I didn't regret; I'd looked cute yesterday! Philip looked away from me, and instead of answering, he went back to the subject of Jon Slate.

"Didn't know Slate knew how to talk to people who don't know the Big East schedule by heart."

"Shut up. It was his way of apologizing, I guess. He was trying to do a nice thing. I don't even know why I'm telling you this." Why was I telling Philip Kim *anything*? He was standing there in his annoying polo with his annoying bomber jacket with all the annoying pins stuck on it. The morning sun glinted off the shifting pins as he shrugged.

"I don't know, man. So, he took you to lunch and now you have to duck between our cars like you're on the run after a bank heist?"

I opened the back door to my car and sat, legs hanging over the edge. "I thought it was a date, and he thought it was a great time to set me up with his other random brown friend."

"Oh . . . *Yikes*." Philip had stayed leaning against the driver's side. The open door was between us. "That's . . . shitty."

"Yeah." It was surprising that Philip was being nice. I didn't trust him. "Look, it was humiliating, but please don't use this against me." He moved to throw his arms over the door and leaned down, resting his chin on his crossed arms. There was a small bemused smile on his face.

"Against you? I'm not your enemy, Mehta."

I looked up at him and was immediately disoriented by the angle. His cheekbones looked like they could cut glass. "Aren't you?" I had to ask. We'd been competing forever. He tilted his head to the right.

"Feels like Jon Slate's more of an enemy than I am. That was a fucked-up thing he said to you."

"You don't think I'm overreacting?" More cars were pulling in, and the lot was starting to fill up. Soon Neil would get in and find me so we could dissect the entire afternoon. But for some reason, I wanted to get Philip's perspective. He wouldn't lie to me, because he had no reason to spare my feelings.

"No. Look, Mehta. I know we screw with each other over grades and shit. But I am telling you that that wasn't cool." It was a strange kind of relief, being validated by someone you constantly disagree with.

"Thanks, Philip." I put my fingers through the handle above the window and pulled myself up. After shutting the door, I turned to look him in the eye. "But if you say anything about this, I'll take you down, cool?"

His cheek indented in a telltale sign that he was biting the inside to keep from laughing. The scar under his eye disappeared as his eyes scrunched with suppressed mirth.

"Philip! Seriously!"

He raised his hands in acquiescence. "Okay, okay. I swear that I won't say anything." He pulled his phone out of his pocket to look at the time. "And now that we've spent the whole morning talking about your boy issues—"

"Hey!"

He continued as if I hadn't spoken. "We don't have time to go over the experiment. Lunch?"

"Payal!" Neil was waving to me from the stairs to the school. I pulled my backpack onto my shoulders and nodded at Philip.

"Yeah, that works. Let's meet in the media center." He shot me a quick thumbs-up before rushing off to do whatever it was that Philip Kim did before class started.

"Well, now you can put Slate into the thanks-but-no-thanks column, right?" Neil had been trying to find the bright side of yesterday's fiasco since I met up with him at the school steps. It was exactly what I did *not* want to go through.

"I guess."

I took stock of the people we passed in the hallway while we walked to class. It was South Florida, so it wasn't like there wasn't a decent number of non-white kids at the school. That didn't stop so many of us from feeling the *minority* label pretty hard. When I was little, I'd endured taunts about weird smells or being dark or ugly, but as I'd gotten older, it seemed like people had realized that those jokes weren't that funny. Or maybe it was the mainstream proliferation of yoga and chai? Who knows. Whatever the reason, they'd stopped, mostly.

At the very least, I'd stopped hearing them.

If I was being honest with myself, I did always wonder if there were cliques where the jokes continued. I took another look around. Was it just me or was the hallway more monochromatic than I remembered? I'd spent my whole life knowing I was Indian, but it had rarely felt like a reason for me to be an outcast at my high school[26]. I mean, there had been that month in ninth grade when Kevin Miller had called me Curry Pie for a week, but he was kidding, and it was harmless. At least that was how my teacher had described it when I told on Kevin. So I brushed that kind of stuff off. And it wasn't like the real world, where the words I feared were *terrorist* or *un-American*. Honestly, I'd take *Curry Pie* over *terrorist* any day of the week.

"Payal, are you listening to me?" I looked to my left in surprise to find it vacant of my best friend. Neil had stopped walking and was several feet behind me, tapping his foot. He was unconcerned by the crowds of kids trying to get around him. My kingdom for that confidence.

"Umm, no. But I've had a very trying day and it's not even eight o'clock yet."

He gave me his best uncle look. "That's not an excuse, but I will agree you've had an eventful few days." He shook it off and resumed. "What I was saying was that Slate's as beige as I thought, and we are moving on from that silly little crush. Come on." He grabbed my hand and pulled me back into the walk to our classes.

"It sucks that what he said isn't even about me. It's about some

---

[26] Even when people were being trash in the real world, the microcosm of my life was fine. Is this what they mean when they say "rude awakening"? Because this was rude as hell.

garbage preconception. That *sucks*. It's like *I'm* not involved at all. I don't like feeling like nothing I do matters." My shoulders slumped, and I dropped my head.

"Oi, mere jaan[27], let's pull back a little. He's a sheltered, myopic, ignorant dude who, honestly, isn't good enough for you."

I rolled my eyes. "Okay, Mom."

"No, seriously. You're too good for him." We reached Neil's homeroom, and he paused a few steps away from the door. "I'll see you at lunch?" he asked. I shook my head.

"I can't. I have to meet up with Philip Kim about psych."

Neil grimaced and walked backward into the door to push it open. "Ew, okay, well, text me when you're done." With that, he disappeared into Dr. Raiford's classroom, and I was left to make the rest of my way to class on my own. I stretched out the straps dangling from my backpack and held them taut while I headed to my own homeroom. The crowd around me was shrinking as kids dropped into their classes, but I still kept my measured pace, thinking and thinking and thinking.

The whole situation really was unfair. Why should I give up on a crush I had for the entirety of my high school experience because Jon didn't see how great I was for someone like *him*? If he didn't like me, or my personality, fine. But he what? Didn't know Indian people could date white people, I guess? He assumed, without any of my input whatsoever, that because of where my parents were from, I was not a viable option for his dating life.

I stopped short.

How was *that* acceptable?

---

[27] A beautiful sentiment because we are each other's lives . . . and not because we are dangerously codependent.

70

You know what? It wasn't! I felt my eyebrows tightening, in a way that my mom said would give me wrinkles, at the injustice of it all. Jon didn't get to categorically decide who was appropriate for me to date. What kind of modern woman would I be if I let him? No one could make that decision but me. I was in charge of my own destiny! As I reached my class door, I squared my shoulders and made a decision.

Jon Slate was going to fall for *me*.

CHAPTER NINE

Philip and I were sitting in the media center trying to work on our psych project. Usually, the center was a hub of activity, but since it was lunchtime, there were only a few scattered groups in the room and it hadn't been difficult to get a table to ourselves. He'd started talking as soon as I'd sat down, and I wasn't sure he'd even taken a breath. I was, to my immense frustration, having trouble focusing. His words blurred while I absentmindedly doodled. All of a sudden, a hand slammed down on my notebook, breaking through the seventh flower I was sketching out along the border. My head shot up, and I glared at Philip. He met my annoyed expression with one of his own, the corners of his mouth down turned far enough to almost be comical.

"Mehta! Would you please pay attention? I don't want my grade dropping because I got paired with someone who won't pull her weight."

I looked at him in disbelief. "Okay, relax, no need to be hyperbolic. You know I'll handle myself. Stop pretending like I'm bad at this class; we have the same grade."

"What chapter did I just tell you we need to go over before we write up our hypothesis?"

I winced. Philip waited with mock patience for an answer to his question that I knew he knew I didn't have. His dark eyes surveyed me, and there was a tiny condescending quirk to his lips. The jerk!

"Umm." I held out the sound longer than was necessary to see if my subconscious had picked up anything Philip had said. But of course not. Gods forbid my brain ever actually came through for me. "Twelve?" Philip's eyes closed, and his head fell back, like his irritation with me was so overwhelming he had to shut out the world. Then he pinched the bridge of his nose, shook his hair out of his eyes, and took a deep breath before replying.

"I said chapter seven, because that's the one that mentions the Stroop effect and that's what we should test, Mehta." He picked up his notes and started flipping through the pages. Philip wanted to work on psychology. Unfortunately for him, all I wanted to do was get started on planning how to make Jon Slate less casually racist in his perception of potential romantic partners.

Wait, what did Philip say?

"Did you say the Stroop effect? That's so basic. We'd just be handing out surveys to lowerclassmen and seeing how fast they get mixed up when the word *green* is in a red font color."

"No, it's not, and people who aren't paying attention don't get to have an opinion." Valid. Annoying, but valid.

"Look, I'm sorry I'm so distracted. But . . . Philip . . ." I tapped my pencil against the table in a quick staccato. "Jon Slate thinks he can't date me because I'm brown." Dropping my chin into my clasped hands, blatant frustration bled into my voice. "That is completely unacceptable."

Philip dropped his binder to the table, scattering dust motes into the sunlight streaming through a window over his shoulder.

"What? Okay?"

"He thinks I'm cute and funny, and only good enough for his Indian friend. If he wants to reject me because he doesn't like me, fine! But . . . he does! He thinks I'm *cute* and *funny*." I punctuated the adjectives by stabbing my pencil into my notebook.

"Well, he's not the best judge of people," Philip said, his tone bored. I shrugged off his insulting interjection. "Also, I don't care." He looked back down at the open book in front of him, frowning slightly.

"I have two questions: Who made him the boss of my dating life? Where does he get off?" I ticked off the thoughts against my fingers as I spoke.

"Probably the bathroom?" Philip was idly flipping pages of our psych textbook and looking at me with definite disinterest.

"Dude!" I slammed my notebook closed. "This is not a joke, Philip! This could be a revolution."

He groaned and quickly glanced around, presumably to see if anyone had heard my outburst. "Whoa, whoa, whoa. I know we had a moment this morning, but I do not want to get pulled into some wacky adventure with you, Mehta. The only thing I want is to get an A on this project."

He pushed his chair back and made as if to get up. A light bulb went off in my brain, and I put an arm out to stop him. This was perfect. Philip was perfect!

"Wait, no, you're exactly the partner I need for this. You can analyze it without thinking about my feelings because, like you said, *you don't care*. This is . . . actually ideal." He really could help me make this happen! Neil had spent the morning telling me to move on, plus, he and Divya would treat me with kid gloves. They'd probably pretend to help while they were actually pushing me to get over it all.

But Philip . . . If I could get his buy-in, he'd *have* to get this to work out if only to show that I couldn't do this without his help. If nothing else but the spirit of competition! Our rivalry[28]! Philip stared at me for a second while I bit my lip and waited for his answer. His expression was strange, at first thoughtful, but it quickly shifted into something more opaque. Under the table, I crossed my fingers. Then he sighed and mechanically started packing his things into his canvas messenger bag. Apparently, Philip was unwilling to recognize my—frankly—inspired idea.

"I'm not going to be a part of *Operation End Racism with Love*. I am not interested."

I scrambled for something to make this more appealing to him. Philip Kim was the ticket to making this work. I was sure of it. Oh, right! What did Philip want more than anything?

"Wait, if you help me, we can do whatever project you want for this psych thing. You can take the lead. And *when* we get an A, I'll say it was aaaall you."

He stopped buckling his shoulder bag closed. His deep brown eyes looked right into mine, a clear calculation whirring behind them. I gritted my teeth to keep the smile off my face.

"Whatever project I want?" he repeated, tone leery.

I didn't look away. "*Whatever* project you want."

"And you'll tell *Mr. Lutton* that I came up with it and you followed my lead?"

I took a deep breath. It was worth it. It was worth it. It was worth it.

---

[28] Once, in tenth grade, we accidentally made eye contact across the lunchroom and immediately got into a who-could-finish-their-lunch-faster contest. He fell and sprained his wrist on the way to the tray dump trying to get ahead of me . . . so, I won.

It was totally worth it.

"Yes."

He waited a minute. I could see him arguing with himself in a way I'd seen him do a dozen times before, eyes shifting back and forth between the pros and cons happening in his mind. Then he sat back down and pulled his psych binder out again.

"Okay. I'm in. *But* first we work on this project and then I will help you plan this disaster of a romantic comedy."

"As long as it's not a tragedy, am I right?" I raised my hand for a high five, and that asshole left me hanging.

Neil was already waiting for me at my car after the last class let out for the day. Massive headphones covered his ears, and his hands hammered against the roof of my car, playing an imaginary tabla. I grinned. He looked like he didn't have a care in the world. I knew that couldn't be true, because statistically there is no such thing as a teen who is perfectly at ease with themselves.

He stopped drumming when he saw me coming and settled his headphones around his neck. Then he greeted me with a song and a dramatically outstretched hand.

"Eh ajnabi, tu bhi kabhi, avaaz de kahin se[29]."

"Ha ha. You are very funny. I'm not even late." I opened the car with a click and slid behind the wheel. "Also, why am I giving you a ride? Where's Finn?" Neil flopped into the passenger side and immediately buckled his seat belt. I hadn't even turned the car on yet.

---

[29] Ha. Ha. Ha. Neil had waited so long at my car for me that I was now a literal stranger, if I was interpreting his *Dil Se* reference correctly.

"He had to stay late for Key Club." His tone suggested there was more to it, but Phantom Neil *and* the closed-off look on IRL Neil's face told me I should not pursue that line of questioning. The sounds of the Joy Crookes song he must have been listening to burst out of the speakers as I hit the ignition button. Best friends already have their Bluetooth attached to your car.

"Ooookay." I absentmindedly drummed my fingers on the steering wheel to the beat of the song while I thought about how to change the subject. After turning out of the lot and onto South Quad Street and passing by the Islands of Adventure billboard—the one that featured something called Dagwood and Blondie on it—I finally asked, "Did you see Divya today?" I hadn't seen her that day; we didn't have classes that overlapped, and lunch had been, well, busy.

"Yeah, she said we needed to do a video chat later."

"'Kay, I'll probably be free after dinner. Will you text her and let her know?" Lightly pressing down on the brake at a stoplight, I clicked on my blinker to turn right. I glanced in Neil's direction and found him tapping a message into his phone. He didn't stop typing to ask me his next question.

"How was your lunch date with Philip Kim?"

I snorted and shot him a look. "It wasn't a date. And it was uneventful, though I think he's going to institute an obnoxiously intense schedule for this psych experiment. Because he's obnoxiously intense." I tried to keep the lie off my face. I wasn't ready to share my plan with Neil, and I didn't want him to try and talk me out of it yet. Phantom Neil had been doing a great job of that all afternoon, ever since Philip had agreed to help me.

Yes, he had. And he would again. This is a bad idea.

Anyway, if I waited for our virtual hangout, that way I could tell Divya and Neil together. It'd be perfect.

"Typical Kim." I was surprised that he didn't have more to say. I'd been complaining about Philip to Neil for years, and I usually got more than two words in response. I looked at him out of the corner of my eye again, but he was facing away from me, staring out of the window.

"You're being weird."

So much for not getting into it. The light turned green, and I turned onto Belvedere.

Next to me, Neil shrugged without turning to face to me. "Maybe you're being weird."

"Neil."

"Payal."

Without taking my eyes off the road, I reached into the cup holder next to me to grab a few soda-sticky pennies that I could throw at him.

"Do not throw those disgusting coins at me, Payal."

I closed my fingers around them and brought my fist up to my shoulder in the most threatening of fashions.

"I can't take off a chappal[30] to hit you with because I'm driving, and also I'm wearing sneakers, so this will have to do. Tell me what's going on or I'll throw these at you." I slowed to a stop as we pulled up to another red light. I turned to stare at Neil, who was clearly facing away from me on purpose. "Neil, what is going on?"

"I tried to talk about your thing with Finn today and he did not get it. He didn't understand why you were making such a big deal out

---

[30] Was there anything more anxiety inducing than an auntie holding her Panchgani-made brown sandal in the air ready to bring it down on your head?

of it. He said that sometimes things don't work out."

I cringed. And then turned right onto Neil's subdivision. We were quiet for a few minutes as I followed the winding neighborhood streets.

"Oh." I didn't know what to say. We were coming up to his house, a two-story salmon stucco eyesore as familiar to me as my own. I turned into his driveway and put the car in park. Before I could open my mouth, Neil started talking.

"I didn't go into this like some naive nothing. I'm Desi, I'm gay, and it's not like I didn't know prejudice exists. And I know he knows it. We're both out teens. In *Florida*. Our government would probably throw a parade if all of us . . . ceased to exist. Like, of *course* we get it. But this time, it was like we weren't even speaking the same language?!" His hands were on his lap, twisting up together in knots in clear exasperation. "He kept saying it wasn't a big deal. It was just a little thing. It wasn't like he called you a racist name, or told you were ugly because of your skin."

I flinched and asked, "How'd it end?"

"It didn't. He had to go to Key Club, and I left to meet you. God. I feel so small." He slouched down into his seat, his hair flopping down and over his eyes so I couldn't see them. It wasn't a look I liked seeing from him. I was surprised that Finn didn't understand where Neil and I were coming from.

"I'm sorry." It sucked when you didn't know how to make something better.

He finally turned back to me and gave me a half grin. "Me too. But it's fine."

Now I scoffed. He stretched his shoulders back, straightened, and immediately seemed more like himself. He curled his fingers around the door handle but paused before pulling it.

"No, seriously. It's fine. Or it will be fine. We're too hot to let this get in the way of a good thing." He was leaning on bravado and we both knew it. But I wasn't about to blow up his spot. So all I could do was nod. Neil did pull the handle then and swung the door open.

"Can't argue with someone when they're right. But, Neil . . . do you think Finn might have a point?" He stalled, one foot out of the car, and turned back to me.

"Because it might not really be a big deal?" he asked.

"I don't know. Like, we know it made me feel crappy. But at the end of the day, the only thing that happened was that I feel bad, and I'll get over it."

"But why should you feel bad about something you can't control, something that's just a basic truth about you?"

"I don't know," I said, now understanding what Neil meant by feeling small. "I mean—" I stumbled. I didn't know what I wanted to say, let alone how to say it.

"I'm definitely going to talk to Finn again, but don't obsess over this, okay? You didn't do *anything wrong*."

"'Kay, I'll talk to you online." As he shut the car door, I saw his mom at the entrance of his house waving him in. I threw my hand up in greeting as I backed out of their driveway to head home.

CHAPTER TEN

"Yikes, that sounds awful." Divya's voice coming through the speakers was lagging a bit behind her video, and it was really distracting. I'd finished giving her a rundown of the date from hell while we were waiting for Neil to sign on. Then I'd definitely tell them about the plan and working with Philip Kim. One hundred percent. I shook my head. I needed to focus. Divya's mouth was moving, but no sound was coming out. She flung her hand up, and the video froze. All of a sudden, her words flew out of the speakers in a rush.

"Where-does-he-even-get-off-with-his-you-need-to-meet-Rohit-garbage-like-he-can-spot-a-good-Desi-dude?" Her hand finally came back down as the image and audio reconnected. "You know Rohit probably sucks anyway."

"Divya, that is not the point, and you know it." I grabbed a pillow and hugged it to my chest. I was sitting on my bed, hunched over my laptop like some kind of gremlin[31].

"I know, I know. I'm really sorry you had to go through that, and I think you acted like a freakin' queen, considering I would've absolutely asked him what exactly he meant by that."

---

[31] Making fun of someone's angles during a virtual hang when they've had a bad day? Red flag. My friends would never.

"I wish you were there so that you *could* have, to be honest." I was about to continue, but the telltale ding of Neil signing on interrupted my thoughts. "I'm adding Neil to the call, Div. Give me a second." She nodded and clearly clicked over to whatever else was open on her desktop.

"Hey! Sorry I'm late. I was on the phone with Finn." Neil's face popped up, splitting my screen into three. His hair was standing straight up like he'd been pulling at it, and I could see glimpses of colorful album covers littering the wall behind his head.

"Oh yeah? Are you guys okay?"

He waved my questions off. "Yeah, yeah, we're fine. Div, you caught up on this one's latest drama?" Neil's eyes glanced at where, I assumed, I was sitting on his computer screen. He was changing the subject.

"Ugh. Yes. There's a fifty-fifty chance that I'll confront Jon tomorrow to see what he expected to come out of that experience," Divya said. I choked on my own spit. No, she would not.

"DON'T YOU DARE, DIVYA . . ." I paused. May as well rip this Band-Aid off and tell them now, before I lost my nerve. "Anyway, I have a plan."

Neil narrowed his eyes. "Well, that gives me a bad feeling." He leaned forward and gave me an intense look through the camera, his dark eyes wide and searching. I tried to remember my conversation with Philip so I could convince them this was a good idea. But the more I thought about it, the clearer I could hear their reactions. Divya would look at me with pity, which she was doing now, but somehow it would be *even more* pitying, and that was the opposite of what I wanted. Neil would sigh and tell me that I shouldn't be partnering with Philip on anything because he'd for sure sabotage it.

82

Like Phantom Neil had been telling me throughout the day.

And would continue to do.

"No, no, don't get a bad feeling. It's nothing, really. I might . . ." What, what would I do? How did I get out of telling them? I did not want them to talk me out of it. This was a good idea. They wouldn't be able to see that. I searched through my thoughts for anything.

"You might . . ." Divya prompted. They were both looking at me expectantly.

"Uh . . . write him a letter. I might write him a note to explain to him why I acted so weird on the way back to school."

"Payal, I love you, but that is a *terrible* idea." Neil rested his head in his hands and covered his eyes. As if *I* was causing *him* stress. Then he looked up again sternly. "Just let it go and move on. Who needs him? There are so many other people in that school to talk to and look at and crush on. He doesn't have anything particularly amazing to offer."

"He's handsome and nice. Last week, that guy Nick was bullying Eric, and Jon made him stop," I said, only slightly petulant. Neil rolled his eyes.

"What a high bar—" he started, only to be cut off by Divya singing.

"*Let it gooo, let it gooo.*" Ironically enough, she was frozen again, but her voice came through loud and clear. I wished for the reverse.

"I don't know. We'll see." I shrugged noncommittally. "I haven't decided on anything yet." I frowned. Lying to people you loved was not a great first step in an epic plan . . . Although, by preemptively telling me to move on, they were not being supportive of my plan, so . . . really, they were asking me to lie to them. *Good one, brain. Way to be on my side, for once.*

"Divya!" Divya's door banged open behind her, and her dad, Prem

Uncle, flung himself into the room. "Su kare che? Jamvanu che[32]."
Divya turned to her dad, completely unfazed by his unnecessarily
dramatic entrance.

"Dad, I'm almost done. I'll be down in five minutes."

"Accha, accha, who is there?" He squinted at the screen over the
tops of his glasses, mouth frowning under his mustache before he
straightened and grinned when he recognized us. "Ah! Payal! Neil!
Kem cho! Tame be store nathi avya."

"Hi, Uncle," Neil and I spoke in tandem. But then Neil kept going.
"Let us know when you start serving pani puri again, and we're
there!" Divya's dad laughed in response.

"Okay, okay, ji." He patted Divya's shoulder and waved goodbye
to us after giving her a look[33]. Divya's parents ran one of the local
Indian grocery stores. There was a six-month period that we ate
there constantly, but then a Starbucks opened up next to the movie
theater and that became our go-to hangout spot. Honestly, there's
only so much bhel that a girl can eat. But her dad missing us was
almost enough to make me feel guilty. On the other hand, Starbucks
had the added bonus of no aunties coming and telling my mom that
I was ruining my appetite with kachra food.

"I gotta go. Mom's probably going to call me for dinner too, in,
like, two seconds." I wasn't lying, but sometimes it was nice to have
an overbearing Desi mother as an excuse get me out of things.

"I've only been here for, like, a second!" Neil exclaimed. By
which I mean he whined. "I need five minutes so you two can tell

---

[32] My mom's great sadness is that I don't speak Gujarati and can only sort of
understand it. But who was the one who decided we'd start with Hindi, hmm?

[33] The patented I'm-cool-but-seriously-it's-time-to-eat look that somehow every
Indian parent knew how to do.

me which kurta to wear to Divya's dance recital this weekend."

"It's not a recital; it's a *performance*." Divya gave us her best wide-eyed Bharatanatyam facial expression with one thick eyebrow raised that probably meant *You're both being assholes. Quit it.* "But okay. Show us the options. Fashion. Show."

Neil grinned. "You got it."

He disappeared off-screen.

"Are you ready for your . . . *performance?*" I asked Divya while we waited for Neil to show us his new outfits. She shrugged and pulled at the braid hanging over her shoulder.

"I don't know—it's a big deal because I think this might be my last one as a student, although I might do something for Anjali Auntie's cousin in Orlando if we go there for Holi. But it won't be the same. *And* Vikash is at his Masi's in Toronto this weekend." She frowned. Vikash was Divya's boyfriend and probably her biggest cheerleader.

"Oh man, I'm sorry, Divs. That sucks. Neil and I will cheer *extra* hard to make up for it, even though I know we can't fill his tiny shoes."

She smiled. "His shoes are not *that* tiny; he's our height. And thank you. I love you." All of a sudden, the familiar beats of Arijit Singh's latest hit sounded off in Neil's room, and I couldn't help but smile. Fashion show.

Divya laughed and clapped her hands. Neil popped onto the screen wearing a long-sleeved black tunic with a maroon embellished vest over it.

"Oh my god, that detailing. This is the one, Neil. The Nehru collar looks so good on you. I wish my neck were long enough for it."

"That's a weird thing to say, Payal, because your neck is . . . a normal length." Divya frowned.

"Shut up."

"You've got to stop listening to Rajeshri Auntie," Divya said. "Now that Sumit's at college, she doesn't have anyone to complain about."

"Hey, I have another option, you guys," Neil interrupted.

"Sorry, sorry, sorry. Please continue." I raised my hands in apology. Neil glared and walked off-screen again. "Ugh, guys look so good in Indian clothes."

"Seriously. Did you see that picture of Shahid Kapoor walking in a fashion show last year?" Divya fanned herself. I pretended to faint.

"Yes, oh—" Neil had come back on-screen, this time wearing a cream-colored kurta top, long-sleeved with a subtle print. He wore a plain dark blue Nehru vest over this one, but this time there was something more. "Neil . . . is that a pocket square? So *fancy*."

He smiled widely. "It is indeed. And I think it classes me up. I could be a *prince*."

"Sure, yes. A prince. From Palm Beach County, Florida. But this is actually better than the last one. I vote this," I said as I looked over the fit.

"I agree." Divya nodded. "The only person who will look better than you is me, and that's only because my mom is making me get my makeup professionally done for this performance." She'd barely gotten the words out of her mouth when Neil responded.

"Yeah, I'm coming to that for sure."

"Payal! Khana!" My mom's voice rung out as Neil was making his plea to join Divya for her makeup session.

"Okay, I have to go for real. I'll see you tomorrow!" I shut my laptop before they responded and pulled me into another conversation.

Alright, so I didn't tell them about the plan. To be honest, they had moved on pretty quickly from the whole situation. I wondered how much of the moving on had been from Neil and how much had been Finn talking.

I didn't really know the answer, but somehow I couldn't stop the thought from festering. This afternoon Neil had been as angry as I'd been, and now he was telling me to move on?

For the hundredth time, I cursed Jon Slate for putting this in my head. I'd been fine crushing on him from afar. Not only fine—I liked it! I liked the anticipation of wondering if he'd notice me; I liked thinking about how cute he was when he wore his baseball jersey to school. If he didn't like *me*, I could at least get over it. But he had to give me a chance.

Maybe the key was to stop thinking of this in terms of Jon Slate and more in terms of a sociological experiment. My hypothesis was that I could get the ignorant yet pleasant hot guy in my class to see me as an actual girl he could date using behavioral conditioning and maybe better clothes. I needed to sit down and work this out.

My phone buzzed next to me. I saw Philip's name and slid the lock screen open to read the text.

PHILIP KIM

> I sent you a google doc link with our psych stuff in it. I sent you a separate one for your disaster life plan. Take a look.

I opened my email on my phone as I got up to head downstairs for dinner. Two new emails, as he said. I clicked on the plan. The document was titled *Payal Mehta Makes Bad Decisions*. I rolled my eyes. In it, he'd only written two things.

- Step one: watch *She's All That* (1999)
- Step two: do the movie in real life.

How in the world was some old movie supposed to help me? Also, wasn't there a newer version of that same thing? Or maybe it was called something else?

"Payal!!!" I started, my mom's voice shaking me out of my digital haze. I clicked my phone off and headed into the kitchen to join my parents for dinner.

CHAPTER ELEVEN

The next few days passed uneventfully. There were papers due and math problems to answer. It was the final semester of my senior year. I couldn't slack just because I was crafting my own revenge-romance movie. By the time I finally had a second to breathe, it was Saturday afternoon and my mom was bustling around getting ready for aunties and uncles to come over to our house so we could go to Divya's performance in the evening together.

I had on a new salwar kameez that my masi had sent down from New Jersey. I pinched the hem along the bottom of my green salwar to keep it out of the way as I ducked to pick up one of my textbooks that had somehow ended up under the living room couch. The Anarkali-style top was so long that the tight churidar pants underneath were almost completely hidden.

"Payal! Are you ready? Arjun Uncle will be here in a few minutes," my mom called, her voice getting louder as she got closer to the living room.

"Yeah, Mom, I'm ready. I'll answer the door when they get here."

She finally appeared, and I was surprised to see her hair half-done and sari unpinned.

"Mom! Why aren't you ready?!"

"Chawal to jal gaye because your dad wasn't watching, and I had to redo it!" She was in full panic mode, which was not great.

"Mom, go finish getting ready." I gestured to the space behind her, where she'd come from. "I'll watch the rice and finish tidying up down here." She nodded once and hustled back upstairs to her room. I headed into the kitchen to take over pot-watching duty.

Is there anything more boring than watching a pot boil? Over the last few days, I'd managed to keep busy enough to not think too much about nonsense, but this seemed like a prime opportunity to wallow.

Ding-dong.

Or not. I lifted the lid and was immediately hit with the scent of ghee and cloves. Inside the pot, tiny pits had decompressed in the surface of the grains and the ghee had soaked completely in. A telltale sign of perfectly finished rice. After covering the pot and turning the flame off, I ran to get the door to greet our guests. I could see two large shadows bracketing two smaller ones through the frosted glass of our front door. As soon as the door was open, Arjun Uncle came in, belly first, followed by his family, followed by a wave of heat from the outside breaking into our air-conditioned safe haven.

"Ugh." I grimaced at the brief feel of sticky air before shutting the door closed behind them.

"Payal! Kya baat hai, yaar[34]. Your salwar is"—Arjun Uncle clicked his tongue and waved a hand at my outfit in a flashy gesture—"first class!"

His wife, Anna Auntie, smiled and nodded, too busy wrangling their tiny kids, Aman and Anya, for anything else.

---

[34] I think in his own mind, Arjun Uncle was the heir apparent to Aamitabh Bachchan, but really he was more of a Govinda.

"Thanks, Uncle. Hey, Auntie, do you need help?" I reached down to grab Anya, who was *maybe* three years old but *definitely* the *most* adorable in her little red-and-white ghagra choli. I saw that Anna Auntie had put kohl on both the kids, making their already huge eyes seem even bigger. It was painfully cute. Anna was dressed in a salwar kameez but with a shorter blue-and-yellow kameez and wide blue pants. Her dupatta was flung easily around her neck, probably to keep the kids from pulling on it too much. She shot me a tired grin and pushed her dark braids back behind her shoulders.

"Thanks, Payal. They are hopped up on something today. Hopefully lunch will settle them down before the show later." Anna was from Trinidad. She and Arjun had met while they were both in the Caribbean at med school years earlier. It was a love match, which set a really amazing example for our community in South Florida.

"Of course! I love hanging on to this puppet!" I pretended to swing Anya up like I was going to let go, and she screamed and laughed. "Let's sit in the living room. I think my mom will be down in a minute." I led them to the couches and settled Anya down on one before helping Aman join her.

"Arjun! Anna! So good to see you both." My dad came into the living room as Aman was getting settled and pulling at his sister's dupatta. Dad went in for the handshake with Arjun Uncle immediately. I shook my head; he was always so proper. He glanced at me. "Payal, did you offer them anything to eat or drink? Go, chai le au, and the snacks. I think Mom put a tray together."

Nodding at him, I headed back to the kitchen while the adults started talking about whatever it is adults talk about. Stocks, maybe? Stepping into the room, I found that my dad was right—somehow,

I'd completely missed the tray sitting on the counter next to the fridge. I pressed a finger to the side of one of the white ceramic mugs to check the temperature—lukewarm and definitely in need of a nuke. No one wants room-temperature chai. I put the cups in the microwave to heat them up. The sounds of kids squealing and adults laughing carried into the kitchen. I could picture Arjun Uncle with his arm around his wife, beaming.

Anna and Arjun somehow made it work despite not being from the exact same place culturally. He was Indian and she was Black, and they were deeply, deeply in love. My mom had told me once how difficult so many of the other aunties had been when Arjun Uncle and Anna Auntie had announced their decision to get married—there were a lot of issues in the Indian community with racism. But there'd also been a wonderful welcoming from some of our people who understood that we shouldn't fall back on old patterns and old biases. I'd been extra upset hearing about it because Anna was basically the kindest person on the planet and all of it was deeply, deeply unfair. In my mind, I couldn't understand who *wouldn't* want her to be a part of our community. Why were people so obsessed with this idea that only like can like like?!

On the counter, my phone vibrated with a notification. It was a text from Philip asking if I'd looked at the doc yet. I rolled my eyes. I still hadn't looked into whatever the heck *She's All That* (1999) was, so I googled it and brought up the Wikipedia page. The more I read, the angrier I got.

"A dorky, solitary, unpopular art student . . ."

Excuse me? So Philip Kim's idea was for me to cut my hair, put on some makeup, and wear a tight dress? As much as I would love

my own makeover montage, I was insulted that this was his big
plan. *How dare he?* I swiped back over to my messages and started
typing.

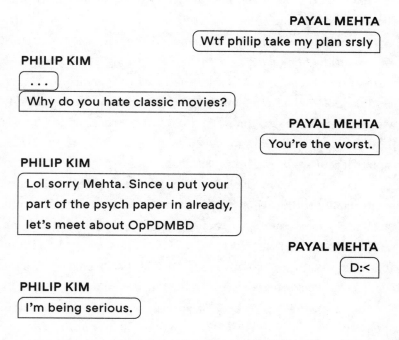

PAYAL MEHTA

Wtf philip take my plan srsly

PHILIP KIM

. . .

Why do you hate classic movies?

PAYAL MEHTA

You're the worst.

PHILIP KIM

Lol sorry Mehta. Since u put your
part of the psych paper in already,
let's meet about OpPDMBD

PAYAL MEHTA

D:<

PHILIP KIM

I'm being serious.

I started typing a snarky response and then paused. This had
been my idea. If I wasn't going to trust Philip, then I should just walk
away from the whole thing.

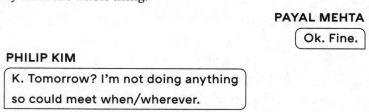

PAYAL MEHTA

Ok. Fine.

PHILIP KIM

K. Tomorrow? I'm not doing anything
so could meet when/wherever.

PAYAL MEHTA

> Let's do it at my house at like noon.

Conveniently, my parents were heading to a Desi doctors' luncheon, so I'd have the house to myself.

The microwave beeped, and I opened the door, then carefully returned the cups to the tray. The smell of ginger and cinnamon with a tinge of cardamom, anise, and black peppercorn wafted up from the hot chai. Leaving my cell phone on the counter, I carefully wrapped my fingers around the handles of the serving tray, bit my lip in concentration, and managed to bring the chai to the living room without spilling a drop. *Skills, baby.*

Anna Auntie, Arjun Uncle, and my dad had settled themselves comfortably on the living room couches. I cringed slightly as the metal tray scraped the glass of our coffee table when I set it down, but no one else seemed to notice. I passed along a cup to each of the adults and left one on the tray for my mom. The kids had been moved to the den; my dad must have gotten some old toys out for them.

"So, Payal, how is school? Almost done, yeah?" Anna Auntie asked, tucking a few thin braids behind her ear and readjusting her dupatta. She never had to ask to remember how old I was or what I was interested in, which I thought was very cool.

"It's going okay, and yeah, just a few more months."

"So that means prom is right around the corner, right? Are you going?"

My dad didn't even let her get the whole sentence out before answering on my behalf. "Payal will be with Neil and Divya. She knows she has no time for boys." Anna and I made eye contact, and I rolled my eyes. She hid a smile behind her cup.

"Arvin, kya baat karraha hai? Let them have fun, yaar." How did some kids end up with parents like Arjun Uncle or Divya's mom or even Neil's parents, but I got—

"Eh, Arjun, don't put thoughts in her head! She's a good girl. No boys-woyz nonsense." And there was my mom, as if summoned. She came into the room finally ready, with her hair pulled back, bindi sparkling between her brows, and gold jewelry dangling from her earrings and around her neck.

"Falu! That sari is beautiful." Anna lifted a hand to feel the silk of my mom's pallu[35]. The fabric was a deep, rich peacock color, with threads of gold outlining deceptively simple-looking embroidery along the bottom.

"Thank you, Anna. My cousin sent us a package of new clothes from their shop in New Jersey. We're excited to have an opportunity to show them off!"

"Well, it's stunning. You'll have to give me the name. We have Arjun's niece's wedding coming up in New York next year. They're doing fully traditional, so I need . . . what was it?" She looked over at her husband, who laughed.

"Oh, nine outfits? Ten? All these kids want to have the biggest Bollywood-style weddings these days." Arjun Uncle shook his head. "Wasteful. Though the dancing will be good."

"Ten outfits." Anna put her head in her hands in mock pain.

My mom started laughing. "Well, we'll limit Payal's wedding to one week, okay?"

I closed my eyes and shook my head. That was my cue. My skin

---

[35] I dreamed of the day that I'd be visited by the sari-draping fairy so I could stop looking like a burrito and move on to ~perfect elegance~ .

had started itching the second Anna said the word *wedding*[36], and sure enough, my mom had come through.

"Oh, do you smell the rice burning again? Better go," I said drily. Their laughter followed me out of the room as I made a break for it.

---

[36] My mother had the incredible ability to get from the first mention of a wedding or marriage to discussing my marriage or wedding within two sentences. It was like the worst version of Six Degrees of Kevin Bacon.

CHAPTER TWELVE

A few hours later—an embarrassing amount of which was spent navigating the parking lot since my dad was *always* convinced he could find a better spot—we filed into the large auditorium that Jeevan Ji owned and regularly rented out whenever children needed to dance to Bollywood music[37]. The function hall was loud in tone *and* color. There were conversations happening in a dozen different languages among the brightly attired guests. We'd only been there a few minutes and I'd already heard snippets of Gujarati, Punjabi, Marathi, Urdu, Hindi—the South Asian community was vast and varied down here. I spied Hasan Uncle, who provided halal meat to Prem Uncle's store, walking his family to the front row. He caught my eye and waved. My dad noticed and lifted his own hand in response. My parents, Arjun, Anna, and their kids moved to find seats near Hasan Uncle in the front, but I hung back, craning my neck over the crowd to find Neil and his cousins. Divya was likely already backstage. There were enough brown people milling about that I couldn't immediately find Neil, so I pulled my phone out to see if he'd texted me. I was about to pull up our text thread when a voice interrupted me.

---

[37] We celebrate literally so many holidays and events with kids dancing to Bollywood music. Like . . . an excessive amount.

"Hey, Payal. You looking for Neil?" I turned around to see Josh Patel standing behind me with a few kids I didn't know. Josh went to our high school but was in the athletic circle, which meant he was friends with Jon. I groaned internally and hoped Josh wouldn't bring it up.

"Yeah, have you seen him?" Josh rubbed at his close-cropped hair and nodded to a few rows behind him in response. I looked over and saw Neil with an open seat on one side and his little cousin Dhruv on the other. "Thanks, man."

"No problem." I took a step around him, intending to join Neil, but then Josh started speaking again. Hesitantly, I stepped back to where I'd been standing in front of him. "So, I heard you and Jon went to lunch last week." Josh didn't usually take an interest in my schedule, but then again, I didn't usually have lunch with anyone in his friend group. I took in a deep breath before responding.

"Uh-huh . . ."

"How'd it go?"

"It was fine?" I shrugged noncommittally. But Josh's query was rubbing me the wrong way. I narrowed my eyes. "Why are you asking, Josh?"

"No reason, just curious. You've never hung out with the dude before, so . . ." His eyes flitted to something behind me. "Anyway, Sarthak's here and I gotta grab something from him. I'll see you later."

"Uh, later." My brows furrowed at his retreating back. That was weird. What had Jon said to his friends about our disaster of a lunch? I wondered. Something to dig into next week when I was back at school. I made my way through the crowd to Neil and settled into the seat he'd saved for me.

"What up? Good choice on the top," I said. He'd gone with the fancier option, of course.

"Thanks. Loving your outfit too, Payal. Your Bhavna Masi knows her colors." He gestured at something behind me. "What were you talking about with Josh?" I shook my head like it wasn't anything important.

"I was asking where you were." I didn't want to get into the Jon stuff here[38].

Before Neil could ask me anything further, the overheard lights dimmed and the sounds of people talking lowered to a murmur before finally quieting entirely. The lights hit the stage, and Divya's teacher, Anjali Patanjali, came out to welcome everyone to the event. She was a tall, stern-looking woman with her hair pulled back in a severe bun at the nape of her neck. I took a single class with her when I was much younger and never went back because I was afraid of her—at least that's what my mom said. Divya always swore she's super nice. I wasn't sure I bought it.

"Namaste, everyone. For those of you who don't know me—" Some light laughter interrupted her here. Who didn't know Anjali Patanjali? "My name is Anjali, and I am the director of the Palm Beach County School of Indian Classical Dance. We're so thankful everyone could make it to celebrate the school's dance showcase tonight. I won't go on too long, but I ask that everyone please silence your cell phones." She paused here and glared at the crowd. "I don't want a repeat of what happened last year." The sound of rustling erupted in the auditorium as people hurried to double- and triple-check that their phones were, in fact, on silent. She went on for a few

---

[38] There is literally nothing on earth faster than the auntie gossip chain. From my mouth to my mom's ears in less than two milliseconds.

minutes after that before finally wrapping up and announcing the first performance, by a group of some of the younger students.

I leaned over to Neil and whispered, "How many things are there before Divya?"

Neil didn't take his eyes off the stage, where eight middle school–aged kids were dressed in their Bharatanatyam finery chum-chumming across the stage into their starting positions. The dancers' costumes matched; they were wrapped up in red-and-green saris, with gold belts shining around their waists. Thick rows of bells ran up their ankles, and white flowers adorned their braids.

"She's next and last, I think," he said back.

A deep tabla beat thrummed out from the group of musicians sitting off to the right side of the stage—*dhum, dhum, dhum, thakh, dhum*—and the kids stepped forward gracefully onto their right feet, hands poised and clasped at their hips. I sighed and settled back into my seat. Bharatanatyam *was* beautiful, but I had to be honest—I was not particularly interested in the rhythmic beats and droning music. At least there was only one dance before Divya's.

The first dance finally ended, and it was time for Divya's performance. The curtain rose, and next to me Neil clapped his hands gently in anticipation. Divya's silhouetted pose was stark against the lights behind her, every line so crisp, I could even see her individual fingers spread out in one of the intricate mudras. They looked like they were blooming out from the crossed wrists tight over her head. Her knees were bent, and the fan of her orange-and-gold sari stretched between them. A tabla started beating out from the side of the stage. The uncle playing was mopping his brow from the energy that the first group of dancers had required.

Even if I didn't care about dancing so much, I did care about Divya, and she *rocked* it—at least to my untrained eye. Her feet were hard-hitting on the stage, her payal[39] chimed loudly, and I could see her dramatic expressions even from back where we were seated.

About ten minutes into the dance, out of the corner of my eye, I saw something light up to my left. I looked toward it, and Neil was hunched over, trying to shield everyone from noticing that he was *on his phone.*

"*Neil!*" I whispered, scandalized. Anjali Auntie was not playing with her warnings. His eyes darted toward me, and he shrugged helplessly.

"Sorry—it's Finn."

"And?" I asked.

"Eh, chup!" an angry voice to our right said, and I slid down lower in my seat.

"I'll be right back." And then Neil got up and sidled his way into the aisle and out of the theater doors.

What the *hell?* I looked up at the stage and at Divya dancing, then twisted my neck back to look at Neil's retreating figure.

I sat through the rest of Divya's performance, buzzing with anxiety. This wasn't something Neil would have done lightly—leaving in the middle of something so important to one of his best friends. I tried to focus on Divya—this was her night, after all—but the *minute* the curtain dropped on Divya's once-again-static figure, dark against

---

[39] *Payal*, as in loud decorative anklet with bells on it, not as in loud . . . me.

the lights behind her, I jumped out of my seat. Apologizing to the other people in the row, I awkwardly shuffled my way to the aisle, trying not to step on anyone's feet.

"Sorry, Uncle—Auntie, eesh—"

"Beta!"

"Sorry!"

Throwing that last apology behind me as I rushed up the aisle to the exit, I focused on trying to find Neil. He wasn't in the back of the theater, so he hadn't made it back inside. The theater doors were heavy, but I pushed hard and slipped out. Onstage, Anjali Auntie was speaking into the mic, thanking everyone for attending. As the doors closed behind me, the pressurized valves let out a hiss of air. I didn't immediately spot Neil, but then I heard a series of low tones somewhere near the exit. I walked forward across the black linoleum tiles of the lobby, and as I got closer, I could tell those tones were frustrated to say the least.

"*Finn,* how can you even say something like that? Of course she has a right to be—" There was a pause here as if Finn had interrupted Neil and was saying his piece. I finally got close enough to see Neil sitting on the floor behind one of the big pillars in the lobby. He looked up at me when I got closer and rolled his eyes. "No," he said, glancing at me again. But this time there was something else in his gaze that I couldn't quite place. Discomfited, I looked away. I could usually read Neil really well.

But then I sighed and took a seat next to him, ignoring the way it would wrinkle the back of my kameez. I stretched my legs out and tapped my fingers against the floor. Neil had gone quiet again, but the muscle at the corner of his jaw was twitching like he was grinding his teeth. Finally, after a curt "Sure. Fine. See you tomorrow.

Bye," he tapped the screen to hang up and immediately leaned his head back against the pillar to stare at the ceiling.

"Soooo," I started. "Is everything . . . okay?" I wasn't sure if Neil wanted me to get involved or not, but I would if he needed it. *No one hurt my best friends.* Neil's eyes were closed, and without opening them, he shook his head lightly.

"It's fine, just having a minor disagreement with my boyfriend over stuff."

"What stuff?"

He brushed aside the question, looking away from me before answering.

"Oh, nothing. It's no big deal. We'll figure it out." The lobby was empty and quiet around us, and I kept my voice low.

"If you're sure . . ."

There was something in the way he wouldn't make eye contact with me, though. And in the way he was twisting his fingers together when he told me it was nothing. He was lying, and I didn't know why. I tapped a finger against his shoulder.

"Actually, well . . ." Neil closed his eyes. "Finn is still being weird about your shit with Jon."

I scooted away from him. That was *not* what I was expecting. "Like, how?" I asked.

I heard the door behind me open, and the chatter from the auditorium spilled into the lobby. There was movement behind us as people started heading out to their cars. I knew Neil and I had time, though. Our parents were probably talking together in the aisle.

Neil ran a hand through his hair, messing up his coif and not seeming to realize it. This must be bad.

"I don't know. I tried to explain it to him again. But I guess it was bugging him because he still didn't really understand what I was saying."

I could feel my irritation rising. Who cared if Finn didn't get it? Finn didn't *have* to get it. I had to get it, because I was the one who went through it.

"So what?" I asked. "If he doesn't get it, maybe that's something you should think about."

Neil's eyes went wide, and he turned to me. "What does that mean?"

I shrugged.

"I don't know. Like, I—I know you thought it was a big deal and you were on my side when I was feeling bad, and then you talked to Finn. After *that*, it didn't matter that much anymore. How are you guys supposed to be together if he can't understand why someone who looks like *us* might be frustrated over this?"

Neil frowned and shook his head.

"That's not fair."

I shrugged again, not sure what to say.

"It's not," he said. "It's not like Finn decides how I'm going to feel about this. And it's not like I can't talk to him about it."

But I didn't want to hear it. My earlier frustration with Neil's dismissiveness came back with a vengeance.

"Oh, the kid with no skin in the game doesn't get it and now his boyfriend gets to tell me it wasn't that big of a deal," I said with a bite. I could feel my voice shaking. Neil's head snapped toward mine, those beautiful brows angled downward, and his dark eyes stormy and furious.

"What the *hell*, Payal?" He sounded hurt, and *that* tone—one that I so rarely heard and never wanted to be the cause of—cut through my anger. I pressed the heels of my palms against my forehead. This wasn't going how I wanted it to go. I'd handled this badly.

"Argh. I'm sorry. I didn't mean that," I said, putting a placating hand on his arm and hoping it'd be enough. "I'm just—"

"Payal, I'm sorry if you felt like I was brushing off what happened. But it's not because of *Finn*." He sounded less sure than he looked, glancing at me and then back down to his phone. I dropped my head down onto his shoulder. "It's fine." He sighed. "I'll call him later, and it'll be fine. And you're fine. And we're fine. It's all *fine*," he said a little too forcefully. "We should go back inside. I know my mom wanted to get home earlier rather than later." And without waiting, he stood up and moved back toward the theater.

Ding-dong.

I was sitting on the couch catching up on a week's worth of sitcoms the next day when the sound of our doorbell echoed through the house. Startled, I stared in the direction of our front door from my spot in the living room like I could see through walls and find out who was there. Lifting my phone from where it was sitting face down next to me, I found several texts from Philip sent over the course of the last ten minutes. There was also one from Neil that he'd sent last night. I'd asked how he was feeling, and he'd said, Fine, P. I'll see you tomorrow. With a sleeping emoji. I figured that meant we really were fine. He wouldn't use emojis if he was still mad, right?

PHILIP KIM

I'm outside

Payal

I'm standing outside

You're gonna make me ring the doorbell

Oh my god.

Damn it.

Fine.

I grimaced. My bad.

I got up and pulled the door open to an already irate Philip standing on the porch. Behind him, the light spatter of a sun shower glittered in the air, a well-timed counterbalance to the stormy look on Philip's face. There were dark spots of rain on his shirt, and my stomach twisted with small amount of guilt.

"Sorry sorry sorry, my phone was on silent and the vibration was off because I was at Divya's dance thing last night and people can hear when a phone vibrates, and I totally forgot and—"

He pushed past me with a terse "It's fine."

"Uh, welcome to my home? We can work in my dad's office." He kicked his sneakers off and followed me into a smaller area off the side of our living room. There was a wide wooden desk, a love seat, and not much to distract us. I curled up on the love seat and dropped my phone down next to me on the light fabric. It bounced once, and I awkwardly grabbed at the air to stop it from falling while Philip sat at the desk and pulled out his laptop and a notebook. Then he put a pen down, settled both hands on the keyboard, and paused before typing anything.

"What's your Wi-Fi password?"

"Oh, give me a second . . ." I dragged my finger across my phone screen before tapping into my gallery to find the picture I'd taken of the bottom of the router. It took me a moment to find it, but after swiping through a couple dozen images, it popped up—in between a picture of me and Neil at Taco Bell and one of my cousin's Pomeranian, Tuffy, walking on its hind legs. I grinned at the puppy.

"What are you looking at?" Philip asked in a surprisingly genuine tone. Still smiling, I held the phone up for him to see, and the corner of his mouth moved the tiniest bit before he schooled his features into their usual indifference. "Cute," he said, and then raised his eyebrows at me. "The password?" I rolled my eyes and started reading the password out in a monotone voice.

"XsFSS78YxqoTLV9856vVwZc997sKfn." I guess it was my mistake to assume Philip was listening, because when I looked up at the end, he was staring at me nonplussed, hands flat on his laptop keys.

"Are you joking?"

"My dad doesn't know how to change it, so it's the factory one." I tried to keep the defensiveness out of my voice, but couldn't help adding, "Sorry it's not *W0wPhilipKimIsSOCOOl* all one word, with zeroes instead of *o*'s."

"Well, I thought you were joking, so can you repeat it."

I rolled my eyes and texted him the image. The hum of air-conditioning kicking in broke the silence while Philip typed the password into his computer. He finally let out a satisfied sound, and I took that to mean his internet was working.

"Okay, in our doc—" He narrowed his eyes at his screen and then shot a dirty look my way. "How come you're not in—wait, where's your laptop?" he asked, and I could hear the subtext of *How are you so unprepared, Payal, we are barely a week into this project and are you even serious about Jon Slate?* I pushed up from the couch with a grunt.

"Yes, I am serious about this, and I will go get it. I didn't *realize* that you were going to treat this like a research paper."

"Serious about what?" He had the audacity to look confused.

"Nothing!"

A few minutes later, I returned with my laptop in tow. Philip was writing notes analog style, with a bright purple pen scratching along the paper. I settled back on the couch, opened my laptop, and logged into our *Payal Mehta Makes Bad Decisions* shared doc. First things first. I typed in a few words and then—

"Ha. Ha. Very funny. '*Payal Makes Great Decisions and Philip Knows Nothing.*' Very good, Mehta. Top marks." But that corner of his mouth was up again, and this time I spotted a tiny sliver of teeth. I felt a little proud at getting a second almost smile out of Philip.

"You are the worst, and I thought our doc should reflect as much." I'm sure he could hear the smile in my voice too, even while I fought to keep it off my face. He grinned and wrote something else in that notebook of his. I stretched up in my seat, trying to see if I could read whatever he was putting down in the book, but it was too far away.

"What are you writing down anyway?" I asked. Instead of answering, he shook his head and shut the book.

"Nothing, I use this notebook when I think of something for my other classes. Anyway." He started typing. I looked down at my screen, where Philip's cursor was moving across the doc at a frightening rate.

What we know:
• Jon Slate has some internal biases.
• Payal needs to get a handle on her awkwardness.

"Hey!"

He ignored me and kept going.

• Jon has the potential to be an okay guy (TBD).
• Jon likes sports, dirty jokes, drinking, and '90s rom-coms.

"Wait, how do you know that?" I interrupted Philip's flow of click-clacketing keys. His hands stilled.

"It's why I put watching *She's All That* in here. I overheard him tell his friends that he saw it on TMN last year and identified with the lead jock, 'like, a lot.'" He lowered his voice and air-quoted the last three words, in a terrible impression of Jon Slate. But I was surprised that he was genuinely trying to be helpful.

"You weren't teasing me because that movie's about a nerd makeover?"

"Okay, that was an added bonus and so I ran with it. But it really seems like he loves that movie, so it could be a topic of conversation? I don't know." He pushed back from the desk a few inches and shook his head, looking frustrated. His bangs fell across his forehead and into his eyes, and I found myself ducking my head a little, trying to catch his gaze. He made an annoyed sound and pushed his hair back before continuing. "Mehta, as much as I appreciate that helping you with this means I'm controlling our psych project . . . I feel like I should tell you that I also don't know what I'm doing."

My jaw dropped. Never in a million years would I have thought that Philip Kim would sit in front of me, in old basketball shorts and a weird pun T-shirt, in my home, and tell me that he didn't know how to do something.

"Uh . . . what?" was the only reaction I could come up with, my head tiling in tandem with the question. Philip scrubbed a hand through his hair *again*, and with a jolt, I wondered if that was actually a sign of nerves from Philip.

"I mean, I've had exactly zero girlfriends and I've cultivated the personality of a condescending nerd. I am not some kind of Nice Guy Jock. I have no idea how to win a guy who sees you as, like, a giant samosa." Philip looked nervous, or at least more nervous than I'd ever seen him before. He was avoiding my gaze, and his hands were fidgeting on the desk. I almost wanted to say, *Awwww*.

I stared at him, considering.

"I think calling me a giant samosa might be racist?"

His eyes snapped back to mine, and he scoffed, but there was no bite in it. A small giggle escaped me. He pretended to glare.

"No, it's absurd," Philip said. "Because that's what his micro-aggression was: *absurd*ly racist."

"Fair point . . . Actually . . . you know what? From now on, this project is called *Payal Mehta Is Not a Giant Samosa*." I digitally cemented it by typing it into our shared doc. "Okay, but back to you not knowing anything—"

"I know *things*, just not about getting the guy, Mehta." Philip folded his arms and looked at me with a patronizing glint in his eye. Something in my chest settled. There was the nemesis I knew and did not love.

"I know," I placated. "But that's why this is brilliant. You are *so* difficult."

"Thanks," he interjected with a snort.

I ignored his interruption, wanting to get this out. "Which is part of the reason I wanted you to do this with me. You don't do anything halfway and you won't lie to me even if something might hurt my feelings. If you really didn't think this would work, you never would have agreed to it."

Philip scrunched his nose in the telltale sign of someone who doesn't like being analyzed. I almost laughed in recognition but stopped before I could because I still needed him to agree with me. With my luck, he'd totally think I was laughing *at* him.

"Okay, fine, well. Uh, I might need to actually do some research." Philip's fingers started flying across the keys again, and I watched words unfold as the cursor moved forward on my screen.

- Find list of rom-com tropes
- Figure out how to teach a white boy about mild-to-moderate racism

My left eyebrow hiked up to my hairline at that. "Mild-to-moderate racism? Pretty clinical for a romance plot."

"Well, what do you want to call it?" he challenged.

I tapped a finger against my chin, thinking for a moment before it came to me.

"Baby racisms."

Philip outright cackled and gave me a delighted look before clicking that phrase into digital stone. His open-mouthed smile was so big, I could probably count all his teeth. Part of me relished being the person to put that expression on his face; the other part of me was unnerved. *Philip Kim* was giving me a genuine smile.

"Baby racisms it is," he said, bringing me back to the moment.

"Well, I know how to fix it, at least." I typed the letters *L O V*, but as I was hitting the letter *E*, Philip groaned so loud, I missed and hit the number four instead.

Payal Mehta Is Not a Giant Samosa

What we know:

- Jon Slate has some internal biases.
- Payal needs to get a handle on her awkwardness.
- Jon has the potential to be an okay guy (TBD).
- Jon likes sports, dirty jokes, drinking, and '90s rom-coms.

> *Comment from PAYAL MEHTA: I know you overheard, but, like, really, though. Does he like '90s rom-coms in general? Or only that one with the faux-ugly hot nerd girl? And is it only '90s, or does it seep into the 2000s?*

> *Reply from PHILIP KIM: We are too early into this for you to be questioning my sources already.*

> *Reply from PAYAL MEHTA: Fine. FINE.*

A: Offer to help Jon study for his history final: lots of one-on-one time.

B: (Or Plan A, part 2) Use study sessions to teach Jon about baby racisms*.

C: Go to see a sports game, aka attend Jon's baseball matches and learn how to talk about the sport.

D: Befriend more white people, show Jon how "American" Payal can be.

> **Comment from PAYAL MEHTA:** *Did my dad write this one?*

> **Reply from PHILIP KIM:** *ha ha, jokes. I have them.*

F: Go full *She's All That:* Wear a small red dress to the next party. Maybe cut hair short?

> **Comment from PAYAL MEHTA:** *No!!!!!!!!!!!!!!!!!!!!!!!!*

*Baby racisms research: http://www.entiropedia.com/microaggressions

CHAPTER FOURTEEN

"Hey, Payal!" I was hitting the button to lock my car in the school parking lot when Divya's voice rang out behind me. I looked back, lifted my hand to block out the sun, and found her lightly jogging her way through the pockets of students trudging toward the entrance. Her hair was out of its usual braid today, hanging down her back, and she had on a bright pink blouse with deep blue shorts[40]. I smiled at her and paused near the little Honda of Death, waiting for her to catch up.

"Hey, Divs. How'd the rest of the night go?" I asked her when she was close enough. There had still been a ton of people at the auditorium when we'd left. My dad had claimed a headache, but I think he wanted to watch the episode of *Grey's Anatomy* he'd been saving since Thursday night. Divya beamed in response.

"It was *amazing*. Dilip Uncle said he'd sponsor my trip to India over the summer to go to Anjali Auntie's mom's school for a special workshop." She squealed, and I felt a surge of affection for her and leaned into it, throwing my arms around her shoulders and hugging her close.

"Holy crap, that's amazing!" We spent a second jumping in excitement before I noticed the crowd was starting to thin around us.

---

[40] Bless our ability to wear the brightest colors on the planet.

"Come on," I said, pulling at her wrist. She let herself be led, and we both headed toward the doors. "What did your mom and dad say?" I asked as we stepped through and into the halls.

"They're thrilled, of course." Her voice dropped the slightest bit. "Honestly, they weren't totally sure they'd be able to cover it, so this is awesome. They don't want to tell me, but I know they've been stressed about it."

"Well, then I'm extra glad, di." I bumped against her shoulder with mine, and she grinned. "Also, I know I told you already, but you killed it. That was the best performance I've seen you do. I think. To me. I mean—"

We stopped at my locker, and Divya cut me off before I could dig my own hole any deeper.

"Don't worry, I know your dance IQ is not the highest—"

"Hey!" I said, mildly affronted, as I twisted my combination into the lock.

Divya ignored my outburst. "But I love that you said that anyway." She turned around and leaned against the closed lockers next to mine while I grabbed my chemistry textbook. "Did anything interesting happen in the hall? I heard something about Shanti Auntie throwing a mango lassi in someone's face? But that sounds fake." I turned my head from where I was stuffing my books into my backpack to gape at her.

"I hope not, because if I missed that, I'm going to mad."

We headed to Divya's locker a few feet away, and I thought back to the show. The only mildly weird thing for me had been the interaction with Josh Patel when he'd mentioned Jon. I told Divya about it, and when she tilted her head and said she didn't think it meant anything, there wasn't really anything I could say. But it did make me feel better about my plan with Philip Kim. That was for sure. It was a little frustrating that my best friends were so ready to put everything to rest when I clearly wasn't in the same place as them—and it had happened to *me*! I should get to decide when I was done have feelings about it. I thought about saying something, but it honestly felt like too much work. So instead, an awkward silence settled over us while she got her own things out for first period. I didn't like it. She finally closed her locker and looked at me, about to say something. But then she stared quizzically at something over my shoulder.

"Yikes—is that Neil and Finn fighting?" I followed her line of sight and saw the two of them standing close together near the boys' restroom and having what seemed to be a heated conversation. Neil's brows were low over his eyes, and Finn was frowning. I grimaced. I still hadn't had a chance to talk to Neil about his phone call with Finn any further, and I felt bad for not pushing harder on Sunday to see how he was doing.

"It does sort of look that way," I started, twisting my hands together with worry. "We should probably talk to him. I think he didn't want to bring us down when I asked about it the other night. And I tried talking to him after your show, but . . ." I trailed off. Did Divya know that Neil had walked out of her dance early? If not, I wasn't about to tell on him. He could tell her himself.

We both watched Neil and Finn for another minute. Neil's hands were moving faster than I could keep track of, and Finn had shoved his in his pockets while he stared at the ground. It looked bad.

"Yeah. I agree," Divya said. And then a huge smile bloomed on her face, throwing me for a moment before I realized why. "Oh, there's Vikash—Vi-KASH!" she yelled out, heedless of people who might start staring. I turned to see Vikash striding our way, grinning the whole time. He was Divya's height, so on the shorter end of our friend circle, but loud enough to make sure everyone saw him. His dark curly hair was a halo around his head, and it looked like his glasses were fogging up from the air-conditioning. I took in Divya's expression out of the corner of my eye, and there was nothing but joy. Vikash and Divs were *another* good match—I was beginning to notice that, at some point, my friends had figured out how to connect with people romantically and . . . I hadn't.

Vikash wrapped his arms around Divya and swung her in a circle before I could even say hello. He was grinning in a way that was also *loud*.

"Divya, Divya, Divya, Divya!" he sang before putting her down. "Remind me to never go to my masi's house for two whole weeks ever again, unless you come with me. But no amount of fresh pav bhaji in the *world* can make up for missing you—"

"Hey, Vikash. I am also here," I said wryly, shooting him a single sarcastic finger gun.

Divya laughed, but her arms were still locked around his neck. I turned my head, searching out Neil again to see if he'd join us, but he and Finn were already gone. I promised myself to find him later and find out what was really going on between the two of them.

"Ha ha. Hey, Payal," Vikash said, pulling my attention back to him and Divya. He moved his head to the side, with an expression I couldn't read.

"I heard you and Jon Slate—" Before he could finish his sentence, Divya shoved him lightly and gave him a dark look. I stared. Jon Slate and I *what*?

"*Vikash*," she whispered like I couldn't hear her. "Did you not *see my text?*" She glared at him, poking his shoulder with one painted red nail.

He looked back at her blankly and asked, "What text?" but at normal volume. My brows furrowed. *Yeah, what text?* Divya's eyes widened and she shook her head, her hair flying into a big, fluffy cloud of curls.

"Nothing, nothing, nothing," she said, grabbing for Vikash's hand. The first bell interrupted anything I could have said, and I swore Divya looked up at the ceiling gratefully. She smiled brightly at me and started backing away with Vikash. "*Anyway*, we should get to class." She waved, and they both set off for their shared home-room before I even had the wherewithal to react to the bell.

"What text!" I *definitely* did not yell at their retreating backs. "What text?!" Someone jostled my arm, and I realized the hallway was rapidly emptying around me, with people rushing off to their classrooms now that the first bell had gone off. Great. I could not be late *again*. The rubber soles of my sneakers squeaked against the tile as I rushed around a corner a few doors away from my own home-room. I was reaching for the door when I heard Neil's voice loud and clear coming from a classroom to my left.

"—what I've been saying! You *don't* get it! And I thought *you* would." I took one step backward and then another. Slowly, I peeked through the narrow window on the door. Inside, I could see Neil standing with his arms crossed, looking out of the windows over-looking the empty football field. Finn was sitting in one of the desks several feet away, closer to the classroom entrance. He was looking at Neil, though, so I couldn't see the expression on his face.

He must have said something kind in response at a much lower volume that I couldn't hear. Neil's shoulders fell, and he nodded.

Finn got up and walked over to him, then put his arm around Neil's waist and pulled him tight against his side. Neil turned his head and kissed Finn softly, and I stepped away from the glass, feeling suddenly ashamed for having basically spied on my best friend.

The sound of a door opening had me turning around in surprise. Dr. Myers was leaning against it, looking at me expectantly.

"Well, Ms. Mehta? I believe you're supposed to be in this classroom."

Mildly embarrassed at being tardy, I nodded. "Sorry, Dr. Myers." I walked past him into the room, resolved to find out what was going on with Neil the second I could.

"Okay, so I'll get permission to do the test with Mr. Lutton's freshman history class, and you'll handle Ms. Díaz's sophomore pre-calc class?" Philip said.

I looked up from my phone at him. I'd just hit send on a text to Neil to check in while Philip was pulling his notes together. My psychology and scheming partner was currently sitting across from me at a table in the media center. There were a few other students scattered here and there, but otherwise it was the regular lunchtime quiet. Philip had his black bomber jacket on again—the wrists were trimmed in a deep red, and I could see he had a habit of pulling at them by how stretched and worn they were. A sign of frayed edges that I could recognize.

"Don't you get hot wearing this thing every day?" I asked instead of answering his question, poking at his jacket sleeve. Philip looked down at himself and then back up at me.

"What? No, I'm fine, Mehta. Don't worry about my sartorial choices." He rolled his eyes and pushed his hand against my finger lightly. A brief and bright pain immediately danced across my skin, and I snapped my hand back, frowning.

"You shocked me!" I said, rubbing the offended spot on my finger lightly.

"I have been called 'electric' in my time." He grinned wolfishly. I could admit it was a little more pleasing than the condescending smirks I usually got.

"Oh my god." I let out an exaggerated groan. "Who's got bad jokes now?" Philip's lips opened, but I hurried to continue before something else ridiculous could come out of that mouth. "Yes, I'll handle Ms. Díaz's pre-calc class."

Philip nodded, his expression shifting back to something serious, and collected a few stray papers. I could see the word *blue* written in a red font beside the word *green* written in a purple font near the margins on the top sheet. I had an identical sheet in my stack. This experiment really was *so* basic.

This was our deal, I reminded myself—Philip got to choose the experiment. But *god*, the Stroop effect? What was this? First grade?

Another sharp smile cut across Philip's features like he knew what I was thinking. "You have anything you want to add, Mehta?" he said, his eyes narrowing without the smile ever leaving his face. I felt a tap under the table and looked down. One of his dirty white basketball sneakers[41] had knocked against my Keds.

I glared at him. "No. This sounds very manageable and *very easy*, Philip," I replied, shoving the papers into my psych folder and tucking my feet under my chair. Philip snorted, choosing to ignore my

---

[41] He didn't even play sports!

clear contempt for our topic. He pulled out his laptop and opened it.

"Okay, on to the other thing," he said. "I have Operation Samosa up—by the way, can we meet somewhere that has samosas next time? I get hungry every time I load this thing up." I couldn't help but laugh at that. Philip leaned back in his chair and looked at me, appraising. "That might be the first time you've laughed at something I said and not *at* me," he mused. I thought back to our meeting over the weekend and how I'd had almost that exact thought.

Was Philip Kim in my head?

No, Phantom Neil replied. *I'd know if he was in here.*

"Alright, don't get too ahead of yourself. Even a broken clock, etcetera."

Philip snorted again.

"Whatever you say, Mehta." He focused on the document again, and his long fingers flew across his keyboard as he typed. I don't know if I'd ever noticed how elegant his hands looked. I shook my head—what was *that*? I didn't need to be thinking about Philip Kim's *hands*.

I didn't usually bring my laptop to school, so I opened my notebook to a blank page. As I stared at it, I went through our list mentally.

"Alright," Philip said. "I think what we're missing—if we treat this like an academic project, which I think we should—is a goal."

"To get him to recognize me as an actual human girl worth considering as a romantic option. Because I *am* and I deserve to be treated as such. Duh," I said.

Philip rolled his eyes and ran a hand through his hair, and I wondered if he was nervous about something before immediately dismissing the thought. I was, however, gratified to see that his action made his hair stick up and out on the sides so he looked like he slept funny and came to school without brushing it. I didn't tell him, though.

"I *meant*," he said, emphasizing the word like I was five years old, "that you need a *tangible* goal. What does that even mean? How do we quantify 'considering you as a romantic option'?"

I had to admit that that was a good point. I hadn't really thought about what this would mean beyond the, well, intangible idea of Jon Slate falling for me. I just knew that I needed to be able to participate in his idea of me instead of letting him base his decisions off assumptions about me.

But Philip's question made sense. Did it mean dating? Did it mean Jon asking me out? I tapped my finger against my notebook while I considered my options. On the wall nearby, one of those ugly school clocks ticked loudly. Philip was still looking at me expectantly.

I glanced around the media center at the other students sitting and working during lunch, as if it would give me some inspiration. I wasn't sure what I was hoping for, but when I spotted Will Gardner, it hit me!

"I think Jon should take me to Will's End-of-Year, Summer's Here bash," I said with as much certainty as I could muster. Philip took a deep breath and pinched the end of his nose. He was muttering something. I leaned closer.

"*I will not mention how pedestrian that is—I will not mention how pedestrian that is—I will not—*"

"OKAY," I said loudly. "That's enough. This is officially a judgment-free zone, Philip! I already feel awkward about every part of this."

He had the decency to look chagrined. He raised his hands up in apology.

"Alright, alright, that's fair. Sorry."

Philip's fingers tapped against the keyboard as he typed in the end goal of the plan. There was a loud noise of the door slamming open from the front of the media center as a crowd of kids walked in. Philip and I both turned to look. It felt like the blood drained completely out of my face when I saw who it was. Philip's voice cut through my anxiety.

"I think this is the first time I've ever seen Jon in the library."

I turned to face him, which luckily enough was *away* from the door. Philip gave a start at whatever look was currently on my face. I must have looked deranged.

"Mehta, what is wrong with you?"

"Nothing! I mean, I haven't technically talked to him since that disaster of a lunch."

"At all?" Philip looked surprised. His brows were raised, and I could see that he was calculating something in his head. "You should fix that now. Why not start immediately? The sooner you talk to him, the sooner this thing"—he waved at the space between the two of us like there was some kind of literal thread connecting our bodies—"will be over."

I shook my head vehemently.

"I am *not* ready for this."

Philip's eyes shifted to look at something over my shoulder.

"Well, you'd better be, because I think he's coming over here."

"What?" I somehow whispered and yelled at the same time. Did I just invent whisper-yelling?

Philip leaned back in his chair, the corner of his mouth quirked up.

"Yup. Time to jump into the deep end, Mehta. You watched the movie, right?"

I had not, in fact, watched the movie. I still had *actual* homework to do and other things, and this could not be the sole thing I was working on, and anyway—

"Time to shine!"

I did not like how gleeful Philip sounded. It was as if he knew I was going to fail and couldn't wait to watch it happen. We'd see about that! Frowning, I quickly looked around to see what my options were. I turned to see that Jon had paused at a table to chat with Will so that Jon's back was to the two of us. He started turn, and I freaked. I shot Philip one last panicked look, and said, "I'm out!"

And then—I am somewhat ashamed to admit—I slid from my seat, ducked under the table, and started crawling toward an alcove that I could hide in a few feet away. The rough carpet hurt my knees, and I was fully regretting my decision to wear shorts to school[42], but at least I was getting away.

"Mehta! Stop!" I heard Philip hiss out behind me, but I didn't stop until I was comfortably tucked between two beautiful, beautiful bookshelves. I was still close enough to hear what was going on at my abandoned table.

"Hey, Philip—was Payal Mehta sitting here a second ago or did I imagine that?"

"Jon. Do you think you imagined a seventeen-year-old Indian girl who we've both gone to school with for almost four years?"

"What?"

"I'm joking. Yeah. She was here, but she . . ." There was an uncomfortably long pause, and then Philip continued. "She got dragged away."

"Oh. Uh." There was some kind of knocking sound, and I think

---

[42] In my defense, it was literally eight thousand degrees outside.

Jon Slate must have start tapping against the wood of the table. Philip was going to hate that; he'd glared at my own tapping fingers plenty of times for me to know how much the noise annoyed him. It went silent again. My spine was pressed against the shelf behind me, and to my right was a magazine rack. I couldn't believe they still made school-only magazines. How did something like *that* stay in business?

I shook my head. I needed to pay attention! Had it been quiet long enough to be safe? I started to rise when Philip spoke up again.

"Is there anything else?" He sounded impatient, which meant the entire time, Jon Slate was probably standing there staring in silence. Oh my god, that was so uncomfortable.

"Oh, uh . . . nah. I was—anyway. I'll wait in case she comes back. What are you doing?"

There was a loud sound of a chair being pulled back. Jon Slate was going to join Philip at our table?! I leaned my head back against the shelves behind me and closed my eyes. How was I going to get out of this? I was going to be stuck here until after the lunch bell rang. And then I'd be late for class, and then they'd probably call my parents because this would be my third tardy, and then my dad would ground me for the rest of my life or something—like, well into my forties.

The sound of another chair brought me back to reality.

"No, I'm not doing this. She's not here, Slate. And I'm leaving, and . . ." His voice went up a few decibels. *"If anyone else is listening, I'll add notes to our doc on how to avoid screwing up a simple assignment!"*

"Uhhh, okay, Philip." Jon sounded confused, which was fair considering that entire last bit was clearly directed at me. Who Jon could not see. And would not see. "I guess I'll head out too. Check you later, Phil."

"It's Philip." Philip sounded farther away now; he was already moving toward the exit. A few moments later, a second pair of footsteps followed, and I dropped my head to my hands in relief. Before I realized what was coming next.

I was not looking forward to reading Philip's notes.

Payal Attempts to Talk to Jonathan Slate
A history, cataloged by Philip Kim

ATTEMPT NUMBER ONE POST–TACO BELL DEBACLE (heretofore referenced as Taco Debacle): Wait near Jon's locker to "accidentally run into him"

    STATUS: Failure

    REASON: Payal doesn't know which locker is Jon's and waited near Eric Smith's the entire time instead. Eric doesn't know it, but he rewarded her failure by giving her cookies, because he is the nicest guy in school.

ATTEMPT NUMBER TWO POST-TACO DEBACLE: Park next to Jon and say hi when you're both leaving for class

    STATUS: Failure

    REASON: Payal hid. Again. I'm going to quit this soon, fyi. It is not worth it. I swear to god.

ATTEMPT NUMBER THREE POST-TACO DEBACLE: I don't care. Just say hi however you can. Just say, "Hello, Jon. How are you?"

STATUS: SOMEHOW A FAILURE

REASON: Would you believe laryngitis?

Payal, get out of this doc. I am in charge of typing up notes.

Slander, verb: make false or damaging statements about

SOMEONE. Me.

DELETING

CHAPTER SIXTEEN

YAARON SUN LO ZARA

PAYAL MEHTA

I want to see your faces TOGETHER.
Catch-up call? Now? Tonight? Soon?

DIVYA BHAT

Can't! Working at the store!

NEIL PATEL

same

I mean I'm doing homework, but I can't
either—dad's super on me about these
essays too. def catch up later, tho

I sighed and clicked the button on the side of my phone to turn off the screen. And then again to turn it on to see what time it was. My background flashed back at me, a picture from last year's Holi celebration. Divya, Neil, and I had our arms around one other, and we were *covered* in every color known on earth—there was a bright purple slash down my cheek, and Neil had yellow across one eyebrow, and there was a veritable rainbow in Divya's hair. The only thing still pure white was our teeth, gleaming out from our Rang Barse faces.

I *still* hadn't had a chance to talk to Neil about him and Finn—Neil had been super busy with his extracurrics all week, and so we hadn't had any one-on-one time. I had seen the two of them chatting amicably at school the day before, though, so maybe everything was okay? I didn't like that we hadn't talked about it. It made me weirdly nervous for some reason. Like, I *should* know what's going on his life.

And he should know what's going on in yours. Shut up, Phantom Neil.

Plus, I was pretty sure Divya was lightly avoiding me so she wouldn't have to tell me that she talked to Vikash behind my back. Okay, fine, I wasn't even irritated about it anymore. I was mostly annoyed that I didn't have anyone to hang out with on this Thursday night. I eyed my phone again, hit with sudden—possibly terrible—inspiration. I swiped it open and typed a new message to Philip Kim: Hey—wyd?

I looked down at the words and at the cursor blinking on the screen; my thumb hovered over the send button. Wait, what was I doing?! I wasn't so hard up for friends that I was going to text Philip Kim for *fun*. I backspaced and dropped the phone onto the bed.

Philip had been a nightmare lately anyway. Excuse me if I might need some time to *prepare* to actually speak to the kid who unilaterally decided he couldn't date me. I tried so many times over the last three days, I should honestly get some kind of girl-tries-really-hard medal. There was a buzzing right next to my head, and I jumped before realizing it was the phone. Then I grinned. *Finally,* someone was coming through. The screen glowed bright, and I picked it up to see who had messaged me. *Oh.*

"Thank you, Screen Time, for telling me I have an hour left to look at YouTube. Super cool. Thanks," I said out loud to my phone like it could hear me. Actually, it probably could hear me, if those weirdly targeted ads I kept seeing on HotGoss were any indication.

Maybe there was something good on TV.

I headed downstairs and into the living room, surprised to find my mom already sitting on the couch, holding a cup of tea in one hand and a spicy banana chip in the other. She wasn't even supposed to be home. Hindi lyrics set to a rhythmic beat emanated from the TV speakers as a woman in a bright red sundress shimmied her shoulders on the screen.

"Oh, hey, Mom. I thought you were going to the office to help Dad."

"Na, he called, said this Dr. Day's son was coming in after all. So I thought I'd watch the new Rohit Shetty movie." She put her tea down onto one of the red fabric coasters littering the coffee table and then reached for the remote, hitting a button to pause the movie.

"Oh, cool . . . I'll watch with you."

Very cool, Payal. Hanging out with your mom to watch a movie. I immediately felt guilty for the thought when she smiled and patted the seat next to her. I fell onto the plush cushions and leaned back. The screen was paused on a man with deep brown skin and a bright smile, with a bandana tied around his forehead to keep his black hair off his face. He was frozen in the middle of some kind of dance step, his knees bent and hands flung upward toward the sky.

"Chalo, let's go. This is supposed to have good songs. Meena Auntie gave me the print from their grocery store."

I frowned.

"Wait, does it have subtitles? Is this some random person's recording of the movie from an Indian movie theater?"

She waved her hands, and her bangles jingled. "No, no! It's a good print. She told me it's from that Priyanath's son's friend in Bombay—he works for the studio. If it doesn't have the subtitles, don't worry. You can ask me what you don't understand. But why are you so worried? Aapki hindi kitni achi hai."

"I don't speak it *that* well." I nodded to the television. "It's fine, though. You can go ahead and hit play."

She pressed the button, and music blasted through the speakers.

Ek ladki

Voh mujhe nahin dekhatee

Voh hawa mein nachati hai

Ek ladki

I listened to the playback singer croon about this poor guy who just couldn't get the girl to notice him, and *tsk*ed. What did this guy know about feeling invisible? He was like six foot two and shaped like a Dorito. How dare he pretend—okay, fine, *act*. They should have cast a dork! More dork representation! It's important!

My mom must have heard the sound I made, because she paused the movie and turned toward me. She lifted an arm and rested it on the back of the couch, then gestured to the screen with her other hand.

"Kyaa hai? You don't like Srikant?"

I rolled my eyes and shrugged, avoiding her eyes.

"Like I'm supposed to believe that *that* guy"—I nodded to the screen where our hero was currently stuck, open-mouthed, in the midst of pretending to belt out the winning note of this song—"can't get the girl because she doesn't notice him? He's going to sing one song in the rain and then, surprise! They'll be in love."

Unfortunately, my mom thought it was a good idea to laugh.

What about this was funny?! I scowled at the illusion on display in front of us.

"I don't know what you could possibly be laughing at," I said, turning away from her to pick at some lint on the couch. She sucked her teeth.

"*Ish*, I'm sorry. I'm not laughing at you. This is what these silly B-list Bollywood movies are—fantasy. You know this. Why are you so worked up?" She arched one perfectly threaded brow. "Is there something wrong at school?"

"No!" I yelped. Completely believably, I might add. I took the remote from her hands and pressed play. "Let's watch. Forget I said anything."

My mom took the remote out of my hands and pressed pause again. She placed a hand on my head and slid it down until she held my chin and turned my face toward her. *Major* mom move over here.

"Payal, sach much bolo—sab kuch theekh hai?"

For half a second I was tempted to admit the whole thing to her—that my feelings were hurt because of a mean-but-believed-to-be well-intentioned thing a boy said to me, and that my friends weren't around—but that really wouldn't get me anywhere except grounded for going to a party, talking to said boy, and then lying about it.

So instead I plastered a smile on my face and nodded.

"Definitely all good, Mom. Nothing that an evening of absurd storytelling and great music won't cure."

The following Monday morning, I sat in my calculus class, dying. Well, no, not *dying*. But definitely feeling some kind of torture. Díaz was going over functions[43] again today. To be honest, I *was* trying to pay attention, but it was so . . . boring. I glanced over at Caitlin; she was going to have her work cut out for her at our next tutoring session. On my other side, Neil's desk was empty. He'd managed to get a pass because there were admissions officers visiting from one of the state schools and Neil's dad wanted him to test out his interview skills. Not that he'd be going to a state school—Uncle had gone to Yale for his undergrad, and so he expected Neil to go to an Ivy League as well. We'd texted sporadically over the past few days, but his dad must have really been obsessing over this college stuff because Neil kept having to bail on any actual human voice-to-voice interaction. I held in a groan (Díaz did not appreciate interruptions in her class *at all*).

"Can anyone tell me what the decreasing interval would be if this is the function?" Díaz pointed to what looked like a murderer's wall of symbols on the whiteboard. I put my head down and hoped she wouldn't notice me. "Anyone?" she asked again, with a plaintive note of defeat in her voice. *Yikes.* I did not want to feel guilty for not knowing calculus, Ms. Díaz! Fortunately for me but unfortunately for her teaching goals, Díaz turned back to the board and started scribbling more symbols while answering her own question.

I sat quietly in my ignorance and counted the minutes until the bell rang so I could rush to psych. I looked over at Neil's empty desk again—maybe we could catch up at lunch. I'd texted him the night before about it, but he hadn't answered. I looked up at the clock on the pale-yellow brick wall again, and *yes!* Only three minutes left until the bell.

---

[43] This was actually adding insult to injury, because where I come from, a "function" is a *party*.

"Ms. Mehta, you have to care about more numbers than the one through twelve sitting on that clock face." Díaz was staring dagger eyes at me, and I tried pull the most apologetic face I could.

"Sorry, Ms. Díaz. It was just so . . . hypnotic."

My good luck came through then, and the ball rang loudly before Díaz could give me detention for some light sass—those had been her exact words the *last* time I got written up in this class, so I knew she wouldn't hesitate. I grabbed my stuff and booked it out of the room.

In fact, I moved so fast that I was the first person to walk through the doors of AP Psychology, where Mr. Lutton was still sitting on his desk, snacking on some Goldfish. At the loud bang of the door opening, however, he hastily shoved them into a drawer.

"Payal!" he greeted me, dusting some crumbs off his tie. "Welcome. How goes the experiment?"

"Hey, Mr. Lutton, don't stop with the Goldfish on my account." I laughed, heading toward my seat in the middle of the classroom. "It's going okay. Philip wanted to do the Stroop effect—"

"Oh, really? I thought Philip was thinking about something else!" Mr. Lutton said, confusing me. I'd been pulling my book out of my backpack, but I paused then.

"Huh?"

But then a stream of students came into the class, and Mr. Lutton didn't say anything else to me. I frowned and went back to taking my things out and placing them on my desk. Philip must have turned something else in to Mr. Lutton without asking me, that jerk.

I was still frowning when Philip finally walked through the door. He gave me a short nod and then looked confused when I didn't respond in kind. He waited a beat, and when I didn't relent, he shrugged, turned away, and headed to his seat a few spaces in front of mine. He didn't look at me again. And that didn't bother me one bit. Not at all.

Mr. Lutton kept us busy most of class, going through an intense sequence of concepts that he was pretty sure would be on the AP exam coming at the end of the semester. I didn't even realize how long we'd been sitting there until he stopped lecturing and grinned.

"Sorry for being so fast, everyone. I wanted to make sure we could save the last ten minutes of class so that you could work with your partners on your experiments and ask me whatever questions you may have."

Which meant—ugh—that Philip was walking my way.

"What is your deal, man?" he said instead of any sort of polite greeting.

"Nothing—did you have a different idea for the experiment or something? Why did Mr. Lutton think we were doing something else?" I couldn't actually say why this was bothering me so much, only that it was. I rolled my pencil along my fingers while I waited for him to answer.

Philip's eyes went wide for a split second, and then he looked as confused as I was.

"Nope, maybe he was thinking of someone else. I didn't have any other ideas." I searched his face for any sign of duplicity but didn't find anything. Leaning back into my chair, I sighed. Philip took that as a sign to turn the desk in front of me to its side with a loud scrape so he could sit facing me.

"Okay, well . . ." I said once he was finished. "If you're going to make any changes, you still have to tell me even though you're in charge or whatever." I didn't know what it was, but this conversation felt weird. I needed to find my footing. "Anyway, I don't even think we really need an update because, as I've been saying the whole time, this is the easiest thing known to humankind." I reached up to poke at Philip's shoulder, carefully avoiding the array of shiny enamel pins.

"And as I've been responding every single time you bring it up, we'll definitely get A's," Philip said, all fake saccharine and crap.

"Don't you want to do something *challenging*?" I asked. I liked pysch, and that meant I wanted to do something interesting. Philip wanting to do something so boring was kind of blowing my mind, if I was being honest.

"No," he said, matter-of-factly. "I want to do something that will get me the grade point I need. If I want a challenge, I'll do a speed run of the new *Zelda*." He must have seen something on my face because then he added, "I get it—this stuff is fun for you and you're good at it. But . . . I don't know. I just like the getting-the-A part sometimes."

"That's fair," I acquiesced. "Though it is *infuriating* that I know I care more about this than you do and we're going to get the same grade in this class."

Philip let out a bright guffaw and then slapped a hand over his mouth. My eyes grew wide, and I knew that my grin was matching his.

"Oh, was that a *real* Philip Kim laugh?!" I said, overjoyed. "That is the nerdiest thing I have ever—"

"Look," Philip interrupted me, looking back at Mr. Lutton. "Let's get through this. Speaking of *challenges*, we can do the *other plan* at lunch. And for the record, I still think the *other plan* is a bad idea." His cheeks and the tips of his ears were bright red.

A little peeved at having my fun cut off, I shook my head to say no. I was also thinking of my hope to find Neil.

Philip was unfazed. "Alright, it's your rom-com. I'm around to facilitate with no dog in this fight whatsoever." His voice was strained, but maybe he was still embarrassed that I'd just heard his very real, very nerdy laugh. He pulled out his stack of Stroop surveys. "Okay, these are from a few freshman classes—spoiler alert: They had a lot of trouble . . ."

The rest of the class went smoothly, to my surprise. After that first minor disagreement, I fell into an easy rhythm working with Philip, and we got through cataloging his surveys. The bell rang as we were adding the information from the last one to our data pool.

"Okay," Mr. Lutton called from the front of the room. "Thanks for being such good workers today—a reminder that I want to get mid-semester updates from you guys next week on how the experiments are going!"

The class largely chorused out a confirmation, with a few groans scattered here and there from kids who might not have been as far along as they should have been.

"I talked to Mr. Manalan," I explained to Philip while I pulled my things together. "He's letting me come into his French I class on Thursday to talk to the freshmen, so I'll have my stack to go through on Friday."

Philip nodded.

"Sounds good. Let me know when you wanna talk about the

other thing. Otherwise, I'll type this up and get it into the shared spreadsheet."

"Cool." I zipped my backpack up and then fished my phone out of my back pocket to shoot Neil a text about meeting at my car and grabbing something off campus. Next to me, I could feel Philip pushing himself up and out of the desk, his ratty basketball sneakers squeaking loudly as he started walking toward the door.

"See you later, Mehta," he said.

I absentmindedly lifted up a hand to wave and then tapped at the screen, and when it lit up, I was surprised to a see a text from Neil in my notifications.

NEIL PATEL

> Sry saw your text about lunch too late,
> already have plans w Finn—c u later?

My lips turned downward into a deep frown. Why was it so hard to find time to hang out with *me*? But remembering the scene I'd witnessed in the empty classroom, I wondered if maybe he and Finn *needed* the time. And it *did* mean that I could spend lunch working on *Payal Actually Talks to Jon Slate*. I swiveled my head toward the front of the class to see Philip's back as he stepped out and into the hallway.

"Philip, wait up!"

I grabbed my bag and shoved my phone into the back pocket of my jeans, then I jumped up from the desk and sprinted to the class door as I scrambled to catch up.

"Careful, Payal!" Mr. Lutton called out behind me.

"Sorry, sir!" I said as I ran toward Philip Kim—who, it turned out, had heard me and stopped to wait.

"Payal!" Philip hopped backward to avoid an actual collision as I skidded to a halt in front of him. There was a flush across his cheeks again, and his eyes had gone wide in surprise. "I heard you! Jeez. Can you bring the energy down, like, five million joules?"

"Is that a lot?" I asked, huffing slightly. Philip gave me a deadpan look. "Jokes," I said weakly, pretending like I knew the answer to my own question. But then I realized what I'd just heard. "Wait, did you just call me *Payal*?" Philip stared at me for a second like he didn't understand the question. Then he looked down at his watch and shook his head.

"If you didn't ask me to wait for any reason, I'm going to lunch," he said. I shot him a mildly irritated look and adjusted my backpack, which had slipped down and over my shoulders.

"I can actually hang at lunch, turns out. Neil's being weird—I mean, whatever. I can hang." I cut myself off; I didn't need to give Philip Kim my and Neil's whole backstory. He'd taken a step back at Neil's name, and I imagined he was probably thinking the same thing about not needing the details. But when I finished talking, his eyebrows went up and one disappeared under black sideswept bangs. His chin came down in a short nod, and he looked at me in an uncomfortable, assessing sort of manner. His eyes were dark and unreadable, and *that* made me the tiniest bit nervous.

"Oh. Well, then I can put my plan into action."

"*Your* plan?" I asked, suspicious.

"Follow me," he said in lieu of any sort of actual informative answer. Then he turned around and started striding down the hall without waiting to see if I was following. I hurried to catch up.

"Okay—but, hey! My legs are shorter than yours! Please take smaller steps!"

Around us, the hallways were crowded with kids talking and laughing, either heading to the parking lot or to the cafeteria. I thought I heard Eric Smith and Swapna Kool arguing about whether they should go to Wendy's or Pollo Tropical for lunch as we zoomed past. We were almost near the doors to the parking lot when Philip finally slowed his stride a little bit so I could catch up.

"What are we doing?" I asked him as we walked. "What is this plan?"

"You'll see," he answered in the most annoyingly cryptic fashion.

"Could you be any more vague?"

"I could have just not said anything." He shrugged and then looked around like he was waiting for something.

"You're the worst," I said, glaring at him.

"Please remember that in, like, thirty seconds. That I'm already the worst and you're already irritated with me."

"Huh?" I asked.

Then I noticed Philip was slowing down even more, and now I was somehow ahead of him. What was he doing? All of a sudden, I felt his two hands on my back, and that asshole pushed me! Well, he shoved me lightly—but still hard enough that I ran directly into the person in front of me.

"Oh my—I'm so sorry, I didn't mean to—I was—"

"Pie? I have been trying to find you *forever*."

Jon Slate was standing in front of me and looking overjoyed. My stomach turned. I whipped my head around to find Philip and put the blame on him, but Philip Kim was nowhere to be seen. What the actual heck? That bastard had thrown me into the deep end without a floatation device!

"Pie?" Jon asked again, and I realized I still hadn't answered him.

"Oh, uh—I've been really busy lately. Sorry about that. I didn't know. You could have messaged on social or something?"

"I guess—yeah, that would have been smart." He blushed. Why was he so cute?! It was not fair! It was disarming, and I needed to be armed!

"So," I started, taking a side step toward the lockers so we wouldn't be in the middle of the hallway. "You were looking for me?"

Jon followed my lead, leaning his shoulder effortlessly against one of the dull orange lockers to our right. The corner of his mouth was cocked up in a half grin. His chin was moving, and he was opening that very pretty mouth of his, and I realized he was probably going to pull another *talk to one of my brown boys* line. I steeled myself. I needed to cut him off at the pass. He could not be allowed to turn this into a weird bit.

"Actually, I'm glad you stopped me." I interrupted whatever he'd been about to say. "Would you want to study for the history midterm together? I heard you were looking for a tutor."

I had *not* heard that, but if he said anything, I'd chalk it up to rumor.

Jon made an *O* shape with his lips as if he was surprised that I'd had the guts to ask—or maybe just surprised that I'd interrupted him.

"Oh, well, actually, I was going to ask—wait, you *are* good in that class, aren't you? Your hand is always up." He'd noticed my hand?! Thank you for being so aggressive, Philip Kim! If for nothing else, for this moment alone. I didn't trust myself to speak, so I nodded my head slightly. His brows furrowed in what I guessed was thought, and then he gave me one short nod. "Okay, yeah, let's do it. Is it okay if you come to my house?"

I tried to stop whatever embarrassing thing my face was probably doing and adopted a calm expression. I needed to be cool. I still didn't think I could actually say words, so I gave him another nod in agreement. His smile widened.

"Great! Can I see your phone?"

I wordlessly unlocked it and handed it over, and then Jon . . .

Jon

Put

His

Number

In

My

Phone.

He handed it back to me and added, "Okay, I texted myself, so I've got your number now too. Let's start tonight? I'll message you the address!"

My brain was officially button mashing. Just nonsense streaming from my hypothalamus or whatever directly to my mouth, because what came out was "Buh-uh-huh okay—will see you or, okay, yeah."

Luckily, he'd been in the midst of heading off as soon as I'd grabbed my phone back, so he didn't hear any of that. But even if he had, *who cares?* I was going to Jon Slate's *house*. Gods bless you, Philip!!!

CHAPTER SEVENTEEN

I pulled up to a modest two-story house. The slats outside were a deep blue color, and the door was cherry red. It looked like it could be straight from a colorized 1950s sitcom about the American dream. More like something out of, I don't know, Connecticut instead of Florida. That is . . . if you ignored the incredible pink flamingo statue that served as the family's mailbox. I stared at it for a few minutes, entranced.

Jon had sent me a text during last period warning me about the flamingo and telling me he was "looking forward to the study sesh." *Looking forward to it! It* being hanging out with *me*. Kid wouldn't know what hit him. Granted, I was too much of a weenie to write anything back aside from "Got it!"

My phone buzzed in my hand, and a text notification slid down from the top of the screen.

PHILIP KIM

Don't screw this up, Mehta. Remember points A and A-2.

A: Offer to help Jon study for his history final: lots of one-on-one time.

B: (Or Plan A, part 2) Use study sessions to teach Jon about baby racisms.

I rolled my eyes. *Yes, Philip, I do know how to do homework.* I had already done part A anyway! I was here, wasn't I? Ostensibly to study history? I held my thumb down against the screen and selected the thumbs-up reaction. I wasn't even going to give Philip Kim a full emoji; he got a bubble reaction[44]. I got out of the car and leaned down to grab my backpack from the passenger seat. By the time I straightened back up, the front door had opened to reveal Jon standing there, silhouetted by the hallway light behind him. He had changed into a T-shirt and loose athletic shorts. Not exactly the most romantic outfit, but that's okay. It was early. We'd get there.

Will you? Phantom Neil said in my head as I waved to Jon. I flinched. I hadn't texted Neil or Divya about my plans. I still hadn't mentioned my deal with Philip to either of them. And in my defense, they didn't exactly seem to care. Neil never sent a reply after I'd written to him asking about lunch tomorrow. He was the one bailing on me to hang out with his boyfriend—and I understood, I did. But then it wasn't my fault if he didn't want to know what was going on with me. I ignored Phantom Neil and the pang in my gut, painted a smile on my face, and walked to meet Jon at the front door.

"Hey, Pie!"

"Hey, Jon," I said. Something about how casual this was made it easier for me to be myself. Most of myself anyway. "You weren't joking about that mailbox." I nodded toward the monstrosity behind me.

"Oh yeah, there's this guy in our neighborhood who makes them. My dad swears he commissioned it as a favor, but I think he really loves flamingos and doesn't want to admit it." He was grinning as he

_____

[44] Look, digital reactions are a fighting language fraught with symbolism and meaning.

said it, and I . . . giggled in response. Who was I? "Thanks for meeting me at my house, by the way," he added as he stepped aside for me to enter. "I know your parents probably aren't down with you being at a guy's house."

My nose scrunched and my brows knit. That might be true—my parents did think I was currently at Divya's—but that didn't mean Jon could make that assumption. But, hey, a prime opportunity for point A-2!

"Actually, a lot of Indian parents are super cool and would be totally fine with it."

There was a quick shift of surprise across his face. "Oh, sorry—I, uh, assumed your parents wouldn't be. Because . . ." He trailed off awkwardly. I winced internally. I didn't want this to be *awkward*. I wanted it to go smoothly!

"No, you're right in this case," I said. "My mom definitely thinks I'm at my friend Div's."

Jon put a hand against his chest and laughed. My heart felt like it got dinged. Maybe to get a step forward, I'd have to move backward just a tiny bit.

"I knew it! So, this is where I live." We'd moved inside by now, and I started toeing my shoes off. "Oh, you can leave your shoes on. My mom doesn't care. Follow me." I realized Jon still had his on. Oh no, was I being *weird*? He'd started moving toward a staircase I could see at the end of the hallway. "We can start working in my room."

"Oh, okay, yeah." I shoved my heel down into my sneaker and grimaced lightly when my sock ended up halfway down my sole. I hitched my bag higher up on my shoulder and stepped forward. Wait—did he say we'd be working in his room? I hadn't been in a boy's room other than Neil's in . . . well, ever.

I stepped onto the light carpet of the stairs and started up them, my eyes following the impressions of Jon's sneakers up to where he stepped off the last stair and into a doorway on the right. I hurried up after him, my sock bothering me all the while. When I got to his room, I wasn't sure what to expect. Neil and Philip were right, sort of—I didn't know too many literal "facts" about Jon. I had a crush on his *vibe* and was excited to find out more. And to be honest, I was pleasantly surprised by what I found. His room was pretty clean, with a few things scattered around, and the same tan carpeting that covered the hallway and stairs. There was a phone stand with an attached ring light in the corner.

The eggshell walls were barely visible behind a total chaos of posters covering them. There were ads torn out of magazines, players from every kind of sport, some bands I didn't recognize . . . I thought I might even see some inspirational quotes stuck here and there. Jon was standing at a desk in the corner of the room. After clearing away some space, presumably so we could study, he stepped back and seemed to realize something.

"Oh, you know what? Let me grab an extra chair from my sister's room." Without waiting for me to respond, he jogged out of the room, and I could hear him heading down the hall.

I didn't even know he *had* a sister.

I walked closer to the wall and ran my finger along some of the pages stuck there. There *were* inspirational quotes in here! One said, NOTHING MATTERS, SO WHO CARES?

Actually, I had to admit, I kind of liked that one. There was no attribution, so I made a mental note to ask Jon where it came from. I took a step back to get a wider look at the whole thing and nearly tripped over something on the ground behind me. My hands flung outward to break my fall, but to my surprise, I . . . didn't hit the floor.

Instead, I fell backward into a hard, flat surface, and then there were two hands gripping my arms firmly, and something smelled really, really clean.

"Whoa!" came Jon's voice from directly behind my head. I was leaning against his chest.

I WAS LEANING AGAINST HIS CHEST!

In a panic, I sprang forward and twisted around.

Jon was already kneeling down and lifting whatever it was I'd tripped over off the ground. He hid it behind his back before I could get a look at what it was. I noticed he was blushing again, bright red spots blooming across his cheeks and over the bridge of his nose. It was cute.

"Oh, sorry, it's super messy in here. I should've cleaned or—" he said haltingly, glancing around the chaos in his room.

"No, no, you're fine. I mean, I'm fine. I mean, it's fine! Let's sit down." I was talking too fast, and my brain needed to slow down so I could think about what I was saying. Jon turned to let me pass, and I couldn't help but notice that he still didn't want me to see whatever was behind him. Oh . . . oh, he was *embarrassed*! There was something embarrassing *him*? Jon Slate? I'd been crushing on him for years, and I don't think I'd ever seen him even remotely embarrassed. I didn't think he could even get embarrassed, considering how easily he'd posted that thing admitting he threw up on someone.

Now John was grinning at me, and my own cheeks went hot. Even in a loose T-shirt and wrinkled gym shorts, he looked *extremely* good. His hair was wet and curling at his ears like he'd just gotten out of the shower. His skin was so shiny, and his cheekbones were high and wide. I avoided looking at his mouth. I took a deep breath to calm myself down. It only kind of worked.

I stepped away and toward the desk, laughing a little to fill the space.

"Sorry about that," I added, and dropped my bag onto the floor beside me. I sat down in the chair he'd taken from his sister's room and pulled out my history binder, trying to forget the feel of Jon's chest against my back. *Okay, it's fine. Think about history, Payal.* My notes were pretty thorough, so we shouldn't need both of our textbooks. I tried not to react when I felt Jon sit next to me. He was *very* close, and I smelled the same clean soap scent I had a few minutes ago. Opening the binder, I glanced at the top page and immediately slammed it shut.

Jon jumped a little next to me and asked, "Is everything okay?"

"Ah, sorry! Yeah, I thought I saw a . . . bug. But I think it was a piece of lint."

Good save, Payal. Completely believable. But Jon seemed to take me at my word. He grabbed his own notebook out of his duffel bag and the book from class. I peeked into the binder again.

Somehow, Philip Kim had gotten into it and left a present for me. I skimmed the top blue-lined sheet of notebook paper:

ACCEPTABLE CONVERSATION TOPICS:

- HISTORY OF THE AMERICAS
  - You are supposed to be studying.
- ROMANTIC COMEDIES
  - Find a way to bring up the fact that you like this genre, especially oldies from the '90s.
- SPORTS
  - I refuse to research this one for you, but I guess

you could talk to him about Serena Williams or Naomi Osaka? They're two of the best athletes in the world, right?

UNACCEPTABLE CONVERSATION TOPICS:
- DO NOT BRING UP ANY WEIRD, NERDY SHIT. YOU KNOW WHAT I'M TALKING ABOUT. DO NOT BLOW THIS FOR US.

Even his handwriting was condescending. I resisted the urge to tear the paper out, crumple it up into a ball, and maybe even set it on fire. But only because Jon Slate was sitting next to me. Instead, I turned to my notes on the Panama Canal and laid the binder flat on Jon's desk.

"Okay, so where do you want to start?" I asked him. He leaned forward to look at my notes, and his arm grazed mine. I swear there was electricity. Like, actual electricity. And not in the painful static-shock kind of way. Plus, other than that thing at the beginning, he hadn't said *anything* to make it weird! This was . . . going kind of okay? My body relaxed a little, and I settled into the chair.

"Your handwriting is really nice, Payal. Now I definitely can't show you my notes. They look like a toddler wrote them."

I found the laughter coming out easily again. It was like at Taco Bell, before he'd ruined it. It could be *easy* to hang out with him if I didn't have to be on guard all the time.

"Well, now you *have* to show me."

He cracked a sideways grin and shrugged, and I was near enough to see a thin, pale line on the side of his nose.

"I bet I know how to distract you." He pulled his phone out of his pocket and unlocked it. What was about to happen? "Mack sent me this list of the best animal photographs taken in the year, and you *have* to see this eagle running into a tree branch."

"That is maybe the last thing I expected to come out of your mouth," I said, somewhat incredulous but already leaning forward to look at his phone. There on his screen was our majestic national bird doing the bird equivalent of a face-plant directly onto a massive tree branch. It was like real-life *Looney Tunes*. I couldn't help it: a loud belly laugh erupted out of my mouth, and I immediately slapped a palm over it in horror. Was this karma for making fun of Philip earlier?

But then Jon was laughing loudly too. Like, really loudly. Loud enough that I stopped feeling self-conscious. He looked at me with that universal expression of *I am sharing something I think is funny with you, and, god, I'm glad you think it's funny*. It was *familiar*. He swiped again, and we huddled over his phone looking at animals being ridiculous, and laughing, our history notes forgotten on his desk in front of us. Jon leaned to his right, and his shoulder hit mine and he didn't move away. My skin was tingling, and something in my stomach was doing major garba moves, but I didn't mind.

It was still pretty early by the time I left Jon's house, barely five o'clock. It had mostly gone really well! There had been some slight weirdness when his mom came in to say hi and did a double take when she saw me. She seemed nice enough, but I think she thought Jon was paying me to tutor him. Okay, I *know* she thought that, because on my way out the door, she asked if she needed to write me a check. First of all, lady, who uses checks anymore? And second of all, I am not the nerdy girl tutoring your child[45].

But that was manageable. I unlocked my car and door and slipped into the driver's seat. I lifted a hand to wave goodbye to Jon, who was standing on his front stoop. He'd actually walked me to the door. Pretty sure it was superhuman of me not to have fainted.

The minute my engine started up, a ding came through on my phone.

PHILIP KIM

So? Are you done? How'd it go?

PAYAL MEHTA

Omg so good

PHILIP KIM

Did you leave already? Let's meet up real quick—I wanna show you this thing I found for psych.

I looked at my phone in surprise. Philip wanted to do something in person? I didn't know what it could be that he needed to show me that he couldn't show me over the internet. But he also wasn't usually one to make frivolous requests. I hummed for a second, looking at the clock on my dashboard. I still had an hour or so before I needed to get home . . . and honestly, if I was late, I was "studying at Divya's," which could turn into "dinner at Divya's" as long as I texted first . . .

Decision made, I typed back a quick reply to ask where, then plugged the address into my GPS once it came through.

Ten minutes later, I pulled into the parking lot of a small coffee

---

[45] Okay, I kind of am. Dang it.

shop in a strip mall directly off Okeechobee. I parked and got out of the car, pausing as I glanced up at the sky. The air was heavy, and the clouds were dark—after a brief consideration, I pulled a small umbrella out of the side of my door and looped the band around my wrist. *Always* keep an emergency umbrella in your car when you live in Florida. Sunshine State, *my butt.*

I could see Philip seated at one of the tables outside, typing away on his laptop and with a tall, dark drink beside it. He was so engrossed in whatever he was doing, he didn't see me until I was already dropping into the seat in front of him. His hands stopped moving, and he jumped a little in his chair.

"Whoa, hey, warn a guy, Mehta."

"Don't be so unaware of your surroundings, Philip," I answered. "So, what's up?" I nodded to his laptop. "What'd you want to show me?"

Philip pushed his laptop to the side and leaned an elbow on the table, cradling his chin. There was a small crumb stuck under the right corner of his lips.

"You've got something . . ." I started, gesturing to my own mouth. Philips eyes darted downward to my lips before he hastily brought a hand up to wipe his face. When he opened his mouth to speak, strangely, I thought he looked apologetic. But then the expression was gone, and he was back to business.

"Well, wait, tell me how it went first. I need to record any data points."

I grinned and started going through the hour and a half I'd spent at Jon's house moment by moment, and for a second, it was like it would've been with Neil and Divya. Except instead of squeals and requests for more details, I just heard Philip typing and going,

"Mmmm. Mmmm," or, "Can you extrapolate on that?" It didn't *totally* suck the fun out of it, but—

"Okay, so he started with a baby racism, and then got cool, and you called him on it, but then you softened it so he was comfortable and you were uncomfortable?" Philip asked once I'd finished. I expected him to be giving me an assessing look, but instead he looked kind of irritated.

"You don't have to put it *that* way." I glared at him. He wasn't wrong, but he also wasn't right. I *had* corrected Jon. "Plus, the rest of the night there wasn't a single B.R., and we got along *super* well," I said, cheeks warming as I remembered the feel of Jon shaking with laughter next to me, his shoulder touching mine.

"I guess that still counts toward the end goal." He gave me a short nod and typed into the document again. I drummed my fingers against the table while I waited for him to finish writing. But then his fingers stilled on the keyboard, and he cut a glance my way before looking down at the screen again. "Wait, did he apologize for the Taco Debacle?" I folded my arms across my chest and screwed up my face into a glower. Philip stared in what I assumed was disbelief. I looked away. "Wait . . . he didn't say sorry?"

I bit my lip and took a deep, calming breath before saying, "Philip, he doesn't even know he has something to be sorry for. I've gotta work up to that, don't you think?"

Philip closed his eyes and rubbed at his forehead. Like *I* was being the annoying one. What did he expect me to do? Walk into Jon's house and be like, *"Hey, that thing you said was fucked up and hurt my feelings and let's do a course in the sociological implications of language"*?! And then what, I get thrown out the door before I even have a chance to wriggle inside of his heart?!

That was a good line, actually. So I repeated it out loud.

"Obviously not," Philip said when I'd finished my incredibly cogent argument. "But . . ." He paused like he wanted to think through what he said for once instead of giving me one of his usual cutting remarks. "I don't know. It sucks that you have to pretend that you're fine." I leaned forward and put my folded arms on the wrought iron table. Philip being frustrated because I had to pretend was . . . not what I'd been anticipating, to be honest. He was looking at me with a softness that I wasn't used to seeing on his face. Or was it pity? It was probably pity. Frowning, I started to ask him why he cared about my feelings, but he wasn't finished. "Have you talked to Neil about this? Or Divya?"

The abrupt change of subject threw me, but I shook my head in answer. Philip's eyes darted this way and that, and now I was beginning to suspect he'd been body-snatched. Since when did Philip Kim make small talk about feelings and check in on my friendships?

"Ah," he said. "Well, they'd probably be better at this than me."

Oh, that's why. Philip clearly cared but was mad he cared and so was passing the buck along to my friends.

"Philip, do you care about *my* feelings?" I grinned, wide and happy and maybe the tiniest bit mocking. Philip closed his laptop and gave me a dirty look.

"And we're done. I'll see you later, Mehta."

—MISSED VIDEO CALL FROM NEIL PATEL—
—DIALING NEIL PATEL—
You've reached the voicemail box of–

CHAPTER EIGHTEEN

"Chalo, Deepa, you have the wine?" my dad asked, glancing at my mom. My parents and I were standing outside of Dr. Day's house the day after my study session with Jon. I guess Dr. Day had invited my dad over to say thank you for his help with Suraj, the blasé med student who was working at my dad's office. Not sure how *I* got roped into this, though. We were standing on their front porch—there was a large statue of a laughing Buddha on one side and two small hurricane shutters leaning against the other. Hurricane season wasn't for another several months, so that was definitely weird.

"Yes, yes, I have it." My mom held the long, thin gift bag up, her dark purple nails flashing in the porch light. I tried not to scowl. I'd asked my mom earlier why I had to come, and I have to say her answer was not exactly satisfactory.

She'd barely heard me while she was digging through the hall closet looking for the aforementioned gift bag, but she still heard enough to say, "Because I said so, Payal, now go get ready," between her mutterings about my dad springing this on her last minute. Which was fair because he had sprung it on her, like, ten minutes earlier.

That had been an hour and a half ago. My plan for the evening *had* been to finally get through some studying for a calculus test and maybe start on my essay for English, but for once my pleas of homework were not enough to get me out of dinner. So now we were here, and I tried to hype myself up to get through what was going to be an extremely boring dinner. It was going to be pretty difficult, considering I was still buzzing from yesterday. Even if Jon hadn't apologized—ugh, *Philip*—it had been *really* fun. At one point during our hang, I'd even managed to sneak in that I liked those movies he was into, and he said we should watch one together sometime!

Sometime! That had potential!

My dad rang the doorbell, and I heard a slew of chimes go off inside. A few seconds later, the knob turned and the door swung open, revealing a plump auntie with a huge smile on her face.

"Hello! Come in, come in!" she said. "It's so nice to finally meet you—I'm Amla, Abhi's wife. He's getting some glasses from upstairs."

"Namaste," my mom said, with her two hands pressed together. "I'm Deepa, and this"—she pushed me forward so I could be on display—"is my daughter, Payal."

"Payal! Such a pretty name," Amla said. And then she lifted her hand. I thought she wanted to shake mine, so I started raising mine to meet her in the middle, but she kept going and then put two fingers against my face and pinched my cheek. The audacity! My dignity! My dad hurriedly pulled me back, and I pressed a hand against my cheek.

"Payal, don't say anything," he whispered as I stepped behind him. Then, in a louder voice, he added, "Amla, so good to see you again. Where is Suraj?"

"Come, follow me—I think he and Abhi are probably in the living room by now. We have wine—"

"Oh, this is for you!" My mom held out the bag to Amla, who took it and peeked inside. My parents and I removed our shoes and left them near the door while Amla Auntie continued moving deeper into the house.

"Thank you. I'll get this in the kitchen. Would you each like glasses of this? We also have whiskey or . . ." I tuned out as she continued to talk about things I wouldn't be allowed to drink. The Days' house was *really* nice. Dad said they'd had it built a few years ago. It was a funny mix of very Indian and very American aesthetics. There were images of gods and goddesses scattered about along with some murtis, but there was also a reprint of a blue-and-yellow Rothko hanging on the wall.

I think Amla Auntie and Abhi Uncle had both been born in the States. I know it used to be that basically no Indian kids would have parents who understood where they were coming from—they were all immigrants here. Actually, Papa-ji's immigration experiment happened when my dad was a baby in India, but the way Papa-ji tells it, everyone was so rude and the food was so bad, he lasted eleven months before he went back home. He still won't come here to visit, and we have to go to India if we want to see him. He was *furious* when my dad decided to move here with my mom. I think they didn't speak for, like, a year [46].

"Payal!" Amla was calling to me, and clearly, she'd been asking me something for a minute.

"Oh, sorry! I was thinking about . . . math."

My mom laughed like I'd said something hilarious. "Payal has a calculus test soon, and she's very studious, as you can see."

Amla Auntie came back over closer to me and made as if to pinch my cheek again. I took a quick step backward.

---

[46] Big *K3G* vibes, to be honest.

"Sorry! Just head in the clouds—what did you say, Auntie?"

"I said, would you like a soda or water? I'll ask Suraj to get it for you."

We'd made it to the living room then; my dad was already chatting with Abhi Uncle. Their son, Suraj, was sitting on the couch looking at his phone, completely disinterested in what was happening around him. He hadn't even looked up when his mom said his name.

"Oh, no, thank you."

"Okay, but let me know if you need anything." Then she turned to her son, and her tone shifted to mom mode. "Suraj! Come talk to Payal!"

Suraj unfolded himself from the couch. He had short hair and a scruffy chin. But the kind of scruffy that was completely manufactured. His lips were turned downward, and he was still looking at his phone when he walked over to us.

"Hey," he said.

"Uh, hey," I answered. "I'm Payal."

"I heard."

He *still* hadn't looked up from his phone. What the hell? Fine. I would abandon what little amount of tact I usually had.

"So, you what, were failing out med school or something?"

At this, his head shot up, and he was already glaring at me by the time we made eye contact.

"I am *on a break*. Not even sure I want to do medicine," he said, gripping his phone tightly at his side by now. I nodded, appeasing. Maybe I felt a little guilty for antagonizing him. "And not because I can't hack it," he added.

I lifted my hands up in apology. "Sorry, sorry. I was just—"

"Being a snotty teen?"

"Reacting to an old who was unnecessarily rude to me."

There was only so much disrespect I was going to take, especially from someone I didn't even know! Suraj finally had the decency to look abashed.

"Fair enough," he said. Then he looked over at the other adults, who were currently chatting about our state's "garbage governor." "This is going to be a long night, huh?"

I nodded. "I think so. Are you really going to drop out of med school?" I couldn't help but ask. I'd never heard of any Indian kids walking away after starting school—there were some who decided not to go even when their parents wanted them to, but leaving after they'd already started? Honestly? Unheard-of.

He laughed, but it was somewhat stilted. Like he meant it but he didn't. Suraj glanced at me but then looked back to his parents and put his phone into his pocket, keeping his hand in there.

"Maybe. I don't know. I'm sure your dad has told you how mad my dad is."

I shook my head. "Nah. I don't think he'd want me to be negatively influenced by you. He's already mad that I won't commit to being pre-med even though I've explained to him that I can't be pre-med if I don't understand numbers."

Suraj laughed that same weird laugh again. "Well, what your dad hasn't told you is that my dad is thinking about forcing me to pay back the tuition they've already spent—my mom is for it, but my grandma says she'll deliberately hold her breath[47] if they make me do that."

"Dang." I blanched. "That is intense."

---

[47] That was a pretty big threat on the Indian grandmother scale. His nani was not playing around.

Suraj shrugged. "She knows I hate medicine—I wanted to go into law."

I did a double take and said, "Sorry, your parents are mad that instead of wanting to get one professional degree, you want to get a different professional degree? What?"

"Don't get me started."

I heard a soft buzz, and Suraj pulled his phone out of his pocket again. While he was typing, I considered what I'd do in his situation. Probably say screw it and do whatever I wanted, though I couldn't imagine my parents ever forcing me into a career—as much as my dad whined and cajoled, he'd never *make* me do anything. Anything big, I mean. Obviously, I'd been forced to attend this dinner. Next to me, Suraj was typing, and I couldn't help but look at the screen—I guess I *could* help it, but sue me, I was bored and nosy—and to my surprise, it looked like he was texting boyfriend-style sentences. From where I stood, I could swear he'd written, No, I can't wait to meet your parents. They made you, I bet I'll love them as much as I love you.

"Hey, Suraj," I said. "Did you ever date someone who isn't Indian?"

For the second time that night, Suraj's head shot up, and he stared at me.

"That's kind of personal. I've known you for three minutes."

"Yeah, but you're my bhaiya now. I have your law-school secret. And that your-grandma-is-your-best-friend secret."

"I did not say that!" he said, aghast. Then his eyes narrowed. "Why do you even want to know, *chotu*?" He tacked that last bit on just sarcastically enough to make it feel like it was coming from a real older brother.

I glanced over at my parents. They were still completely engaged in conversation with Suraj's parents—my dad had his drink raised, and my mom had a hand on Amla Auntie's arm. Should I tell him? This could be my chance to get the perspective on this Jon stuff from someone older *and* Indian *and* unbiased. My gut twisted with nerves, but I thought it was worth the potential embarrassment. I took a breath and told him my story. When I was finished a few minutes later—I couldn't believe the extent of my romantic entanglements could be explained in less than five minutes—I could see a deep indent on the side of Suraj's face, where he seemed to be biting his check.

"Are you seriously trying not to laugh?" He shook his head, but that indent was still there. And I think his eyes were watering. "Is there something about this that is *amusing* to you?"

Finally, he was able to get ahold of himself. He inhaled a deep breath and blew it out slowly. "Sorry, sorry. But it takes me back. I think you should do whatever you want to do and not let this world tell you who you're supposed to be or what you're allowed to do."

"That is surprisingly inspiring." I shot him an appraising look, pleased with his answer.

"Don't forget—I'm basically a twenty-five-year-old med-school dropout. If this blows up in your face, I am not responsible."

And that felt more in line with the level of confidence the universe usually threw my way.

After the universe gifted me that double whammy of advice with the caveat of no responsibility from Suraj at Dr. Day's house, I decided to go full speed ahead with my plan. Sure, there was that annoying little voice in the back of my head that told me I should talk to my actual friends about this and not just rely on Suraj, who didn't actually know me, or Philip, who was only invested in this because I was offering something in exchange.

And by "annoying little voice," I definitely meant Phantom Neil, who had recently started relying on sarcasm to get his point across.

Payal, maybe this will go great and your friends will be happy for you!

Divya was still avoiding me, and Neil was—well, he kept saying he was busy. Logically, I knew he wasn't lying. We'd run into his dad at Prem Uncle's store the other night, and he'd told us how proud he was of Neil's work ethic[48].

But no, I wasn't ready to share with my friends. I wanted to talk to them when I had something concrete to talk to them about. Something they couldn't dismiss out of hand. One study date did not an exciting adventure make!

I texted Jon to set up a study schedule for the upcoming test—a week away, which meant we were going to get together the next three nights. Well, evenings. Okay, *fine*, late afternoons. The only issue really was clearing it with my parents.

My dad was easy—I told him that I had a big test coming up and that I needed to study. My mom, on the other hand?

Wednesday morning, I slipped on a pair of flip-flops and grabbed my keys off the hook by the door. Before I could make it outside, my mom called from the kitchen.

"Payal! This evening, Raveena Auntie is coming by with Sejal— can you watch her while Raveena and I have tea?"

My plan *had* been to text my mom from school and tell her that

---

[48] Only Neil's dad could use the words *work ethic* about a seventeen-year-old.

I was going to Divya's to study. Lying to your parents was *so* much easier over text. I hesitated and then walked back to the kitchen, where my mom was having her first cup of chai of the day. She was seated at the table, scrolling through the news on her phone, still in her nighty.

"Sorry, Mom, I have a study session to prepare for a big history test next week."

She nodded. "Okay, that's fine, bete—tell Divya's parents I said hello and that I'll come by the store soon for bhajia."

Hey! I didn't have to lie. It's not really my fault that she was making assumptions, right?

"Uh-huh, okay, gotta go—bye!" I spit out as fast as I could, booking it to the door before my mom could notice anything weird in my voice or use her bananas mom-sixth-sense to find me out. Literally, the last thing I needed was for her to make a big scene and Jon Slate to forever cement his idea of what Indian girls and their families were like.

Thanks to an accident on Military Trail, I was *late* late to school. The parking lot was nearly full, and I had to park in the back near where the newly licensed sophomores usually ended up. I grabbed my things, pulled on my bag, and cursed my decision to wear flip-flops, since they were the *worst* shoes for running. Hurrying as much as I could to the entrance of the school, I pushed the doors open and wondered if I could get away with sneaking into chemistry or if my teacher would make me get a late pass from the office.

"Payal Mehta, I see you're running late today." I jumped at the voice and then winced, turning to find Ms. Díaz standing in front of her classroom door. She looked at me impassively. "Is it safe to assume you haven't gone to get a late pass from the front office yet?" I nodded. She was quiet for a moment before finally raising her eyebrows. "Well? Go get one. I'm sure whoever has you first period today will appreciate it." Argh!

Groaning, I turned tail and started the long walk to the other side of the school. The front office was close to where the buses came in and to the loop where parents dropped their kids off. My first class of the day was, like, four seconds from the student parking area. This was *very* annoying.

If I was going to be late anyway, I decided to take my time strolling through the halls. For the most part, it was pretty quiet—I did hear the loud braying of trombones as I made it past the closed doors of the band room, but that was about it.

Until it wasn't.

I was about to climb the steps leading up to where the front office is when I heard Neil's raised voice coming from somewhere behind me.

"Are you fucking *kidding* me? I already—No, she wouldn't—Not without—Why are *you* the one telling me this anyway?" And then whatever he said next became unintelligible before he went quiet.

He sounded pissed. Without even thinking about it, I twirled around to follow his voice. I retraced my steps down the short space to where the hallway ended in a T, but then instead of turning back the way I'd come, I turned right. I saw Neil at the other end, striding away furiously. He must have immediately started moving after I'd heard him. Damn! There was no way I'd be able to catch up to him without running and probably getting caught *twice* for not having a pass. I looked back toward the stairs and then at Neil's retreating figure again. No, I needed to get to the office first—if Díaz got me one more time, I think she'd actually call my parents.

CHAPTER NINETEEN

After that, school was blessedly uneventful but infuriatingly long. I'd texted Neil on my walk back to the front office to tell him what I'd seen and ask if he was okay, but he hadn't answered. He'd been mostly MIA all day, and I'd have been more worried if I hadn't seen him laughing with Finn on their way off campus for lunch. I'd honestly be close to slipping from worried to angry if he didn't get back to me soon, though.

Philip Kim missed psych for some reason—he'd texted me to let me know he'd be out since we were supposed to be doing partner work, so at least I wasn't surprised. Unsurprisingly, when I asked why, he'd replied with "none of your beeswax" like it was 1995. I wondered if he was watching some old movies too. The thought made me laugh. I hadn't seen him since the coffee shop, but we'd video chatted to work through some experiment stuff, and of course the Google Doc was *lousy* with information.

The only good thing to really happen before the final bell rang was that I had a few minutes to actually talk to Divya—the frustrating part was that Vikash was there, so the conversation was completely inane. I didn't want to share anything about Neil in front of Vikash—even if Divya might talk to him about it later, it didn't seem right. It did feel nice to talk to her, though. Even if it was about nothing. I made a mental note to be more aggressive in getting together with her *and* Neil. We'd have off times like this before, when everyone was busy or, in Neil's case, dealing with their own shit. I couldn't fault them. Divya was practicing up a storm to prep for her trip in a few months, trying to come up with a new dance—going so far as to use an empty classroom during lunch! And Neil . . . well, clearly, I didn't know. Plus, Finn had been driving him to and from school lately, and I didn't want to insert myself in between since it seemed like they needed the time together. None of that stopped it from feeling super unfair.

Finally, the day ended after the most boring English class *ever*. Seriously, who *cared* about an old white guy who has been dead for two hundred years and what he thought about anything?! I filed out of the classroom among the rest of the students and made it to my car a few short minutes later. I glanced at my phone before turning the car on in case Neil had replied. My gut twisted when it still said *Read* under the text I'd sent to him. I was about to drop the phone into my center console when it buzzed in my hand with a message from Jon—my eyes for *sure* became actual hearts when I read his name—telling me he'd see me soon. Oh yeah, he would.

This time, when I got to Jon's house, I had to actually ring the doorbell. The door opened to reveal his mom—a pretty, blond woman who had already grievously[49] insulted me. But she did look abashed when she saw it was me at the door. She pulled her cardigan tight around her and invited me in.

"Hi . . . Payal. It's so lovely to see you again. Jon mentioned you'd be by—he's upstairs."

---

[49] Fine. Mildly.

"Thank you, Mrs. Slate—"

"Please, call me Corinne."

My eyes went wide. Calling a grown-up by their first name without . . . like, any kind of modifier? Absolutely not. That was not happening.

"Oh, uh, thanks," I said awkwardly, resolved that I would simply never utter her name out loud. "And thank you for having me."

"Of course! Thanks for studying with Joansy—oh," she said as I stepped toward the stairs, "are you staying for dinner? I don't have time to cook anything, but I'll be ordering pizza in about an hour."

I nodded but paused with my foot hovering over the first step.

"That sounds awesome. Thank you for inviting me. I really appreciate it. Who is Joansy, though? I'm here for . . . Jon?"

"Absolutely no trouble at all. And, oh, sorry! When Jon was little, his sister, Margaret, decided he was her new doll and she named him Joansy. Now it's a family nickname." That was the cutest thing I'd ever heard, and I filed it away in the getting-to-know-Jon-Slate file folder in my brain. *Ask me how many things I know now, Neil!*

I get it, I get it, but I still don't like it, Phantom Neil echoed from somewhere behind the file folder.

After thanking Mrs. Slate again, I headed up to Jon's room. I walked in to find him hastily tidying around, picking things up and shoving them wherever they'd fit. I cleared my throat since he hadn't noticed me come in.

"Oh! Hey!" He flipped around, surprise etched across his features. He looked handsome in jeans and a green polo that made his eyes seem brighter.

"Hey—you didn't have to clean or anything . . ." I said, standing by the door.

Jon shot me an aggrieved look.

"Yes, I did. My room was a *pigsty* last time, and I'm still embarrassed about it." Butterflies erupted in my belly, and I felt warm all over. It was nice that he clearly cared about what I thought.

"Okay, *Joansy*," I said, grinning and maybe flirting the tiniest bit with the boost of confidence I'd gotten.

Jon's face took on a horrified expression. He walked to his door and stuck his head outside, yelling loudly into the home.

"MOM! YOU DID NOT TELL HER—"

From somewhere downstairs came a "Sorry!" and Jon came back in, red-faced, and shut the door behind him. Laughing, I moved to sit at the desk.

"Don't blame her. It probably slipped out! I'm glad I got to hear it."

Jon pressed his palms against his eyes and groaned.

"I keep asking her not to use it in front of friends. Everyone on the team knows it too, and it is the *only* thing they'll use in the locker room now."

I *almost* felt bad for him, except for the fact that nicknames are a *huge* staple of Desi culture[50].

"Look, my mom and way too many of my aunties called me Sweetie Payal until I threw an epic tantrum in front of the County Indian Society. To this day, I'm not allowed to go when there's a party at Vela Auntie's house. I feel your pain."

Jon tilted his head to the side and looked at me, consideration in his gaze.

"I'd say you were right to do it . . . But the nickname suits you— come on, you're sweet, S. P. Also, you are going to have to tell me that whole story at some point."

---

[50] There were literal cousins in my family whose real names I didn't know.

He said it so matter-of-factly. I *must* have died and gone to heaven. Why was he so good at complimenting people? No, so good at complimenting *me*? I blushed and tucked a piece of hair behind my ear, more so I'd have something to do with my hands than really needing to get it out of my face. S. P.! He'd nicknamed *me*!

"Thanks." Pulling my notebook out of my bag, I thought about how to move the conversation along to something outside of studying. While Jon set up his laptop and opened it, I looked around his room for inspiration. Unfortunately, there was *so* much going on, I didn't even know where to start. A sound blasted out of Jon's speakers, and he scrambled to find what tab it was coming from, but I'd already recognized it.

"Is that Denzeen?!" I said, completely surprised. Denzeen was one of my all-time absolute favorite streamers. But she was not, like, mainstream. Which is part of what I liked about her. She was also super eclectic—she did product reviews, but also gaming stuff and movie stuff; she did *everything*. I loved it. It was pure chaos.

Jon finally located the window the sound was coming from and closed it. He turned to me, mouth open wide with shock but with a hint of a smile at the corners.

"You know Denzeen?! No one knows Denzeen!"

"Only one of my favorites!" I wasn't lying; I'd been a follower for, like, three years. I wasn't going to tell Jon this because *embarrassing*, but I'd definitely found her through her Percabeth fanvid a few years ago.

"I didn't know you knew, like, cool stuff," he said in the same matter-of-fact tone he'd used to call me *sweet*. It didn't sound as pleasing to my ears this time.

"Ouch." I scooched back in my chair. What did he mean by *that*?

"No, no, I mean, it's, like, a regular streamer. That's awesome." And what did he mean by *that*? "Did you see her latest from last night?" Jon had already turned back to his computer. I struggled, wanting to say something but also feeling like it was too weird to ask him what he meant now that was already clicking through to Denzeen's latest video. Besides, shared interests were *a good thing*. "You're gonna love this one if you haven't seen it yet." He grinned at me over his shoulder before pressing play.

I gasped. It was an unboxing video for the new *Birds of a Feather* cartoon merchandise line.

"I know, *right*?!" Jon said.

"How did you know I was into this show?" I asked, wondering how he'd guessed this would be a video I'd like.

He nodded behind us to my bag sitting on his floor.

"I noticed you had a pin of the cockatiel from the third episode on your bag the last time you were here," he said. "But I didn't want to be, like, too extra last time. I've been told I can be a lot." I wanted to throw my arms around him right then[51]. But I knew that would be too much, so I didn't; instead, I leaned closer and pointed at the related videos to the right of the current clip. I pointed at the screen, careful not to tap it.

"Play that one next!"

He bit the edge of his lip, and I think he was trying not to smile too big. So I smiled big enough for both of us.

We spent the next ten minutes going over our favorite Denzeen videos and what we thought her very best moments were when she was being "candid." It didn't quite erase the sour taste in my mouth from the "regular" comment, but it was hard to be upset when

---

[51] My heart!!! I too had been told that I was a lot!!! Too much sometimes!

things that I had in common with Jon Slate kept . . . popping up out of nowhere.

The next night, when I stepped into his room, there was a stack of books sitting on his night table. The spines were worn and recognizable, with flat gold lettering set against a deep green background. He caught me looking at them, and said, "Oh yeah, I was in the mood to read an old favorite, so I ran by the library during lunch."

"Does that say—" I started, and Jon answered me before I could finish asking the question.

"The Green Trials? It's this—"

"Oh," I interrupted. "I *know* The Green Trials series!" I *loved* those books! Was this a sign? It felt like a sign. I picked up the top book and flipped through it, my eyes skimming and searching. I finally stopped going through the pages when I found what I was looking for. *"And so, young hero, the times are bleak,"* I intoned, *"but you'll find strength in the dark, as—"*

"All heroes do." Jon finished the line. I jumped a little bit and made a *woo* sound.

"I really thought I was the only person who had ever read these books!" I waved the novel in my hand through the air. "I have the whole series at home . . . and the *special editions*." I pretended to dust something off my shoulder.

"You *have* to bring those over when you come back tomorrow," he said, eyes pleading and hands clasped in front of him. "My mom did a mass purge last year and accidentally gave my set away. I've been waiting for the right covers to end up on eBay, but it's been *months*."

"I will!" I agreed. "I promise." I put the book back down on the stack and ran my fingers along the cover before turning back to Jon. He sat down at his desk and pulled his history binder out. His hands stilled just short of opening it, and he looked back at me.

"Okay, *one* more question—count of three, favorite in the series?" he asked, and I nodded. "One . . . two . . . three—"

Our voices, entwined, said, "First half of *The Green*, second half of *A Vengeance Denied*."

"Oh my god."

"OH MY GOD."

"I can't believe you're a nerd. I love this." I fell into the seat next to him, knowing I was probably beaming and not quite able to care if I looked ridiculous. Jon shook his head and laughed at me, pressing a finger against his lips.

"I'd appreciate it if you kept it at least a little bit on the DL, Pie."

Obviously, I said yes. Now we had a shared *secret*.

We never quite made it to our history notes, actually. Most of that night was spent rehashing our favorite scenes and how mad we were that the author had never written anything else, and then falling into a conversation about what kinds of movies we liked and what kind of music we listened to. Before I knew it, it was 8:00 p.m., and I wasn't even sure how the time had gone by so fast. Unfortunately, that was my cue to go home or risk having my mom call Divya's mom. Next to me, Jon was wrapping up a story about meeting one of his favorite musicians at a music festival over the summer. His eyes were bright, and his energy was infectious. I wanted to keep talking to him about stuff that made us happy.

I'd had a crush on him for so long and I hadn't really known him, but I was finding out that Jon was . . . delightful. Plus, there hadn't been any *major* mishaps in the last few days, only a few little comments here and there that were strange. Mostly, he'd been sweet and funny. There hadn't been a single weird comment today anyway. That was proof that the more time I spent around him, the more he was definitely learning that he was wrong about his assumptions.

"Oh man. I gotta go." I sighed, looking at the clock on his computer. I pushed the chair away from the desk and started to put my things away.

"Ah, what a bummer, but I get it—early curfews! My buddy—" If he said an Indian kid's name here, I was going to scream. We'd been doing so *well*! I thought we were fixing this! "—Jordan—" Whew. Okay. "His girlfriend, Reshma, has the *same* thing." *ARGH*. I resisted the urge to face-palm.

"It's the worst," I said instead. "My friends Neil Patel and Divya Bhatt don't have a curfew at all. Their parents *trust* them." Was it too subtle? Was I chicken for not calling him out directly again? I thought of Philip and how I shouldn't have to feel bad. But, I don't know. I didn't want Jon to get defensive if I tried to lecture him. Who wanted to be lectured? I was *not* a teacher. I was just a senior in high school.

"Oh, really?" He rubbed at his chin as if it was *so hard* to figure out how two other brown teens could not have a curfew while his friend's girlfriend did. Ugh. "That's cool," he said finally. So . . . success? I guess?

"Yeah . . ." I stood, pulling my bag up. It was starting to get awkward. "Anyway . . ."

He brightened. Whatever internal monologue he'd been having clearly forgotten.

"Okay, I thought of something we can do tomorrow." He rubbed his hands together anticipatorily.

"Study?" I asked with a slight grin as I dug through my bag for my keys.

"Oh yeah, we are gonna *study*," he said, waggling his eyebrows.

What the hell did that mean?!

CHAPTER TWENTY

PAYAL MEHTA

What did that mean? What do you think??

PHILIP KIM

Uh . . . that he has something for you to do
that is not studying, that's for sure.

PAYAL MEHTA

It was so good tho other than that
last part, but I think he got it.

PHILIP KIM

Yeah, I'm sure he definitely picked up on
your extremely subtle slight push against his
assumptions about an entire community.

PAYAL MEHTA

You can't ruin this because you
helped get me here lol

PHILIP KIM

Omg don't remind me. I still can't believe
he didn't say sry for the taco debacle.

Any way—sry I missed class this week. I'll
make it up later and I'll be back next week.

PAYAL MEHTA

It's fine. What are you doing?

PHILIP KIM

We had to visit my grandma—
she lives near my aunts in PA.

PAYAL MEHTA

Oh where?? My masi's in Jersey.

I mean my aunt

PHILIP KIM

I figured, I woulda said halmeoni
but I know how to code switch
better than u

PAYAL MEHTA

Omg

Shut up. Thats cool that u get to visit
her—my dadi is in india

PHILIP KIM

But at least then u get to visit India. We
haven't gone to Korea in forever. I think my
mom used to go every summer after they
moved here when she was a kid? N the rest
of my cousins go every summer now

PAYAL MEHTA

Why don't ur parents wanna go?

PHILIP KIM

i think it's bc my dad and his bro don't get
along but also it would be rude not to visit
them if we go? idk its annoying

PAYAL MEHTA

omg we totally have family drama too. my other masi and my mom haaate each other tho they pretend not to, so when we go to India we always have to go to their house and it's so awk

PHILIP KIM

ha ha idk which is worse

PAYAL MEHTA

there was like a 3 yr period we didn't go to india but i got mad about it tbh

PHILIP KIM

Lmao oh I can hear it now MOM Y CANT WE GO TO INDIA IT IS MY RIGHT AS A PROUD INDIAN AMERICAN CHILD

PAYAL MEHTA

My mom would get mad if I said indian american lmfao I would have to like recite the indian national anthem or something

PHILIP KIM

Plz tell me you know the indian national anthem

PAYAL MEHTA

Ahahahahaha I know like the first line bc it was in some movie I watched a lot as a kid I think but no sry to disappoint even tho I know u r used to me disappointing

PHILIP KIM

Nah ur alright, I get u—and im not disappointed, ur a good nemesis bud

PAYAL MEHTA

I bet you say that to all ur nemeses

PHILIP KIM

Nemesi*** (and don't worry I only have room in my brain for one nemesis)

PAYAL MEHTA

That is WRONG, it is nemeses, I saw it in Star Trek and Jean Luc Picard is always correct

N same

PHILIP KIM

Top 5 picard moments go and then I'll tell u why janeway is the best bc she's hard as hell

PAYAL MEHTA

Omfg we are gonna fight over star trek now too ok

[Incoming video chat from PHILIP KIM]

PAYAL MEHTA

Hey, maybe we can catch up tmrw?

NEIL PATEL

Maybe idk, school stuff is kicking my butt

PAYAL MEHTA

Oh ok

NEIL PATEL

Sry

PAYAL MEHTA

It's fine but lemme know
when you're free

NEIL PATEL

CHAPTER TWENTY-ONE

The fourth and final night of study dates, I was on my way to Jon's house and still feeling frustrated about Neil—especially since I'd been haranguing him about not talking to me. Chatting with Philip had been a great distraction . . . chatting with Philip, which had gone on *way* longer than I'd realized. I'd panicked when he'd moved us from text to video—but then I remembered that it was Philip. Not a big deal. Next thing I knew, it was past midnight! Just *chatting* with my archnemesis—no big deal. But Neil still hadn't reached back out. I was dying to know what had pissed him off, dying to know how he and Finn had made up, dying to know about his college admissions stuff, dying to know—well, everything, really. But I couldn't *force* him to change his priorities. The only thing I could do was keep reaching out.

I rolled up to Jon's house again and parked. I'd been here three times already, but I still felt a little uncomfortable about it. Just hanging out with Jon was easy enough, but his parents had been interesting, to say the least. When I'd stayed for dinner, I'd offered to help clear the table because I don't think anything would make me feel more uncomfortable than watching someone's mom doing the cleanup while I sat there like it wasn't happening. But they'd resisted every step of the way. Then, when his dad found out my dad was a doctor, he'd leaned back and laughed and said, "Of course he is. I should have known!"

Tonight, though, Jon had mentioned his parents were going to be at some dinner with friends and so we'd have the place to ourselves. I tried not to think of the implications, but there was sweat beading down my back. To be fair, he hadn't phrased it that way, so my imagination was probably going into overdrive for no reason. Although . . . the study dates *had* been steadily becoming more date than study. With this in my head, it was no wonder that my hand shook a little as I opened my car door.

"Relax," I said to myself before taking a deep breath in through my nose and holding it for a count of four before blowing it back out through my mouth[52]. Nerves at least partially settled, I walked up Jon's sidewalk.

I got to the front door and opened it, per Jon's instructions to "come up whenever you get here." The house was quiet, and my short-lived breathing-induced calm was already starting to slip away. I stalled at the decorative mirror near the base of the stairs. A last-minute face check couldn't hurt, right? I looked at my reflection, and my cheeks went bright red. The girl looking back at me from the mirror was *nervous*. My eyebrows were scrunched, and there was fear in my gaze. I tried to smile, but it made me look more uncomfortable somehow. Had I forgotten how to *smile*?

Damn it, Jon, why weren't your parents home?!

Finally, I couldn't stall anymore and had to hope my face would look marginally normal by the time I got to Jon's room. When I got there, he was sitting on the edge of his bed with a big booklet of what looked like CDs lying across his knees.

---

[52] Something tells me this was not why my mom taught me breathing exercises.

"Hey," I said, standing in the doorway. Jon turned and looked at me, smiling before nodding for me to join him on the bed. While my brain began to short-circuit, he started speaking.

"Hey! Okay, so, you admitted to me yesterday that you've only seen *She's All That* when it comes to primo classic nineties rom-coms, I thought I'd contribute to your education since you've been contributing to mine. This is my mom's old collection of movies."

Huh?

He pulled out one of the discs and held it up so I could see. It was white, with a neon font spelling out *10 Things I Hate About You*. Oh my goodness, we were going to watch a romantic comedy together. *Right now.* Goose bumps erupted along my arms, and I quickly clasped my hands behind my back before Jon could notice.

"Oh! Okay, yeah," I said, hoping my voice wasn't shaking. "I've never heard of that one."

Look, if you talked to me about Bollywood movies from the nineties and the early aughts, I could definitely hack it—American movies from before I was born, though? Not so much. It wasn't something that played in my household. I thought about saying as much out loud, but I bit my tongue. I didn't want him to say I was weird or make some other comment about how *regular* I was or was not.

"Man, pop culture has failed you. We are definitely going to do this." He scooted back on his bed and patted the spot next to him.

Right, I still needed to sit down. My stomach twisted.

"We're not going to watch it on the TV downstairs?" I asked. I didn't see one in his room.

"Nah, if it's cool with you, we can watch it here on my laptop. It's old enough that I have a disc drive on it." He opened the laptop up and rested it on his lap.

I took a hesitating step forward. His bed had a dark green comforter on it that looked soft and welcoming. Jon shifted so he was sitting closer to the wall, leaning against one of his pillows. He was cross-legged at least, but if he unfolded his legs, he'd basically be *lying down* and I'd be sitting next to a boy in his bed while the boy was *lying down*. I could feel my cheeks go hot at the thought. I *hated* blushing; it emphasized how round my cheeks were. Jon patted the space next to him again.

"Is this cool?" he asked. And I could feel the implication of *for you, as a brown girl, specifically* hanging, unsaid, at the end of that question. My stomach did another funny little flip. But I nodded brightly and unclasped my hands. Luckily, at least I didn't have goose bumps anymore. I moved to sit next to him like I didn't have a care in the world, hoping he wouldn't feel how tense I actually was. I matched his posture so when we were settled, we both were kind of hunching over the laptop between us. There was a headphone splitter plugged into the port so we could both listen at the same time. Jon saw me looking at it and added, "It might have a disc drive, but the speakers are kind of busted, so we'll have to use headphones." He gave me sheepish grin, and I tried not to think about why he decided this was better than watching the movie downstairs. "*She's All That* is great and all, but it's *10 Things I Hate About You* that is *the best*," Jon continued while I pulled my earbuds out of my bag and set about detangling them. A hand entered my vision while I was struggling with the white wire, and Jon's fingers grazed mine as he took the buds out of my busy hands, and I nearly yelped in surprise. "Let me. You're going to break it if you pull that hard." He laughed.

"Oh . . . thanks," I said. My heart was *dhak-dhak-dhak-ing* in my chest, and I subtly tried to take in a deep breath to slow it down into a normal rhythm. Watching him work at the wires, I couldn't help but be thrown by how quickly this was moving. *Was it really just a few weeks ago that this kid threw up on me at that party? How did I even get here?* Then Jon was passing my earbuds back to me and plugging the end of them into the splitter. He slid the DVD into the slit on the side of the machine and leaned back . . . straightening his legs. Okay, we were definitely going to lie down next to each other and watch this movie.

I really needed my heart to calm down because this was totally no big deal! It was super cool and something teens did every single day in America, and if Random American Teenager Number Forty-Seven could get through this, then so could I! Making a deliberate effort to appear as casual as possible, I mimicked Jon's movements so my legs were parallel to his, heels digging into the comforter. I regretted wearing shorts—I should have put more lotion on. My knees were definitely ashy. But if I tried to move or cover them now, would it call more attention to them? Jon was busy fiddling with his laptop, so I decided to deflect instead.

"Alright, let's see this magic movie that is the best cinematic experience of all time," I teased lightly, trying to get back some of that ease of conversation we'd had when we were pretending to study. But he paused before hitting play and looked at me seriously.

"Okay, I don't want to *over*hype the movie, so please lower your expectations. It's still from, like, over twenty years ago, so there's some, uh, problematic stuff in there. I should warn you. It's not as bad as, like, what my mom watched from the eighties, but it might shock you a little."

"Consider my expectations managed," I said, grinning and hoping it wasn't coming across as weak as it felt.

Turns out when Jon Slate meant "watch a movie," he literally meant watch a movie. We were halfway into the movie, and no moves had been made. It was just a pretty fun story that I was surprised to find out was based on a Shakespeare play called *The Taming of the Shrew*[53].

The shrew showed up to the epic high school party that her little sister wanted to go to, and then a fight broke out on-screen. Jon and I laughed together at the creepy guy screaming, "Ooh, fight!" and running off to find the action. But then I noticed . . . well, like in a lot of older movies, there were, like, twenty to thirty people on-screen and the vast, vast majority of them were white kids. And nearly every one of the leads was a white kid. Definitely not a single South Asian among the bunch. Honestly, I wanted to laugh. If I'd been with Neil or Divya or probably even *Philip*, one of us would have definitely made a joke about it to cover the slight burn of not being included. I looked at Jon out of the corner of my eye. Was it worth risking it?

The beats of an old hip-hop song interrupted my thoughts, and Jon said, "This part's a little hard to watch."

I followed his eyes to the screen, where the angry girl was drunkenly dancing on a table while everyone watched. I cringed. He was right, it *was* hard to watch. But then she *literally* fell into the arms of the romantic lead, and I *literally* felt Jon sigh next to me and lean

---

[53] Maybe I should have paid more attention to Shakespeare in class. I doth regret that choice . . . I am definitely not using that right.

a little closer. It had taken me a good chunk of the movie to calm down, but my nerves came roaring back. My heart was pounding, and I felt jittery inside . . . but in a good way this time. I grinned. I was *not* going to disrupt this moment.

A few minutes later, I was screaming with laughter. "Did she— Did she *just*—"

Jon was in a full-body cringe; his hands were over his eyes, and he'd paused the movie. He was muttering something under his breath, and I leaned forward to catch it.

"Oh my god, oh my god, how did I forget—"

"That she *threw up on him!*" I yelped, a giggle bursting out of me right afterward. Jon pulled at his cheeks with his fingers as he scrubbed his hands down his face, uncovering his eyes. He was tomato red. I pursed my lips, trying to hold it in.

"I know I already said sorry, but I am seriously *so sorry*. I was embarrassed for *days* after that happened." I'd never seen him quite so earnest. I wasn't sure what to do with it. Philip's question of whether or not Jon apologized for what he'd said at Taco Bell hit me, but I ignored it. Jon clearly was feeling terrible about the party, and I didn't want him to feel *even worse* by adding another thing he needed to apologize for.

"It's—I mean, it's okay. Things happen. Like, look." I pointed at the screen. "I bet *they'll* be fine."

Jon shot me a massive smile. "Thanks for not making me feel like a huge tool even though you totally could have if you'd wanted to, S. P." He pressed play, and if I scooted an inch or two closer to him when the movie started, who's to say[54]?

So far, the movie was not bad, if hilariously, *hilariously* specific

---

[54] I am. I am to say. I did it.

to the experiences of the kids it portrayed. Even saying the words *teen pregnancy* out loud? My father would *never*. Go out with a rugged Australian teen and play paintball? As if. I looked at Jon sitting next to me and grinned to myself. Maybe next time, Jon and I could play paintball.

As the movie went on, I realized how quickly I could spit out a joke I knew Jon would get, so it couldn't matter much that he wouldn't get some of my references, right? Our rapport was starting to feel like second nature. Didn't everyone adapt to the people they were with? I was adapting.

Assimilating? I frowned at the intrusive thought from Phantom Neil.

That wasn't what I meant. Ugh, *assimilating*. Ew. Whatever. It didn't matter! What mattered was I was spending the evening with someone I liked, someone I had things in common with, even if it wasn't *everything*, and it was really nice. My hands were still tingling from where our fingers had brushed together earlier! And I was pretty sure the sweater I was wearing was going to smell like his pillow when I left.

Was that weird? Maybe it was a little weird.

On-screen, the shrew was crying as she read a poem she'd written, and I was wiping at my own eyes. I looked over at Jon and found that he wasn't even pretending not to be misty-eyed. I grinned a small smile. This was totally worth it.

Walking through the halls in between classes at school a few days later, the only thing I wanted to do was gush about this wild thing that was happening to me. Serendipitously, I saw Neil at the end of the hall chatting with Divya near her locker.

"Neil!" I called out, standing on my tiptoes and waving, not caring at if people in the halls started staring. Jeremy Owens actually stalled his usual dashing through the halls to glare at me for getting in his way, but I was not to be deterred. I was going to talk to my best friends!

Ahead of me, I swear I thought I saw Neil twitch, but he didn't look my way.

"Neil!" I tried again, speed-walking to get closer.

Still nothing. Now that *was* weird.

He was turning away from Divya now and walking off to his next class, and I could see Finn near the doorway waiting for him. By the time I caught up to Divya, they were both out of sight.

"Hey," I said, huffing and bent over with my hands on my knees.

Divya looked at me in consternation. "Did you . . . run here?"

"I was trying to catch up to you *and* Neil," I said, the slightest bit pointed. "What's going on? I'm starting to think he's mad at me or something. It feels like he's been ignoring me for weeks. The only thing I can think of is missing his call."

"He's mad?" Divya asked. "He hasn't said anything to me, and I know his dad has been on his back because Neil hasn't gotten his Harvard application in yet. I think his parents told him he's spending too much time with Finn." I winced. I knew Neil's parents usually were okay with Finn—but I could definitely see his dad blaming "the American" for stealing Neil's attention. Divya looked back the way Neil had left. "That's weird, though. Why would he be mad at you?"

"I've been *trying* to ask him," I grumbled. I thought about the many times I'd reached out to both of them. "I feel like I'm the only one who ever asks about chatting or doing things in the group chat, and you *both*"—Divya flinched—"keep blowing me off. How is that my fault?"

"I'm sorry! I felt bad because I told Vikash about your whole Jon Slate thing and I didn't tell you I told him and I don't handle conflict well and so I didn't know how to talk to you plus dance has been—" She was getting frazzled, digging her toe into the ground and looking away from me.

"Divya!" I interrupted. "It's fine. I don't even care, I promise. I miss hanging out with you. Like, seriously, I do not care at all. I just want to hang again." It's possible I didn't care because I was riding high on the Jon Slate front now anyway, and so the old me who was mad about what Jon had said? She didn't even exist anymore. Mostly. Divya was beaming by the time I'd finished talking.

"That makes me so happy to hear, Payal!" she exclaimed as she flung her arms around me. I laughed, hugging her back, and then immediately coughed and pushed her away for a second after getting a mouthful of her hair.

"Blech." I gagged.

"Sorry!" Divya pulled her hair back and opened her arms again. I fell into them, happy to have at least one of my friends back to normal. I'd have to figure out what to do about Neil at some point, though.

"Ehm." Somewhere behind me, someone was clearing their throat. Disentangling from Divya, I turned to see Jon standing there holding a book in his hand. He had his baseball jersey on and a pair of jeans, and I remembered he'd mentioned something about a scrimmage later to prepare for the game over the weekend. I wasn't entirely sure how a scrimmage was different from regular practice, but I guess it warranted dressing up.

"Hey!" I said, hyperaware of Divya behind me. I could practically hear her thoughts, wondering what was going on and why Jon was talking to me.

"Hey, S. P., here's that book we were talking about. I knew I had it somewhere. Get it back to me whenever," Jon said, passing me the graphic novel he'd told me about a few nights earlier. I took it from him and smiled, hoping to move him along before Divya said anything.

"Thanks—I'll see you in class later?"

"Definitely! We're gonna ace that test even if we didn't study as much as we should have," he said with a wink. A wink! And then he turned and walked away.

"Good luck with the scrimmage!" I called to his retreating back.

He turned around and cupped his hands around his mouth, "Thanks, S. P.!"

Divya's hand gripped my arm and spun me around as soon as Jon was out of earshot, pulling me close enough that I could see her eyeliner wings were the slightest bit uneven.

"And *what* was that?!" she asked. Her voice was too loud! I stepped away and smiled even though I knew it probably looked super awkward and fake as hell. "S. P.?! He has a *nickname* for you?!"

"Nothing! It was nothing," I said. "Nothing at all. We were studying for the history test today. That's all. No big deal. Really."

Divya could see through my bullshit, I could tell. But I wasn't ready to tell her until I had *something* to say. More than *Oh, we hung out a few times and watched a movie.* I wanted a real moment of triumph. I wanted to, as Philip might say, "get the goal." And I wanted to talk to *Neil* about it too.

"Did you guys . . . talk about what he said? Did you write that letter?" she asked, and I could hear a beat of mortification in her tone. It took me a second to even remember what she was talking about before it came back to me—the lie I'd told them about writing Jon a letter explaining myself. I'd said it because I hadn't wanted to mention the plan with Philip. I gave her a disbelieving look. I couldn't believe she thought I'd actually do that.

"No! We just . . . I don't know. He's fine. He's a nice guy. We studied and we had some fun. That's all." The hallway was rapidly emptying around us at this point, and I saw my out. "Anyway, we'd better go before the late bell rings. I'll, uh, tell you more about it later." I started to walk away before stopping, mid-realization. "Oh, also, if my mom asks, I've been studying at your house this week!"

CHAPTER TWENTY-TWO

PHILIP KIM

There's a baseball game this weekend.
You should go.

YAARON SUN LO ZARA

PAYAL MEHTA

Tryin 2 diversify my interests—
baseball game this wknd??

DIVYA BHATT

Can't! Performance in Tampa for
my cousin's sangeet!

PAYAL MEHTA

K have fun! Neil???

. . .

Ok cool whatever

PAYAL MEHTA

Ok but u gotta come w me

PHILIP KIM

Ok but you're buying me a hotdog

PAYAL MEHTA

Maybe one popcorn kernel

Maybe

CHAPTER TWENTY-THREE

I'd been going to this school for almost four full years, and I could honestly say this was the first time I'd attended any sort of sporting event willingly. The Florida sun was *very* hot on the back of my neck, and I was pretty sure I smelled like sunscreen. I looked up at the sky, blinking into the bright light, and I couldn't help but think of sitting in the backyard with Neil and joking about our moms just weeks earlier.

But I didn't *want* to think of Neil. If he was going to shut me out, then I'd shut him out. *And* Phantom Neil.

Hey!

"Okay, so that guy"—I gestured to the player standing at bat—"is going to hit the ball. And I bet that that guy"—I pointed at one of the other players standing in the outfield—"is going to miss catching it."

Philip had leaned back on the bleachers and tilted his face up toward the sun, which only highlighted his grimace. I could see the sheen of sunscreen shining above the sharp cut of his jawline too, but somehow he didn't smell like it. How was that fair?

"This is completely inane. I do not care, this is not making this game more fun, and I *fully* regret coming to this with you." His eyes cut sideways to look at me, softening the words.

I grinned. Philip was good at complaining, but he rarely meant it. He was next to me on the ribbed, metal seats, wearing a basic short-sleeved burgundy T-shirt and ripped jeans—but not the fashionable kind, the kind where he'd probably had those jeans for eight million years and the rips were authentic. Even though his bomber was a pretty light jacket, it was definitely way too hot out for it. He looked good in what he was wearing anyway. Comfortable. I mean he looked *comfortable*. I shook my head and looked down at my own outfit, regretting my fashion decisions. I was wearing a random school T-shirt I'd found in the back of my closet from eleventh grade[55] so I could actually support the Brighton High Knights.

"Whatever," I said, banging his knee with mine, "this is fun. I got you a hot dog."

"That was an hour ago."

I dug my phone out of my back pocket to check the time. "It was *literally* eleven minutes ago. You inhaled it. I'm not buying another one. Here," I said, holding up my half-finished carton of fries, "do you want some of these?" He looked at them disdainfully.

"You mean those soggy sticks you refused to add hot sauce to?"

"I don't like vinegary hot sauces!" I said, petulant. "I *can* handle heat. I'm going to put raw serrano peppers in everything you eat." I put the fries down on the seat next to me, but in doing so, my phone slipped out of my fingers. I yelped and reached for it, missing by a hair. Philip was already moving by then, his body leaning into my lap as he grabbed for it, taking advantage of his longer limbs. He managed to get ahold of the phone before it fell between the open bleacher seats and onto the ground below.

---

[55] I actually don't even think I was the one who bought it. It might have been Divya's. Or Neil's.

He let out a quiet "Whew!"

But I was too busy noticing the *entire weight* of his torso across my legs to appreciate the save. A sliver of bare skin between his T-shirt and jeans was pressed against my thigh, and I think my brain was short-circuiting a little bit. Philip seemed to realize his position just then because he hastily pushed away from me and back into his own space, cheeks aflame and gaze averted. He settled back into his spot and held the phone out to me, still studiously avoiding looking in my direction.

"Ah, thanks," I said, taking the phone from his outstretched hand. I could feel my own face heating up—even though I hadn't done anything! *Not cool, body.*

There was a beat of awkward silence between us, but thankfully a loud sound from the field offered a distraction.

"Oh, someone hit the ball really far," I said, forcing my tone to remain even.

Thankfully, Philip just tilted his head back up to the sky and groaned loudly. I heard an older lady behind us mutter something about "rude teenagers." Holding in a laugh, I elbowed Philip in the side.

He opened his eyes and looked at me balefully. "Can we *please* pretend to watch the game and talk about anything else at all? I thought that was the whole thing with baseball. Everyone agrees it's boring, but they come to the game to hang out."

"Well, you were the one who said yes to this, okay? You can't complain about it now." I shot him a grin—whatever weird energy had been between us a second before was gone now, making me wonder if it had really been there at all. I looked at him out of the corner of my eye. Philip's cheeks *were* still flushed a deep red . . . I shook my head at my own ridiculous train of thought and bit back a hysterical giggle. It was just the heat.

"Why did I have to come with you anyway?" Philip asked, and I was *extremely* glad he wasn't a mind reader because he would never stop making fun of me. Then I realized what he'd just said.

I frowned and tried not to think about my friends. "Because Neil and Divya didn't want to. And I knew you'd want to *hang out* with me," I said, aiming for teasing but not quite landing it. Philip's face took on an unreadable expression. But before I could ask him about it, I noticed movement from below us. "Oh, look, Jon's waving from the bench!"

"The *dugout*, I'm pretty sure?" There was something else behind the boredom in Philip's voice, but I couldn't put my finger on it. Honestly, if he wanted to be snarky about baseball, no skin off my nose.

"Whatever," I said, waving back at Jon, who'd looked surprised to see me, but happy, I think.

"Okay, Jon has seen you—we can leave now. That was what I really thought needed to happen," Philip said once I'd brought my hand back down.

"Oh, come on, I've never come to one of these before—"

"You've never come to a high school baseball game? Wow, what kind of sheltered life have you been living as a super-traditional Indian teenager who has clearly just come over to America?" he joked in that dry way of his that I was really starting to appreciate.

I laughed and elbowed him lightly in the side again. He squirmed but didn't move away, instead sending a long finger into my side in response.

"Ah!" I squealed, laughing. "Okay, okay, shut up—you're right, this *is* boring, and I've only ever been coerced into going to wrestling matches with Neil because his boyfriend's on the team. But maybe something happens at halftime?" My voice went up at the end because I wasn't really sure what a baseball halftime looked like. Then something horrific occurred to me. "There is a halftime, right? They have halftime entertainment? Like, there will be music or *something*, right?"

Philip shrugged. "I have no idea; I haven't come to one of these either."

I looked away from the field, where it seemed like not much was happening. If I couldn't get into *cricket*[56], I was definitely not getting into baseball.

"Okay, fine, if we do leave, where would we go?"

Philip shrugged again. "I don't know, home? Or"—he paused, and when he started again, his voice had that weird tenor to it again—"there is this movie playing that I was thinking about seeing . . . *The Ghosts*—"

". . . *of Nara*???" I finished. Philip gave me an approving look.

"Alright, Mehta. I'm going to have to start taking notes on what we both agree is quality shit, because I have to be honest, it is really throwing a wrench into my nemesis plans. Actually, I bet that's why we're nemesi."

"Nemeses," I said instantly.

"Nemesi," Philip said again, but there was no heat in it. Just that mild irritation and condescending tone I've learned is simply how

---

[56] My poor dad tried *so hard* to get me to care about cricket, he bought me bats and a tiny jersey when I was a baby, but legend has it that every time he turned a match on, it was the perfect way to get me to fall asleep. My mom still laughs about it, and, honestly, cricket still makes me tired.

Philip sounds. He looked down and started typing into his phone. "Okay, I'm looking up showtimes. We can go do that instead, right?" Philip asked, and I nodded in agreement. Then I leaned backward and stretched my body out to work any kinks out from the horrible seating. Philip was smiling down at his phone, swiping through the ticketing app.

"Admit it, you don't regret coming to hang with me today, right?" I asked, a few laughs breaking my question up. Before Philip could say anything, though, there was a heavy movement next to me when someone sat in the unoccupied seat to my right. Looking over, I was surprised to see Josh Patel. He was clasping his hands and grinning; his knee was bouncing.

"'Sup, sports fans?"

"Hey, Josh," I said, still unsure of why he'd come to sit with me and Philip. I could see his regular crowd seated several rows closer to the field. "What's going on?" Philip gave Josh a taciturn head nod and then turned down to look at his phone.

"Man, Payal, I don't know what you did, but bless you," Josh said. Philip shifted in his seat next to me, and I could tell he was intrigued, but I had no idea what Josh meant.

"What are you talking about?" I asked him. Josh unclasped his hands and stretched them high over his head. He had on a pair of dark sunglasses and was facing the field, so I couldn't get a read on his expression other than it was a happy one.

"You don't know?" He answered my question with one of his own, and he sounded surprised. "Jon was seriously, *seriously* trying to convince me to go out with you."

"What?!"

Now Philip was silently shaking next to me, and I knew he was

201

desperately trying to hold in his laughter. Oh my god, this was terrible. Josh was still talking, and now I really needed him to shut up.

"Like to the point I assumed you asked him to ask me? But when you barely said anything to me at Divya's thing, I figured he was being a freak."

"I would not—" I started, my face now burning more from embarrassment than from the heat around us.

"I know, I know!" Josh faced me, finally. "I *know*. But it was so weird, I really couldn't figure out why else he'd be doing it. But whatever you're doing is working because last week it totally stopped. He hasn't asked me once if I've texted you yet."

"Why didn't you just—" Philip broke into our conversation, and I already knew what he was going to say before he finished.

"Just tell him to stop?" I said, because I was wondering the same thing.

"Dude does not take no for an answer—he really thought you—" Josh pointed at me and then back at himself "—and me? Would work? So, so misguided. Also . . ." Now he hesitated.

"What?" I asked again. What else could he possibly say that was more embarrassing than what he'd already said? Luckily, the seats around us were pretty empty. Turned out, no one *really* cared about our school's baseball team.

Josh's mouth fell down into a frown, and his eyebrows disappeared behind the frames of his sunglasses. "He may have texted your contact info to every Indian kid he knows two weeks ago—in case you're getting any weird texts. Not that he knows many!" he said, trying to reassure me. I felt my face morphing into a purely horrified expression as he went on.

"You got weird texts?" Philip asked.

I wasn't sure whether it was worse that Jon had sent those messages out . . . or that no one had thought I was interesting enough to message. *No, it's the first thing, Payal. Definitely the first thing.* Philip's question was going to be ignored, though, that was for sure.

"That is . . . so, so . . ." I didn't even know how to end that sentence. Infuriating? Embarrassing? Terrible?

"It was *misguided*," Josh said again. His chin was resting on his hand, his elbow braced against his knee. "Maybe I shouldn't have said anything? I assumed you guys had talked."

And that brought me back to what mattered. Jon and I *had* talked. Maybe this was progress?

"This is *very big yikes*," Philip intoned. I side-eyed him and hoped he could see he was being annoying. His mouth was in an ugly sneer. Why was *he* so mad? I ignored him and refocused on Josh.

"Nah, it's fine. Thanks for telling me, Josh. I appreciate it."

Josh nodded like he'd done his good deed for the day and pushed his hands against his knees to stand up easier on the shaky bleachers. "Cool, see you at Mahek Auntie's house next weekend?"

I nodded and gave him a short wave, which he returned before turning away.

"Later, Phil, Payal."

"It's Philip," my nemesis said under his breath. Once Josh had retreated far enough, Philip's face contorted in irritation, and he blurted out, "You don't really think that's fine, right? Like, that's gross on so many levels."

"It's gross," I agreed. "But he probably thought he was doing me a favor."

"And that makes it better?" he shot back.

"You already knew he was problematic! But he stopped—that's

growth! Right?" I spread my hands out in front of me like I was gesturing toward evidence on a table.

Philip shifted his head to the right, looking at me searchingly, his face twisted up. "Is it, though?"

"Look, obviously it means he's not looking to get me hitched to some random brown dude like he's my mom in an eighties Bollywood movie. Maybe he's starting to be interested in me, for *me*."

"Right," Philip said, deadpan.

"Anyway," I said loudly, ignoring Philip's clear dig, "this is a good sign for both of us! It means the plan is working!"

"I thought the plan was to end racism with love."

"Yeah, exactly. It's working out. Everything's coming up Payal." I smiled wide and bright and gestured around me.

Philip snorted. My smile turned sour.

"Don't make that sound!"

"Don't make excuses for 'misguided' dudes," Philip replied, throwing sarcastic air quotes around the word *misguided*. If air quotes could be called sarcastic. "You should quit this," he said, and I gaped at him. He couldn't be serious.

"Oh, come on. You don't mean that. What about the plan?"

"Maybe the plan is the thing that's *misguided*." He shrugged.

"Whatever," I said again. "You can't back out now. You already agreed to help me."

Philip sighed, and I could see the fight go out of him. "Fine. *Fine*," he said, "but I'm calling in so many favors over this, since I am definitely going above and beyond."

"Whatever it takes, buddy."

CHAPTER TWENTY-FOUR

FROM: Payal Mehta <payalmehta@brightonhs.edu>

TO: Neil Patel <neilpatel17@brightonhs.edu>

SUBJECT: ??

Hey, I miss you can we please talk? I'm sorry I missed your call and I hate that I have no idea what's going on with you and you don't know what's going with me

CHAPTER TWENTY-FIVE

I closed my laptop, leaned back in my chair, and rubbed at my eyes—I'd sent that email to Neil a few weeks earlier. Just after I'd gotten home from the baseball game–movie hangout with Philip, actually. And he still hadn't answered. As some kind of weird self-induced torture, I kept opening it out of my sent folder and considering forwarding it to him with the tag *icymi!* and a smiley face at the end for good measure. But that was pathetic, and I was *not* pathetic.

At school, it wasn't any better. Neil . . . didn't talk to me. He was freezing me out, and I had no idea why. I asked Divya about it again, but she said she hadn't talked to him much either, with all her Bharatanatyam practice. Which was fine! Fair, even! Despite our promises to each other, we hadn't even hung out that much. She was busy with dance, and I was busy with school and Jon and Philip. It was good in one way, since I felt super weird because I still hadn't told Divya—or Neil, though that was more his fault than mine—anything about Philip or Jon or the plan. So there were these Neil- and Divya-shaped holes in my social circle (triangle?) *plus* I couldn't—fine, *wouldn't*—talk about the biggest thing happening in my life right now. And it wasn't because I didn't want to tell Divya! But it felt wrong to tell her and not Neil.

Honestly, even Phantom Neil had stopped popping into my head, which seemed like a very bad sign.

But Neil was the one who was making that choice—to not talk to me and to not tell me *why* he wasn't talking to me. I did as much as I could! I reached out! He ignored me. It was officially not my problem anymore.

Or so I kept telling myself.

My phone buzzed from behind me on my bed, still in the same place I'd thrown it when I walked in from school a few hours ago. Until I'd opened that email, I *had* been very diligently working. Now that I'd been sufficiently distracted by the familiar feeling of frustration, though, I figured I may as well give up. I unfurled my legs from where I'd been sitting crouched in my desk chair[57] and shook my right foot out a little to get rid of the pins-and-needles feeling. I needed to remember to stop sitting on my own feet for so long. Hobbling slightly, I made it to my bed and tapped at my phone screen. It was a text from Philip telling me he'd listened to the playlist I'd sent him and that I was right—it was a perfect complement to the *Trek* book he'd told me about. I grinned; I *knew* he'd be into it. I pictured him begrudgingly typing the words *you were right* to me, and it took everything in my body to not send back a voice text that was just me laughing.

Instead, I typed back a quick note, I told you so, and hit send. Philip wrote back immediately asking if we were still on for the psychology meetup. Before I could answer, he sent another message that said And stop opening that damn email. Patel will reply or he won't.

A month ago, if I would have told myself that Philip Kim would be the friend I'd be talking to about my issues with *Neil*, I would have—

_____

[57] You sit your way and I'll sit mine, okay?

well, first I would have asked about time travel, but then I would have laughed in my own face. I pressed down on the message and hovered between using the exclamation point or the thumbs-up reaction. Philip was right. I was honestly kind of surprised at how cool he'd been about everything. He was totally ready to talk me through whatever was happening, and I didn't even have to negotiate with him for it. Like we were actually friends or something.

Instead of using a reaction image, I tapped on Philip's name and hit the camera button. The screen shifted to dialing, and I had the brief and sudden urge to slam my thumb down on the hang-up button. But then the sound of someone answering brought me back to my senses. To my surprise, the face that filled my screen wasn't Philip's, but that of a rather a pretty Korean woman staring at me. Her hair was long and black and straight, with a few streaks of gray. She had thin black liner on, and her wide cheeks were subtly rouged.

"Hello? Who's calling? Sorry, Philip is in the bathroom," she said. Her voice was low, and I could hear a thread of Philip's cadence in her slight accent.

"Oh, hi—I'm—" I started to say, but another voice popped in, interrupting my introduction.

"MOM? WHY ARE YOU ANSWERING MY PHONE?" Somewhere off-screen, Philip was yelling loudly with a panic I'd *never* heard from him before. It was incredible. The woman, who I now knew was Mrs. Kim, looked over to the side and immediately started speaking in rapid Korean. I cringed[58] at her tone. I heard Philip's voice speaking back to her, but since it was *also* in Korean, I had no idea what he was saying. Wait, did he just say my name? When she turned back to the

---

[58] I may not speak the language, but I did speak immigrant-parent-yelling-at-you-so-your-friends-won't-know, and that was *definitely* happening.

camera with a huge smile, I wasn't totally sure what to expect.

"So you're Payal! We've heard so much about you. But I see that he didn't tell me how pretty you are!" Mrs. Kim said, her teeth shining bright and white against her grinning red lips. My face immediately flushed. That wasn't really on the list of things I thought I would hear when I decided to call Philip. He was talking to his mom about me? She said I was *pretty*? I looked at myself in the smaller square at the bottom of the screen and had to stop myself from grimacing. My hair was in a ponytail, but there were frizzy curls escaping the rubber band, which gave me a strange halo effect, and my skin looked gray in my bedroom lighting. Not ideal, if I was being honest.

Then the camera shifted as Philip grabbed the phone from her, and his face came into view.

"What my mom means is that I told her about the psych project," he said drily. There was a slight tinge of red on his cheeks, but other than that, he looked completely unruffled by everything I'd witnessed. Jerk.

"Sure, though I'm offended you didn't tell her how pretty I am," I teased. The red on Philip's cheeks spread further, and I bit back a smile; at least he could get embarrassed too.

"I'll punish him for it. Don't worry!" I heard his mom say, and I couldn't help but let out a loud laugh. Philip rolled his eyes in what I was realizing was a more good-natured than condescending way before telling his mom he was walking away. The background changed behind him as he walked through his house. "So what's up?" he said while I tried to get glimpses of the space around him.

"Nothing, calling you seemed like more fun than actually working on calc homework," I said—it wasn't exactly the reason, but it wasn't a lie. But I couldn't say, *Oh, nothing, I felt like talking to you.*

He'd *never* let me live it down. His eyebrows went up and disappeared under his bangs as he made it to wherever he was going and shut a bright-white door behind him. It was quiet for a beat while he situated himself on what I figured was his bed.

"Wow, I feel so important," he said once he'd finally sat down. I looked over his shoulder and squinted like it would help me see what I was looking at.

"Is that a Jin poster?" I asked, and Philip turned around to look up at the wall over his black metal headboard.

"Obviously," he said. "You know I had to rep Samurai Champloo."

I looked him at, incredulous. "You're not seriously telling me that Jin is the best character? Like . . . seriously. *Seriously?*"

That was all it took for the conversational floodgates to open, and we spent the next twenty minutes arguing about a series we both ostensibly loved but clearly had massive disagreements about. It was awesome.

"Whatever," Philip finally said. "I can concede—"

"HA!" I cut in and then *immediately* hung up before he could say anything else. I swiped over to our text and wrote:

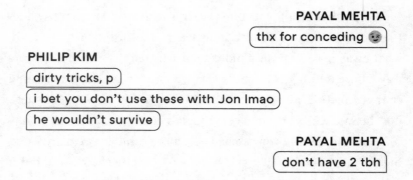

PAYAL MEHTA
thx for conceding 😌

PHILIP KIM
dirty tricks, p
i bet you don't use these with Jon lmao
he wouldn't survive

PAYAL MEHTA
don't have 2 tbh

I flipped over and onto my stomach and rested my chin on my folded arms, grinning at the text the whole time. Me and Philip Kim. *Friends*. Past me's head would explode.

And on top of *that*, if I told my past self that I'd have had not one, but *two* non-school-related hangs with Jon over the last few weeks? Well, okay, she might have fainted. Our history test was long forgotten at this point—my A had been expected, but Jon's C+ was a surprise given the amount of coursework we *hadn't* gone over. Despite no imminent test, we'd continued our study dates even though there was definitely no studying happening.

Okay, one hang was school-related insofar as we'd hung out after school on campus because his practice got canceled and I'd happened to run into him on the way to the parking lot. We'd literally sat and chatted outside his car and watched videos on our phones together for, like, *an hour and a half*. And it was super chill because that was the new me: super chill. The second hang was way more deliberate.

I was at the same coffee shop I'd met Philip at, only this time it was Jon sitting across from me. He was holding a large mug and had a hand over the mouth of it, wafting the steam toward his face. I was staring, fascinated. In a way that told me I was maybe making too many assumptions about him, I was shocked to find out that Jon was kind of a coffee snob.

"I've been here a few times," he said when we sat down at a table next to the floor-to-ceiling windows. "The roast is *okay*." He winced slightly and waved his hand in the so-so motion. "But when you need caffeine, you need caffeine, am I right?"

"You probably have, like, five million joules of energy in you, huh?" I joked.

"I have no idea what that means, S. P." But he laughed as he said it, and I put a mental reminder to tell Philip Kim that his joke kind of worked out for me. He would hate it. Outside, there was a bright flash of lightning, and the side of Jon's face was illuminated in its wake. We'd managed to make it into the shop before the storm really broke, but the thick afternoon humidity had really done a number on his hair. It was sticking up this way and that in haphazard frizzy curls. Because I had been smart enough to assume it would rain today, my own frizzy mess was slicked back into a tight bun on the top of my head.

"So," I said, pulling out the reason we were here from my backpack. It was a signed special edition of the first book of The Green Trials series. Jon's eyes went huge, and I swore I could see my whole face in the reflections of his irises. He lifted a hand over the cover and then hesitated, like he wasn't sure he was allowed to touch it. "Go for it." I smiled, gesturing. "It's, uh, wrapped in a protective film."

"This is *amazing*," he said, running his fingers along the cover before opening it to see the signature inside on the title page. "How'd you even get this?"

"Oh, my dad had a patient once who *loved* him and found out that I was a big fan of the books, and so they passed it along to me," I said quickly. I didn't really want to bring up my family and give Jon an opening to stick his foot in his mouth.

"That's so cool," he said again. "My dad never gets anything cool; he does marketing for, like, home appliances." He grinned suddenly. "I mean, unless you're in the market for a brand-new state-of-the-art dryer that weirdly plays music when your clothes are finished?"

"I think I'm good," I said with laughter in my voice. Jon pushed the book back toward me.

"I can't believe no one's made a movie of these books yet," he said, but then immediately went back on that by adding, "although I don't know if I'd want someone to make a movie of it."

"I know what you mean. There's *no way* they'd get the nuance. And they'd probably try to truncate the whole thing into one movie or something horrible like that."

"Or worse, break the series into more movies than there are books!" He moaned. "Never mind, I take it back. I do not want anyone to make these movies. Although, if they *did*, I know exactly who I'd cast for Torrigin."

I put my elbows on the table and leaned my chin on my closed fist. "Oh yeah?" I asked, "Who?"

Jon looked away, biting his lip. Then he snapped his fingers a few times, and I realized he was trying to remember the actor's name.

"Oh, what was it—James something? He's British, I think."

"Personally," I said, pressing a hand against my heart, "I can tell you that there's this Pakistani actor who would be *excellent*. He's got the dark hair and eyes, and the *beard*. Not to mention that come-hither look Torrigin uses, like, eight thousand times." I typed Fawad Khan's name into the browser on my phone and brought up a picture to show Jon. Once he'd leaned forward to see it, he nodded appreciatively.

"Oh yeah, he *totally* looks the part. And I bet he could learn how to do an English accent easily enough."

"He could probably use his regular accent . . ." I said, but there was an embarrassing meekness in my voice. "I mean—"

Jon had reached forward and pulled the book back again. He was flipping through it now and hadn't heard what I said.

"Thanks again for showing me this. It really is so freakin' cool. The illustrations are amazing."

"Aren't they? The one of the mountain? It's my *favorite*."

"Mine too!" Jon leaned back in his seat and gave me an appreciative look. "Man, I'm so glad you asked if I wanted to study, S. P. I never would have known that we could be here like this. That it'd be so easy? I would've lost out."

I smiled softly, ignoring half the sentiment again and instead focusing on the last part, how *he* would have missed out on hanging out with *me*.

"PAYAL!" Uh-oh, that was my dad's voice. My dad was *never* the one to yell for me unless I was in trouble. I started racking my brain trying to figure out what I could have done—then I slapped a palm against my forehead. Honestly, what *hadn't* I done was the better question. I'd been lying to my parents for weeks—every time I went to see Jon, they thought I was at Neil's house or Divya's house or studying at the library.

"COMING!" I yelled back. I shoved my phone into my pocket and headed downstairs. I really hoped my parents didn't know about the lying.

When I got to the living room, my dad was waiting for me. His hands were on his hips, and he looked furious.

"Payal, tell me why Dr. Day is saying it is your fault that Suraj won't go back to his studies?"

I—*what?*

"Uhhh . . ." I started. I didn't even know what to say. The allegation was so absurd, it was like asking me why it was my fault that someone decided to cancel *Riverdale*. What did it have to do with me?

My dad was tapping his foot now, which meant a lecture was forthcoming. There were plenty of things I would accept being yelled at for—like I said, I have definitely been cosplaying the bad kid lately—but this?

"I didn't do anything. I haven't even talked to him since I met him at that dinner *you guys* forced me to go to." I hated that my voice went higher at the end like I was asking him a question. I wasn't—or at least I didn't mean to be, even if my tone said otherwise.

"Payal—you must have said *something*," my dad said, flinging his arm out and catching his tie so hard that it whipped over his shoulder. He hadn't even taken the time to change out of his work clothes, which was yet another indication of how mad he was.

"I don't know if it's worse that a grown man is blaming a seventeen-year-old for his problems or that you, as another fully adult man, believes him" is . . . what I wanted to say. But my dad would've killed me. So instead I lifted my shoulders in a confused shrug.

"I don't know. We talked for, like, five minutes."

"Arun! Is that ullu ka pattha blaming Payal for something?" Mom yelled from the other room. Thank goodness she'd entered the chat.

My dad's eyes went wide behind his glasses. I stifled a laugh—it looked like he had not actually said anything to my mom before deciding to randomly yell at me for the choices of some twenty-five-year-old. He took a deep breath like he was trying to settle himself.

"Falu, Dr. Day is not an ullu ka pattha!" he finally called back to my mom. I heard her laugh and had to bite back a grin. Then to me, he added, "Never mind, you can go back upstairs." And that was probably as close to an apology as I was going to get. I nodded and turned to walk away. Talk about a close call—out of everything to get in trouble for, something I didn't actually do was a surprise. I was lucky he hadn't run into Divya's parents or something and found out that I hadn't been over to her house in weeks. But where did that kid, Suraj, get off blaming me for anything? I thought we were cool!

I pulled my phone out of my pocket on the way back up to my room, intending to type out a long text complaining about how extra my dad was being, but when I went to fill out the "To:" field, I was surprised to see my fingers instinctively hitting *P* for Philip.

When did *that* happen?

"Hey, S. P.!" Jon's teeth gleamed in the sunlight, highlighting his smile. He was standing on the sidewalk in a loose Brighton High tank top and teal board shorts, waiting for me outside his house. He was actually leaning against that god-awful pink flamingo and somehow *still* looked good. I closed my car door and sent a bright look back his way but couldn't help but feel puzzled. He never waited for me outside. I melted a little bit inside, though, hearing his nickname for me again. I didn't love that it stood for *Sweetie Payal*, but I did love that we had an inside joke!

"Hey," I said. "What are you doing out here?"

"I actually thought we might go somewhere else today," Jon answered, his voice lilting up at the end. "If that's cool?"

"Sure," I said. "Do you . . ." I gestured to my car. "Want to get in?"

"Oh, you know what? Yeah. I haven't seen what your driving skills are like yet." He pulled at the passenger-side door, and I furrowed my brows. Now I was nervous.

"I mean, you can drive," I started, but Jon was already shaking his head, holding on to the handle, and sliding into the seat. Yeah, that was weird to suggest, wasn't it? Ugh.

"No, no, no, no. I'm already getting in. Too late."

I groaned as soon as he shut the door, and then I opened my own, getting in and twisting the ignition. Immediately, one of my favorite Bollywood songs started blasting from the speakers—it's one from the 1940s or something, and it's *beautiful*. I scrambled to turn it off, though, before Jon said anything about my taste in music. I mentally cried. It wasn't like I *only* listened to Bollywood music! Before this song, I was belting a Harry Styles one! My playlist was sabotaging me.

"Do you care if I pair mine?" Jon had his phone out in one hand while the other hovered at the control panel. Did I?

"Oh, uh, sure, that's fine."

That's fine? That was *intimacy*. I mean—not—okay, *whatever*. It means you're close with someone. Paired phones! I drummed nervously against my steering wheel, waiting. This new situation with Jon was clearly throwing me off my game.

The second his phone connected, Jon pressed play on some kind of surfy-rock kind of music, and it was nice. It was pretty. Very chill—much like, I had learned, Jon himself. He bobbed his head and turned the volume up a little bit.

"Okay, where are we going?" I asked, pressing the brake and shifting the car into drive.

"I thought we could go to the beach," he answered, fingers tapping against his knee to the beat of the song.

"Which one?"

"How about Lake Worth? Or Municipal? Either way, the drive's nice—"

"Let's do Lake Worth. I love that drive through the old parts of the town." And I really did; the pier was super cute, if a little touristy. I eased my foot off the brake and pressed the accelerator lightly to get up to the twenty-five-mile-an-hour speed limit in Jon's neighborhood. He was humming along to the song and looking out the window. "Is there any reason we're going there today?"

Jon shook his head. "Not really—my mom has friends over, plus I figured we've done everything we can possibly do in my house."

There was something in his voice, though. He sounded a little weird. I wanted to push, but—what if he got irritated? I was presenting as this super easygoing girl to Jon. Would she push? I wasn't sure. So I played it safe and nodded, flicking at the volume control on the wheel to turn the song up.

"I couldn't help but notice you did not bring your backpack," I said finally, after the song had played for a minute or two. Jon started laughing.

"Yeah, I figured we didn't need to pretend anymore, right?"

I could feel him turning to face me, so I smiled while my insides were doing flips. That was something I was *supposed* to read into, right?

We made it to the beach forty minutes later. Since it was a random Tuesday after school, there was plenty of parking. I pulled into a spot, and we both got out of the car—Jon paused at the back of my car and pulled the trunk open. The corner of his mouth came up.

"I knew you wouldn't disappoint," he said, holding up the twill bag I usually had shoved to the side in my trunk.

Like so many of my fellow South Florida teens, I always kept beach gear in the trunk. You never knew when you'd end up at one. I was glad I'd decided on shorts and a loose white T-shirt. Late spring temperatures were also *brutal*; I could already feel a sheen of sweat on my forehead from the heat. We walked across the steaming concrete and finally made it to the wooden walkway heading out toward the sand. Thankfully, the strange timing meant there was also plenty of space for us to find a spot reasonably far away from other people. Jon took the beach towels out of the bag and spread them out for us. I dropped my flip-flops at one corner and sat, cross-legged, facing the ocean. I pawed at the bag and then dug deeper into it when I couldn't find what I was looking for.

"Ah, shit," I said.

"What's up?" Jon asked as he shifted into a comfortable position next to me, his legs kicked out in front of him and crossed at the ankles.

"I forgot the sunscreen in the car." Jon furrowed his brow.

"Oh, right!" he said after a beat. "Skin cancer is no joke—also, I do not want to burn. I can go grab it?" he asked—reaching for my bag to get my keys. It was very gallant of him. I watched as he awkwardly walked through the hot sand back to the parking lot; I stared for a minute as I appreciated his shoulders in the bright Florida day. Then I took my phone out and texted Philip.

PAYAL MEHTA

Am at the beach with Jon???

The speech bubble popped up, and the ellipsis danced in a staccato rhythm. I waited for Philip to send through what was apparently going to be some kind of extended diatribe. Probably about how the beach was for tourists or something. But when my phone finally dinged, I was not-so-pleasantly surprised.

PHILIP KIM

Huh. That was weird. My fingers danced across the buttons as I typed a question asking why he'd sent such a short response, but before I could finish, Jon was back with the sunscreen. Unfortunately, or fortunately, the sunscreen thing did not devolve into any kind of movie moment where Jon offered to put some on my back or vice versa. Probably because it was the spray kind. He did ask me to spray his back, but there's no way to romantically spray sunscreen on another person—I stood a few feet away after learning the hard way that if you stand too close, the sunscreen *will* get in your mouth.

"So . . ." I started when we'd finally covered ourselves and smelled like whatever it was that sunscreen smelled like regardless of the scent listed on the bottle.

I could see the freckles on Jon's shoulders, and the reflection of the sun on his blond hair was so bright, I could barely look at it. He looked *literally* sun-kissed.

"Relax, S. P. Let's take a breath and chill." He leaned back onto his arms and lifted his face up to the blue, blue sky, closing his eyes against the bright light.

"That's what my mom says." I laughed, mimicking him. The warmth felt good against my face.

"Your mom tells you to relax and chill?" he asked, turning to face me with a bewildered expression.

"Not in so many words. With my mom it's 'Payal, meditate karo,'—I mean, 'Payal, you should meditate . . .'" I stumbled through the words.

"Ooh, yeah, moms are always there with the advice, right?" His own laugh bubbled up then. It was a laugh that was lovely to listen to. Unlike his big laughs, this one was soft and rolling, and I wanted to wrap it around me like a warm blanket. "Anyway," he said when he'd stopped, "she's right, and I'm right. Just chill for a second."

Then he lay back and put his arms behind his head and closed his eyes again.

I sat there for a few minutes, tense as hell. Should I lie back too? Should I stay seated? My knee started bouncing, and all of a sudden there were warm fingers resting on it, firmly stilling it.

"Okay, you have to tell me what is going on," Jon said without opening his eyes. My knee went stock-still.

Just that his fingers were touching my bare knee?! That I was not entirely sure how we got here? That he made my stomach do flip-flops whenever he opened his mouth? That his jawline made me want to cry? I scrambled for anything else to say that would not completely mortify me.

"Just some weirdness with my friend Neil" is what came out of my mouth, surprising me.

"Neil Patel?" Jon asked. "Oh, are he and Josh related? I keep meaning to ask you."

I groaned.

"Not all Indian people are related, Jon," I said, agitated, and some of my nerves settled down quickly.

"Not because they're Indian!" he said, aghast. "They have the same last name!"

"Oh!" I said, and tried to keep the awkward laughter from spilling out of my mouth. "Sorry! I mean—gut reaction."

Jon peeked out of one eye and grinned at me.

"It's fine," he said. "I think I can distract you from whatever's got you stressing out." This should be interesting. I waited for him to pull his phone out to play another surf-rock song. But he didn't. "Payal," he said, his mouth quirked up at the corners and his cheeks raised up into bright apples. "Do you want to go to Will's party with me?"

OH MY GOD.

CHAPTER TWENTY-SIX

I had to say yes. Obviously, I had to say yes. But I couldn't get my mouth to move. Finally, my jaw worked, and it opened.

"I—"

Before I could say anything more, Jon kept talking.

"It's just . . ." He straightened up, back to sitting, so now he was turned fully toward me. His hand was back on my knee, fingers tapping lightly on my skin, causing little fireworks everywhere they touched. I was possibly on the verge of hyperventilating. "You're so cool. And, like, I didn't know—I mean, I said this already, kind of, but I *really* didn't even know I could hang out with you like this, like, totally normal. I'd really like it if you said yes, in case that wasn't clear."

Okay, wow. That was not exactly a compliment.

"What do you mean by—" I cut myself off. It wasn't an insult either. Before, Jon didn't know me. And now he did. This was semantics. He was staring at me, waiting for an answer. I put my hand over his, and he flipped his own so our palms were pressed together. My heart stuttered for a single beat. Semantics were *fixable*. I could fix this. We'd have a talk about assumptions about what was "normal" or whatever, but . . . he'd *really like it if I said yes*!

"Um, yes, yeah. Yeah. I would love to," I said. I could fix this.

CHAPTER TWENTY-SEVEN

PAYAL MEHTA

He asked me to the party!

PHILIP KIM

Woo

PAYAL MEHTA

Why are you being weird?

This is what we wanted

PHILIP KIM

It's what you wanted

The only thing I wanted was
to get an A in psych

PAYAL MEHTA

Gee thx a lot

PHILIP KIM

CHAPTER TWENTY-EIGHT

I took another spoonful of daal from the pot and added it to the katori on my plate so it sat alongside roti, bhindi, and some raw onion[59]. My parents were seated at the table, already starting in on their dinner.

"Does anyone need a napkin?" I asked, waiting for them to decline before joining them. My dad tore a piece of roti and folded it between his fingers before dipping it into the yellow lentils.

"So, Payal, I ran into Divya's dad today. Uncle said you haven't been by in ages—I thought you've been studying with Divya?" He held the piece of roti, using it to gesture vaguely in the direction of outside, like Divya was at our front door or something.

I nearly choked on a bite of bhindi. Did I actualize this by thinking about it the other night?!

"Oh," I said after swallowing down some water to clear my airway. "We've been at the library. It gets a little hectic at her house. And half the time, I'm with Caitlin anyway."

You'd think with how much lying I'd done over the last few weeks that I'd built up some kind of skill at it, but apparently not. I was sure they could see through my shaky voice. But my mom only

---

[59] *Try* not filling up your plate in an Indian household. I dare you. I dare you to cross the mom of the house like that and live to tell the tale.

nodded and started mixing the daal up with the rice on her plate, her fingers taking on a slight yellow tinge of haldi as everything came together. She seemed content with my bullshit answer to my dad's very valid question.

My dad hummed, looking at his phone. "Ah, it looks like Faizal is going to be here next month. He's going to stay with us for two weeks."

I relaxed slightly. Wow, maybe my parents were not as scary and all-knowing as I'd assumed.

"Oh, also, Venkat and Alia are coming over tomorrow—"

"*What?!*" I yelped. My dad jumped; his hand hit his glass, and water spilled across the table in a long arc of liquid.

"Payal! Chup! What is wrong with you?" he said. My mom hurried to grab a towel.

Venkat and Alia were *Neil's parents*, which meant if they were coming over—

"Don't worry, bachu, Neil is coming; it's been such a long time since he's been here—we were going to invite Divya and her parents too. But Prem said he and Ruta are working," my mom said as she finished wiping up the mess and got up to put the towel next to the sink. When she turned around, she was looking at me with concern. "Why hasn't Neil been here lately?" she asked as if it had just occurred to her. "Did something happen?"

I shook my head vehemently. "No! No. Just, you know, college applications, tests, everyone's busy these days," I said, and hoped that it was convincing.

"Ah" was what my mom said. "Okay. Arun!" Her attention had been turned to my dad, who was tapping his phone screen in a burst of dull thuds. "Are you playing that game again?"

"No!"

I let the sound of my parents' light bickering wash over me. I wasn't sure what to be more nervous about—Neil coming over, or my parents finding out through the Desi grapevine how little anyone had seen me over the last few weeks. Hopefully the college thing would be enough to cover me. There wasn't anything I could say to my mom or dad, though. Not without admitting to a million other things. So I swallowed down my food, smiled, and nodded. I needed to talk to Neil. My parents could not find out anything about my Jon Slate stuff before I'd had a chance to make it to that party—they'd ground me *forever*.

What had been a pleasing smell of masala and mango pickle a few minutes before was now making my anxious stomach turn somersaults. Did I mention that I had never been particularly great at handling stress?

I pushed my chair back from the table and stood, picking my plate up. My mom looked up at me. "Khatam? Already?"

I nodded. "Yeah, I've got a lot of work to get through, and I'm not hungry anymore, so . . ." I trailed off. Luckily, she and my dad didn't find anything strange in my words. And they shouldn't—I'd played through this exact scene a million times with them. When in doubt, blame homework, and I'd be scot-free.

As soon as I got back to my room, I sent Neil a text asking him if he knew about our parents' dinner plans. The *Read* tag appeared, but no dancing ellipsis. I dropped the phone onto my desk and clenched my fists at my sides, taking a deep breath in through my nose and blowing out through my mouth. I was pissed off. How were we supposed to fix something if he wouldn't even talk to me? I hammered out another text to him and punched the send button.

> Fine, whatever. Try to find a way to get out of coming to my house tomorrow since it is clearly too much work to ever talk to me again.

NEIL PATEL

> Kinda seems like you're the one not talking to me tbh

What did that mean?!

PAYAL MEHTA

> ????

But he didn't say anything else, and I had no idea how to interpret that. I had *literally* been sending him texts and emails, and I'd even tried calling. Who called on the *phone* anymore?

I had to hope he'd follow through. It was strange having the stuff with Philip and Jon on one hand and then this weirdness with Neil on the other. My life had been so simple for so long—and maybe a little bit boring. But I usually knew where I stood with the important people in my life. Now Neil was not talking to me for who even knows what reason, Jon was asking me on dates, and Philip was . . . you know what? I don't know!!!

He'd barely spoken to me in the last few days since I told him that Jon had invited me to the party. It was like now that my plan was done, our psych experiment stuff could be sorted out through awkward professional emails. The last one he'd sent said, **Updated psych doc. Add intro and I'll revise. Thx.** We'd gone from texting constantly to nearly no communication. I frowned down at my phone. I missed him. I missed having someone I could talk to so easily. We had one more meeting the day after tomorrow, but I had a bad feeling that Philip was going to cancel.

Philip didn't confirm or cancel, but he skipped class. So psych had been infuriating, but school was otherwise uneventful and then I was on my way home. Auntie and Uncle were going to be there in, like, two hours. I still had no idea if Neil was coming or not. We didn't have any shared classes that day, and so I was going in with no intel whatsoever. I hated feeling unprepared. This *suuuucked*. A loud and angry song started playing through my car speakers, and I let out an angry whoop of appreciation for my phone shuffle's ability to understand my mood. I turned the volume up and screamed my way down Belvedere.

Unfortunately, the time really flew by after I made it home, and before I knew it, the food was in dishes, there were snacks on the tables in the living room, a pot of chai boiling on the burner, and the doorbell was ringing.

"Payal! Darwaza!"

"Got it!" I called back, dreading every second as I walked to our front door. I braced myself, reached for the knob, and turned it. When the door opened, it revealed Divya—and my brain went blank while I stared at her in complete confusion. Had I invited her and forgotten? Did my mom call her?

"Hey!" she said, coming in without waiting for an invite because that would be ridiculous.

"Hey . . ." I answered, trailing after her.

"Divya! Hi!" My mom had entered the foyer, already dressed in a simple salwar kameez. She opened her arms to hug my friend. "I'm so glad you could come—I was sad to hear Neil wouldn't make it tonight."

My shoulders slumped, though I wasn't sure why. I was the one who'd told him not to come . . .

"When did—" I started to say, but Divya interrupted me.

"Your mom ran into me at my dad's store while I was on my free period earlier." She turned to my mom. "Auntie, can I grab a cup and then Payal and I will go upstairs?"

"*Ish*, you don't need to ask. Go, it's hot and on the stove."

I was so glad Divya had come. I itched to grab her hand to pull her up the stairs to my room. I would've too, if the scalding-hot tea wasn't a factor. By the time Divya was settled on my bed with a steaming mug of chai between her hands and I was sitting on my desk chair facing her, I still hadn't stopped grinning.

"So . . ." she started. "What's going on with you and Jon? Because I feel like there is *so much* you are not telling me."

I grimaced and leaned back against my desk. Right. That whole thing.

"Well, first, can you tell me what this freakin' text from Neil means?!" I threw her my phone so she would see it. I watched her brows knit as she read through the exchange. She looked puzzled when she gave it back to me.

"I have no idea. I don't even know what it *could* mean. You've obviously been trying to talk to him?" She screwed up her face.

"Right!" I flailed and nearly fell off my chair.

"Like, I know he was going through that stuff with Finn or whatever, but that seems fine now, so . . ."

Ah, that unspecified *stuff* again. My favorite thing. Divya bit her lip as if unsure how to continue. She took a sip of her chai instead of saying anything else.

"I want to know what I *did*," I moaned into my hands.

"Is there anything you could have done . . . ?" she asked. "Like, did you get in a fight?"

I thought back—literally nothing. There was our minor thing at Divya's recital, but I'd apologized almost immediately. Other than that, the only other stuff I'd been doing was my Jon plan with Philip, but that had nothing to do with Neil at all.

"Divya, I'm going to actually scream because I literally can't think of anything that warrants the way he's acting."

She threw her head back and groaned, in what I assumed was frustration. "Well, nothing is making sense and I have no idea what's going on, and you *know* I—"

"Hate that. Yes, I know," Divya said.

I know too.

Oh, wow, after weeks of silence, Phantom Neil made an appearance. *Thanks a lot, Phantom Neil.* Divya put the mug down on my night table, stood up, and walked over to me. Then she leaned down and threw her arms around me.

"I'm sorry," she said into my shoulder, and I softened a little.

"Ugh, I'm lucky you like me so much." I put my arms around her, and I had to admit, it was nice hugging one of my best friends again. She smelled like my mom's chai-and-vanilla-scented body wash and the things I'd associated with her forever. It was safe and comfortable. I hummed in gratitude.

"So," she said, pulling back. "I'm sorry I can't help you—but I promise I'll ask him about it. But it's Neil . . . You know how stubborn he gets when he's upset about something." She was right. Neil and I both had a tendency to withdraw and be stubborn when we felt wronged. "You might have to be the bigger person for a while and keep asking him too." She moved back to her seat on my bed and picked her mug back up.

Instead of responding, I rolled my eyes. But it was easy for her to say. Every time I reached out to him and he didn't answer, a little more of my dignity got scraped away and dropped into a metaphorical trash can. Divya took that as a reluctant acquiescence, I guess, because she didn't wait for me to say anything before she opened her mouth to ask, "So *now* you have to tell me. What's going on with you and a certain hot blond with a sensitive stomach?"

I hesitated. Even if I was mad at him, it felt really weird telling Divya this without Neil knowing. But I also didn't think I could sit here and lie to Divya's face anymore. And I didn't want to! I wanted to tell her about Jon and our dates that weren't dates and about going to the party. And I wanted to ask her what she thought was going on with Philip and why he was pulling a Neil-lite. But . . .

"I . . ." I started, twisting my fingers together. "I want to tell you, but I want to tell you and Neil together. And . . ." I paused, wanting to say something but not sure how to say it. "You know, the last time we talked about Jon, you and Neil told me to get over it. And I wasn't . . . I don't think I was ready to get over it?"

Divya's mouth was open in an *O* shape, as if what I'd said had never occurred to her.

"Payal! We didn't want you to get hurt. You know that!"

"I know! I just—it really . . ." I struggled, trying to find the words in my head. How did I say this without sounding like I was sensitive or a crybaby? I looked away from her and twisted my fingers in my lap.

"You can talk to me about it now, if you want," she said, doing what Divya always did. She tried to find the right thing to say, even if there might not be one.

"Thanks, di—but I still . . . soon." I settled on *soon*. Her face fell a little, but then she plastered a smile over it so quickly, I wasn't sure I'd seen it at all.

"Okay! Then I'll tell you how Vikash's cousin is the worst person I've ever met in my entire life."

See? It wasn't exactly the right thing to say, but it was enough to get us back to a space we were both familiar with, and I was thankful for it.

CHAPTER TWENTY-NINE

Divya ended up staying the night. She borrowed an old T-shirt and shorts to sleep in. The sleepover was perfect. Almost perfect. Okay, not quite perfect. But more perfect than anything else had been with my friends in ages, so I relished it. When we were both lying under my comforter and whispering to each other and watching videos in the dark, I felt more at home than I had in a while. I hugged her tightly the next day before she left. It was early afternoon, but we'd only been awake for an hour or so, having stayed up *way* later than we should have.

"Please can we not wait so long to do this again?" I asked, knowing that some of it was my fault. Divya stepped away and gave me a thumbs-up. Her hair was pulled back in a loose braid, and she'd changed into her clothes from the day before.

"Deal. And as *soon* as you are ready to talk, I am ready to listen. No moratoriums, no pushing you anywhere you're not ready for." As she turned to go, another car pulled up to the front of the house. It was a familiar black Nissan, and when the passenger door opened, I wasn't surprised to see Philip get out of the seat. I could see now that it was his mom driving. Philip nodded once at her and shut the door.

"Oh, you and Philip are still working on that project?" Divya asked, her voice significantly less warm than it had been a second earlier.

"Yeah," I said. "And he's not so bad, actually. He's been pretty cool these last few weeks since you and Neil were, uh . . ." I trailed off.

"Right, sorry," she said. "I'm glad you had someone in your corner, then."

"I mean, I wouldn't go *that* far." I laughed weakly, thinking of how weird Philip had been this week. Then he came up the front stairs to the house, and Divya put up a hand in greeting.

"Hi, Philip. I was about to head out."

"Okay," he said, not giving her anything else to go off of. A month ago, I would have yelled at him for being rude, but now I could hear the tenor of awkwardness underneath the rudeness, knowing the uncertainty he felt when he was around people he didn't know well.

"Okay, then." She turned back to me. "I'll see you later, and I meant what I said! Text me whenever. Or let me know if you wanna video chat later. I can show you the new payals I got."

I nodded in short quick bursts and waved. "Sounds good!"

When she was seated behind the wheel of her car and pulling out of our driveway, I finally turned to Philip. He had his jacket on again and was studiously looking at anything but my face.

"Hey," I said, letting ice seep into my tone and hoping he could feel it. Instead of returning my greeting, he chin-nodded at me and gestured to the door.

"Should we get started?"

"I didn't even think you were coming today." I stepped back inside and didn't wait for him to follow, throwing the words behind me like they didn't really matter.

"We have to go through the results and it's easier to do that in the same room. It's not like I canceled," he deadpanned from behind me.

"Did Divya leave?" My mom's question entered the room a second before she did. I started to answer her, but she saw Philip before I could. "Oh, who is this?"

"Mom, this is Philip—we're working on a psych project for school."

"Hi, Mrs. Mehta, it's nice to meet you." Philip's voice had gone warm and congenial, and I whipped around to stare at him. He had a bright smile on his face, and a hand out for my mom to shake. Who was this, and what had he done with my taciturn nemesis? I tried to catch his eye to mentally ask what the hell he was doing, but he intentionally ignored me in favor of sucking up to my mother.

Who was currently grinning from ear to ear.

"It's wonderful to meet you too, Philip. I hope you and Payal are going to work hard today."

"We've got the highest grades in the class for a reason." This time, Philip didn't sound conceited at all; he sounded plainspoken. My mom *loved* that.

She smiled at him and then put her arm out in an invitation to move to the room to our left.

"Go, you can work in the office. I'll bring some snacks in later." She turned to me, and the smile faded into a stern look. "Payal, darwaza khula rakh."

"Duh," I replied, and followed Philip through the door, which I did, in fact, leave open, with a pointed stare at my mom's retreating back.

"So," I said, falling backward onto the couch. Philip was already seated at the desk, and something deep in my stomach twisted at how suddenly it felt like nothing had changed. We were right back where we were the last and only time he'd come over to work.

There was a deep blue folder that he'd pulled out and was already flipping through.

"I already put together the report, if you want to look at it," he said. There was no question in his tone, only the assumption that I'd walk up there to read something over his shoulder. It was unclear whether or not I was going to be able to make it through this entire afternoon with him without screaming.

Fuck it.

"Why are you being like this?" I asked, hoping I don't sound half as pathetic as I felt. "What? Did you decide that you like being enemies more than frenemies or something?"

"Not everything has to be a joke, Payal," Philip answered without answering. His lips tilted down into a slight frown, but there was an edginess in his eyes, and his sleeve was stretched tight from where he was pulling it at the wrist. I could see him worrying at the fabric with his fingers. It gave me the courage to keep talking, because obviously he wasn't as closed off as he wanted me to think he was.

"Seriously, then. What is up? You just, like, shut down last week."

Philip leaned back in the chair and looked away, opening and closing his hands into fists a few times. Then suddenly he pushed back the chair and stood up.

"Let's go for a walk," he said.

"Huh?" I asked. I had whiplash from the sudden change of topic.

"Come on. I don't want to—Just come on." Philip walked past me, and in a role reversal, didn't even wait for me to follow before heading out the door.

"Philip! Wait! Hold on!" I yelped, heading to the door and slipping my feet into whatever shoes were closest in the shoe closet. The

237

front door was open, and I stepped through it, calling back behind me, "Mom! Just going for a walk. We'll be back in a few minutes!"

"Okay!" I heard distantly as I hopped down the front steps, praying I didn't fall. The shoes I'd put on were my mom's deep red chappals; her feet were at least half a size smaller than mine. Philip was standing on the curb in front of my house when I finally caught up to him. He was balancing on the edge, his dirty sneaks tipping his toes over, nearly touching the asphalt a few inches below. He had his hands shoved deep in his pockets. There was the scent of rain in the air, and I hoped we got through whatever was going on before it started pouring.

"What the *hell*, man?" I asked, shoving him lightly so he hopped down onto the street. In response, Philip clasped his hands behind his head and groaned, his expression pained.

"What do you even actually *see* in Jon Slate, Payal? He is like this cookie-cutter version of a person. He's barely real!" Philip's eyes were wide, and his mouth was in a thin, straight line slashing across his face, giving him an off-putting, stern look. I could see a small muscle twitching at his jaw.

"Huh?" I said again. "What does that have to do with anything? And he's not—I mean—What is going on right now?" I was having trouble finding my footing, and I hated when that happened. But Philip was being so confusing! I watched him now as he kicked at the street. He'd gone from stern to frustrated and angry, if his scowl was any indication. The pins on his jacket glinted every time he moved, the reflections a scattering of bright spots on the street. Why was he even wearing it? It was warm outside. I knew I didn't really care about the jacket, but everything about him was irritating me right now. Then he went still and stared at me, his eyes darting over my face like he was looking for something. Finally, he let out a sigh and answered my question,

"I don't even know what's going on."

He started walking along the edge of the curb but still in the street. I rushed up the sidewalk to match his pace.

"Philip, there's very little you don't know," I said, trying to lighten the mood or get us back to somewhere familiar, at least. He cut a quick glance at me, and I caught a sharp grin before it faded and he was frowning again. We were closer in height while he walked in the street, and I lifted a hand up to rest it on his shoulder. The fabric was hot under my fingers. "Just tell me what's up," I said, tightening my grip and pulling a little to get him to stop walking.

"I . . ." Philip said, and finally stopped. He took a deep breath and squared his shoulders. Then he stepped up off the street and onto the sidewalk so he was facing me. My hand fell off his shoulder, but as it slid down his arm, he caught it in his and held it.

"I like you," he said, and my jaw dropped. "And I think," he continued, looking at me dead in the eyes, "that you like me too." Everything went fully blank for a second as I worked to catch up with what was happening. Philip's voice was much more unsure than I'd ever heard it before, and there was an uncharacteristic tenderness in his brown eyes. "But," he added with his brows knit, and I tried to refocus, "you're so caught up in this beige blank slate of a dude—who says shit that makes you feel small—a guy you pretend you'll be able to fix by being the Indian girl in his life who teaches him how to be a better person. *That's* what you want? Yeah, right."

With every word, my blood boiled hotter. I snatched my hand away from him and stepped backward so there was space between us.

"How *dare* you," I spat out. "Yeah, I *want* this. I am *choosing* this."

Philip's eyes narrowed.

"Is it what you want?" he asked again. "Or were you reacting to a situation you couldn't control by trying to find a way to control it?"

"You don't get to tell me what I'm doing!" I said loudly. A car drove by, and I remembered we were standing outside. I made an effort to compose myself. I couldn't even think about the first part of what Philip had said. I was so angry that after all these weeks, he couldn't see what I was trying to do. "Philip," I said, my voice even, "no one gets to tell me where I'm allowed to be or what I should do. I get to decide."

"Even if that place is next to someone who doesn't even know who you actually are?" he asked, furious. His hands were flailing! "You've dissected every conversation you've had with him *with me.* Ask him to name something about you that didn't start with him or what *he's* into. He won't be able to. But—I . . . Mehta—Payal—I know you. I've known you!"

I moved forward and poked a finger into his chest.

"What makes you think that? When you can't even see why I'm doing this." I sneered, looking up and into his face. Philip didn't even flinch. His hair was falling over his eyes, but I could see them—so dark brown, they were almost black. Like mine.

"I know why you *think* you're doing this. I know you. I do, and you know me. You can't tell me you haven't been paying attention these last few weeks. Is it *work* to talk to me? Because I can tell you that talking to you is the easiest thing on the planet." He gestured between us and let out a little hysterical laugh like he couldn't believe he had to make an argument at all. "I don't have to worry about how you'll take something I say, or that you won't understand me. Does that sound familiar?" he asked. There was a plaintive tone to his question, and my heart skipped. I took a small step forward and closer into his space. I opened my mouth to say—I wasn't really sure what. That he was right?

"Philip, I—" I was close enough to see his eyes flitting back and forth over my face, to see the tight way he was holding his jaw and the way he was pulling at the edge of his sleeve. My eyes darted down to his lips and then back up to his eyes again. Philip noticed—of course he did. He leaned forward. So did I. Then Philip was kissing me. And I was *kissing him back*. My eyelids dropped closed, and everything else around us was blocked out. This was *not* like the time I got hives after kissing a boy in the closet at a party. This was very, very different. I could feel his mouth against mine, welcoming and warm. I draped my arms around his neck, and his hands were at my waist. It felt good—the kissing, the way his fingers curled at my hips. And it felt right. Thunder crashed above us, startling me.

My eyes snapped open.

Wait, we had been *fighting*!

I pulled away and stepped backward in a hurry, unable to hide the shock written over every inch of my features.

"What—What was *that*?!" I asked. My voice was rough and shaky. I twisted my arms behind my back and interlocked my fingers, holding them together out of sight. The air felt charged around us. I was thrown; I didn't know what to do. Or what to say. A paradigm was trying to shift, and I was stuck where I was, with the shifting happening around me. Philip was gaping and—*oh my god*—I'd never seen Philip Kim so flustered. A flush overtook his cheeks, the thin scar under his eye a bright pale line. His gaze was unfocused. He brought a hand up and curled it around the back of his own neck, resting his chin against his arm and looking away from me.

"I . . ." Philip shook his head. "I didn't mean to do that."

"You didn't mean to do that? *I* didn't mean to do that!" I cried. I was starting to panic. I could feel it in my gut, bubbling up. "What did we even do? Maybe we should agree that it didn't happen. Right. Like, what's real anyway? No one has to know. We can pretend—"

"Payal," Philip said, looking more miserable and sorrier than I had ever, ever seen him. "I have to tell you something."

"No, you don't," I said immediately.

His eyebrows scrunched. "I—What? Yes, I do," he said, a slight tenor of anger creeping into his voice. There he was.

"Whew, okay. I didn't recognize you for a second. Had to make sure you were still Philip." I laughed, but the sound was thin and reedy and fake. Philip sighed, and the heaviness was palpable. His shoulders straightened, and he closed his eyes briefly and nodded to himself before opening them and finding my gaze.

"I talked to Neil," he said, which was the last thing on the planet I expected. In fact, it wasn't even in the realm of expectation.

"Okay . . ." I said slowly.

"No, I mean, I told him about you and Jon. I didn't like it, the way you were . . . editing yourself around him. And I didn't know how to—I didn't think it'd be a big deal. I thought Neil could talk you out of it, but then instead he got *really* mad about you not telling him and stopped talking to you . . . and I've wanted to tell you for weeks, but I got scared and I'm sorry! I'm sorry." The last two words came out so soft, I nearly didn't hear them.

I stumbled backward. It felt like every molecule of air in my lungs had shifted into a different state and become solid. Philip's hand was reaching out like he was going to catch my arm. Instead, he slowly dropped it back down to his side.

"You what?" I managed to get out. My hands curled into tight fists, and my voice was low with anger. "You . . ." He'd talked to Neil about *me*. And about Jon. Like this was some kind of—"I knew you didn't care about this whole thing I was working on, but I at least thought we were *friends*." No wonder Neil was freezing me out—he was probably furious I'd been lying to him. That after talking to him about Finn, I was a hypocrite or something. That after—

"I'm sorry!" Philip's mouth was twisted. "I was trying to get you to drop this asinine idea *because* I'm your friend." He smiled, but it wasn't real. "But nothing I said was getting through to you. I thought Neil could help."

I stared at him, and he shrugged. Like he had no idea what else to say. As though simply saying he was sorry could fix this. *He* was the reason my best friend wasn't talking to me.

"I don't—What was your *plan*? All those times I talked to you about what was going on with me and my *best friend*, you'd didn't think to say, 'Hey, I might know what's—'" I started, then stopped. "Actually, wait, no. I don't—I don't even care." Philip opened his mouth to respond, but I held up a hand. "No. No, you don't—You don't deserve to say anything else. You *lied to me*. You're the reason I haven't had my best friend for weeks. You don't—You don't get to kiss me and then tell me you've been lying to me for who even knows how long. Since when?" Philip tried to speak, but I wouldn't let him get a word in. "Actually, I don't care," I said again, trying to make myself believe it. "I—I'm leaving. You stay here. Call your mom, or whoever, to come get you. Do *not* come back to my house. I am—" I stopped. There was something tight inside my throat, and it was getting more difficult to talk. My cheeks were hot and probably bright red. My eyes were starting to sting, and I could feel tears on the verge of falling. I spun around and walked away. I didn't want him to see me cry.

CHAPTER THIRTY

PHILIP KIM

Hey, I'm sorry

I shouldn't have done it

don't even know. It spiraled and then you were you and I didn't know how to feel, except guilty and happy that we were becoming I don't even know what.

Obviously I was wrong. But I wasn't lying. Okay at the beginning, maybe, I thought this was a big joke. But when it really started to matter? I had to come clean.

Payal come on

Okay alright, you're right. Let me know if or when you're ready to talk.

CHAPTER THIRTY-ONE

Bzzzt. Bzzzzt. Bzzzzt.

Stifling a groan, I turned my head to locate the source of the annoying sound rattling through my room. The carpet fibers tickled the side of my ear, but I ignored that minor annoyance to locate the louder one. *Oh.* There, under my desk, my phone was vibrating against the faux-wooden backboard, leading to an echoing buzz that wasn't so much cutting through my headache as it was enhancing it. Twisting my head back, I glared up at the ceiling. I should move to my bed. Lying on the floor felt pathetic. But it also felt like it was the only place I could try and wrap my head around what had just happened. Mostly because I was hidden from anyone who came through the door by lying on the right side of my bed, so I would have time to collect myself. Because right now? Not collected. *Uncollected*, even.

Philip *liked me* liked me. Philip *kissed* me. Philip . . . lied to me?

I couldn't believe Neil knew. Had known for a while. Wait! That day I had to get a late pass—that was . . . That was when he'd found out! When he said, "She wouldn't have"—that was about me. *She wouldn't have kept it from me* is what I bet he was going to say. That was the last time Neil had actually said anything real to me. I fell backward again. Rolling over, I pressed my cheek against the carpet. Everything about this was terrible.

Philip Kim put his tongue in my mouth. I shoved my face into the crook of my elbow and kicked my toes against the floor. The heat coming off my cheeks was downright radioactive. I shifted and rested forehead against my arm, so close to the carpet that it was scratching against the tip of my nose. I let out a deep sigh. I guess the kiss itself wasn't so terrible. As far as my limited experience with kissing went, it was pretty good. The memory of the way his lips *felt* pressed against mine flashed in my head—somehow both sweet and intense, pulling me into him in a way I'd never anticipated.

But! *He'd lied to me!*

The way you lied to me? Phantom Neil asked. I shook his voice right out of my head. It wasn't the same.

This would be the ideal time to talk this through with someone.

I wasn't sure if I was angrier with Philip for telling Neil or for ruining what had quickly become a really great friendship. Like—I *liked* being around Philip. I liked talking to him. I liked arguing with him. I liked—

I liked a lot about him.

Then there was Jon. I searched for that feeling again, of his fingers loosely holding mine and the way my heart pounded when he asked me to the party. But the only thing I could hear was Philip's voice echoing in my head telling me that I was "editing" myself. But everyone did that. *Everyone.* I had a plan. The longer Jon and I hung out, the more *me* I could be. American, Indian, nerd, sarcastic, awkward, loving, joyful—so many things together.

And having someone like Jon wanting to be with someone like

me? It was proof. Proof that I wasn't going to be dismissed because of some bullshit preconceptions, that I could hang at a baseball game, and at parties, and proof that I could control *my* life—god, it *sucked* that I couldn't talk to my best friend about this.

I stood up and started to pace, working through the last few dates with Jon.

There were clearly parts of me that Jon liked! I wasn't *pretending* to be into that stuff. So I had been dialing it back on some of the references he might not understand, and maybe I tried not to explicitly talk about my culture too much.

Or at all?

But was it because he didn't want me to, or was it because I was too afraid?

I reached over and grabbed my phone. My eyes skimmed over the multitude of notifications without pausing to actually read them. Text after text from Philip. I held the socket on the back of my phone with one hand and pushed against the side of the phone with the other, twirling it in a circle while I considered how—or if—to respond to his latest ones. I stopped my movements and settled the device in my palm, then opened the phone to his messages but didn't read any of them. He would see that I'd seen them and chosen not to respond.

Sit and stew, Philip Kim!

Then, before I could talk myself out of it, I opened a blank text, typed a message, and hit send.

PAYAL MEHTA

> Hey u wanna watch a bollywood movie later? I'll bring by one of my favs

JON SLATE

> Oh hey I don't rly like reading subtitles—
> but what if we start w like a clip or two
> on youtube I could check it out?
> send me some links!

I don't rly like reading subtitles. I full-body cringed, and my eyes rolled so hard I thought they might fall out of my head. It wasn't exactly a *no*, but . . . why was he making this so hard?! Whatever. I *would* send him clips. And he'd love them. Or, he'd better tell me he liked them, at least. Disappointed, I pulled up the YouTube app on my phoned and listlessly looked through a few options to pass along to Jon. A notification dropped down from the top of the screen, cutting off the top of Aamir Khan's head for a second.

PHILIP KIM

> I am not going to stress over the fact that
> you read these and didn't respond because
> I know exactly what you're doing.

> It's like I said: I know you, Payal.

I threw my phone back down to the floor and groaned out loud. That *asshole.*

CHAPTER THIRTY-TWO

I didn't respond to that text from Philip. Or any of the ones he sent over the next week. It wasn't hard—we only had one class together, and this week in psych we had been mostly focusing on preparing for the final exams, but unfortunately today that was going to change. It was a work-on-our project day.

On Monday, when Philip walked into class, my breath caught in my throat. He was wearing fitted jeans and what looked like an old comfortable T-shirt with some kind of faded logo on it. And even though there were bags under his eyes, he looked good. I'd tried to prepare for this, for seeing him again, knowing that we were going to have to actually speak. Telling myself that seeing him didn't matter, that I was better off, that I had my plan and I needed to stick to it . . . but apparently preparation didn't do anything. Philip yawned then and rubbed at his face before walking toward his desk. He *did* look tired. I could guess at least some of it had to do with me. My stomach twisted, and I frowned. I didn't want to feel *sorry* for him. He was the one who'd lied to me. Neil hadn't talked to me in *weeks*!

At some point, you're going to have to admit some culpability, you know, Phantom Neil piped up.

I looked away as Philip's head turned in my direction. I didn't want him to catch me staring, but even without seeing, I could feel his eyes on me. I put my head down on my desk. *Let him think about what that means. Let him lose a little sleep.*

I thought I was ready for him by the time Philip claimed the spot right in front of me. Then he shifted so he was seated with his legs hanging over the side of his chair and faced me. His eyes met mine for the briefest second, my heartbeat doubled, and I immediately looked down and ran my eyes over my notebook instead, pretending to read.

"Meh—Payal . . ." Philip started, his voice low. But whatever he was going to say was cut short.

"And how are my top two students doing?" Mr. Lutton had walked over.

"We're fine, we'll have our project in soon," I replied tightly. There was movement happening in the corner of my eye; I saw Philip rest his hand on my desk and start tapping his fingers. The same way I used to—the way that I knew he hated. I shot him a dirty look before turning back to Mr. Lutton.

"Philip mentioned—I'm looking forward to it, kids. Just make sure it's on my desk within the next two weeks." Mr. Lutton grinned, clearly not picking up on the negative energy that I thought was practically vibrating off me and Philip.

When he walked away, I glared at Philip. "Oh, you didn't think it was important for me to know that you'd said anything to Lutton?"

"Well, I didn't think you were looking at any of my messages, considering I didn't see another *Read* tag," he shot back. The truth was I'd eventually turned off my read receipts because I didn't want Philip to know if I'd seen his texts or not.

"Whatever," I mumbled. I hated this. I wanted—I don't know. To be friends again? To get back to that comfortable place we'd been in?

"*Whatever,*" he snarked back. Then he turned away to face forward and scribble into his notebook, and I focused on mine.

At the end of the period, I dropped my folder on Philip's desk. He looked at it with a blank expression before stacking it with his own notes.

"I'll put these together," he said tersely. He turned away and started packing his bag without another word.

It stung. It was probably safe to assume I wouldn't be getting any more texts or messages from him anytime soon.

Which made sense—how many more times was he going to try? Until I told him it was okay, he probably wouldn't try again, honestly. I frowned as I realized what that meant—he was taking *my* lead.

I went through the rest of the school day in a bit of a daze. Finally, the last bell rang, and I stepped out into the hallway. Everyone was scurrying by, heading to their cars or the pickup station or the buses to kick off their weekend plans, and here I was moping outside of a quickly emptying classroom. I didn't want to feel like this.

Cutting my way into the crowd heading to the parking lot, I took stock of the *good* things happening right now.

1) I was going to a party with a dude I'd liked for three years, and *he* had asked *me.*

2) *I* had made that happen.

3) I *was* desirable and I knew it and I'd proved it.

I straightened my shoulders, lifted my head high, and made my way through the exit. It was gray outside, and the air felt heavy with a sticky moisture. I grimaced a little at the gross feeling against my skin. Several feet away, I spotted a head of dark hair tilted toward a lighter brown one—Neil and Finn. They were holding hands and laughing. I picked up my pace for a second before immediately hesitating . . . I should hang back. Neil obviously wasn't ready, and I—I wasn't sure what to say now that I knew he knew. His message from weeks earlier made sense now. Of course, the person I'd been talking to was Philip. And Jon.

Like he could feel me watching, Neil's head turned, and we made eye contact. He said something to Finn and then held his phone up to me, gesturing to it. I pulled mine out and there was already a text from him on my locked home screen. It covered up the top halves of our faces from that day we celebrated Holi, so I could barely see three bright, color-covered smiles underneath it.

NEIL PATEL

> Walking Finn to practice but then
> meet u at ur car?

I looked up and saw him watching me, brows raised. An intrusive thought popped into my head—did Philip say something to him? I gritted my teeth. I *hated* that that was my instinct. Neil's expression was neutral, but I finally nodded once, and he smiled in a tentative sort of way. He turned back to Finn then, and they kept walking.

I was surprised—and thrilled—to see Divya standing at my car by the time I got there. She was leaning against the back door on the driver's side and listening to something on her phone. There was a thermos on the ground next to her feet. Her hands were moving into various mudras, elegant and soft. She was probably practicing for her next dance class. She looked up as I got closer, and waved, then pulled her earbuds out of her ears and shoved them into the pocket of her sweatpants.

"Hey! Neil texted me," she said, preemptively answering the question I was about to ask. "I figured, I'm here, so we can finally find out what the heck is going on!"

I grinned and said, "I'm glad." Then I looked away. "I know most of it, I think," I added. Her eyes went wide, but she waited for me to speak again. "I think we should wait till Neil gets here?" I sort of asked, uncertainty lacing through my tone. Uncomfortable, I tucked a lock of hair behind my ear just for something to do with my hands.

"Is it . . . bad?" she asked in return. "I mean, I'll wait, of course, but . . ."

"No, no, I don't know." I leaned against the driver's door, next to her, the heat of the metal warming my skin through my clothes. "This was his idea, so—"

"So," she said, and then balled her hands into fists and proceeded to do a little dance, shaking her hips and punching the air in sharp movements. "You are gonna make up!" she sang, and punched on rhythm between each of the words. I couldn't help but let out a sharp bark of laughter. She looked *ridiculous*. And amazing.

"I hope so," I said, smiling fondly at her antics. Inside, my stomach was rolling. I *was* nervous about the upcoming conversation. Neil and I hadn't *talked* talked since Divya's dance thing several weeks ago. Had he been sitting there getting more and more resentful every time I didn't come clean, or every time he saw me talking to Philip or Jon? I took a deep breath. This shouldn't be so nerve-wracking. I'd known Neil for *so* long.

It will be fine. I'm pretty reasonable. I silently thanked Phantom Neil.

"Hey, guys." And for the first time in a long time, Neil walked up to my car. His hand was raised in greeting, and he looked . . . sheepish. I don't think I'd ever seen Neil with that particular expression on his face.

"Hi," Divya and I said in unison.

"Hey," Neil said again. His fingers were thrumming against his sides, and he was biting his lip, both telltale signs of nerves. The three of us stood around awkwardly for a second before Divya took things into her own hands.

"Okay," she said, frowning. "This is uncomfortable, and that's *okay*. Let's get in the car and finally *talk about it*." She groaned the last part of her sentence, elongating the word *talk* in a deep tenor. She opened the back door and hopped in behind the driver's seat. I shrugged at Neil and got behind the wheel while Neil walked around the front of the car to take his spot in the front passenger side.

I turned my car on, and a Frank Ocean song blasted out of my speakers, already mid-song. Neil's phone had autoconnected. My heart warmed, and I started drumming against the steering wheel. Out of the corner of my eye, I could see Neil's mouth quirk up on one side. Behind us, Divya was already humming.

"So let's get it out there," Divya finally said, a few minutes after I'd pulled into the parking lot of her parents' store. I could hear the soft taps of Neil's fingers against his jeans.

I took a deep breath and turned to them both. "I am so sorry for lying to you guys."

At the same time, Neil said, "I'm sorry for icing you out!"

And Divya said, "I'm sorry for something I don't know!"

I turned the car off and laughed a little bit.

"Let's go one at a time?" I asked. "And, Divya, you don't have to apologize just because we are." I twisted around in my seat to look at her. She was laughing awkwardly into her thermos.

"Yeah, that's weird, yaar," Neil added, but he offered her a slightly pained grin to soften his words.

She nodded, biting at the lip of her drink, and then added, "Fine, you're right. I didn't do anything wrong except for what I *already* worked out with Payal."

"Oh, the Vikash thing? I told you she wouldn't care," Neil said. I harrumphed in my seat. A slice of sun broke out across my windshield, and I leaned forward to catch the clouds breaking apart in the sky.

"So you *were* talking about me," I said, still craning my head forward to watch the clouds moving.

"Obvio!" they agreed in tandem.

"Look," I said, falling back into my seat and refusing to acknowledge the reference. "I'm seriously sorry I said that thing about Finn not getting it. I have no idea what your conversations were like, and I shouldn't have assumed. But I am *really* sorry for lying, Neil. And I'm sorry you had to find out from *Philip*." I said his name like a curse, and I knew they could hear it.

"I'll admit, that was maybe the most shocking part of it—that Philip knew something about you that I didn't. And yeah," Neil continued, "I was mad that you didn't tell me the truth. But I was also mad that you told me Finn wasn't worth it because he didn't understand, but then you turned around and gave Jon so many chances. Philip told me about some of the things Jon said—and how you didn't call him out on it. How is that fair?"

I could hear Divya hum behind me. I shrunk a little down into my seat and dug my fingers into the upholstery under my thighs.

"I—" I paused. I didn't really even know what to say. He wasn't wrong. "I'm sorry," I repeated. "I was taking out my own shit on you and Finn. I'm glad you guys are okay."

"We're okay." He emphasized the *okay*. "We had a good conversation about it, like, the *next* day. And we'll keep having more of them. I'm still a little hurt, and I think we're both finding out this isn't a situation that can be magically fixed with a single conversation. But that's also *okay*. Finn gets that." I remembered seeing the two of them in that empty classroom and how quickly Finn moved to Neil's side. There was an affection layered over Neil's face now; maybe he was thinking of the same scene. "But for now," he continued, "Finn said he was sorry for invalidating what we were going through. What *I* was going through by not being heard by him. He wanted to understand at the end of the day and asked about it in the wrong way. Ironically enough, I didn't like feeling like I had to, I don't know, pretend like it didn't matter? Like someone making assumptions about you, and you being mad, and me being mad, that all of that wasn't fair. Or unreasonable. Or whatever!" He took in a deep breath. "I don't even know how we're supposed to talk about this."

"Philip and I called them *baby racisms*, which turn into, like, fifty-foot-tall babies banging around in your brain." I scrunched my nose, thinking. "Or at least that's how I pictured it. I'm not sure what Philip was thinking."

"There's that name again," Divya said from behind me, and I whipped around to frown at her. I didn't like her tone.

"Nope!" I yelped. "No, absolutely not." My cheeks were getting warm. I could feel them turning purple[60]. "Anyway, I'm *sorry*. I really am. I didn't *want* to lie to you guys."

"Can someone explain to me exactly what the lie was?"

"Oh, right," I said, turning around fully in my seat so my back rested against the steering wheel and my knees were up against my chest. "I, uh, decided to make Jon Slate realize I was cool enough to ask out on a date to prove that I could fix racism with true love. Or at least make this guy get that 'being Indian' is not a reason to reject someone." There was a snort and a loud, wet sound from the back seat. "Divya, tell me you did not spit coffee out *in my car*."

She ducked down and cried, "Sorry!"

I leaned over to see her where she'd hidden in the back, and she was wiping her mouth against the sleeve of her jean jacket. She pulled a rag that had been living in the one of the seat pockets and started dabbing at the seat beside her, pulling up the dark stain.

"So many apologies in this car today," Neil joked. "But okay, fine, I don't like Finn making me feel like I was wrong for being mad about the *baby racisms*, but I also don't like that you flippantly decided it was okay to cut Finn—who you've known and liked for*ever*—off, and then I find out that you're hanging out with Jon Slate, who started this whole annoying thing in the first place!"

"You're right." I twisted my hands together, nervous about the next part. But before I could start telling them about exactly what happened with Philip, Neil had one more question.

"Okay, so we're . . . accepting Jon's apology?" he asked.

"Oh, uh, he . . . he didn't exactly apologize. BUT!" I rushed forward before they could cut in and be as annoyed as Philip had been. "But he invited me to Will's party this weekend! Like, as a *date*."

---

[60] That's color theory, baby.

Divya's and Neil's jaws dropped simultaneously. It was pretty gratifying. This is what I'd been waiting for.

"What?!"

"Man, if you think that's wild, you're gonna freak out when I tell you that Philip Kim kissed me this weekend." I held in a breath and then heard that sound again. "DIVYA, STOP DRINKING THAT COFFEE WHILE I'M TALKING IF YOU CAN'T KEEP IT INSIDE YOUR MOUTH."

CHAPTER THIRTY-THREE

NEIL PATEL

I'm not saying I'm Team Philip, but I am saying I understand why he talked to me about you tbh

PAYAL MEHTA

Have I told you lately how I'm glad we're friends again? And also in WHAT universe was he right?

NEIL PATEL

He thought I could get through to you about how shitty it is that you don't feel comfortable being *yourself* around Jon.

PAYAL MEHTA

How so????

NEIL PATEL

Has he asked you any questions about your life? Like, does he actually know anything about *you* other than the things you happen to have in common?

PAYAL MEHTA

He will!!! I think.

NEIL PATEL

Will he though? And, again, not saying I'm Team Philip . . .

PAYAL MEHTA

KINDA SOUNDS LIKE YOU'RE TEAM PHILIP NEIL

NEIL PATEL

I'm just saying, I'm not Team Jon. 🙎

PAYAL MEHTA

Whatever, I'm going on this date

NEIL PATEL

Divya and I wouldn't miss it for the wooooorld.

PAYAL MEHTA

Ha ha ha.

NEIL PATEL

Now tell me more about kissing Philip Kim like . . . WAS IT GOOD?

PAYAL MEHTA

Oh, my mom's calling, gotta goooo

🏹💜→

Flustered, I slammed my computer closed and pushed it off my lap onto the bed. My mom was *not* calling me, but answering Neil's question was not a road I wanted to go down right now. Even with the awkward questions, I couldn't deny the happiness of my friends and me being back to normal! I'd dropped Neil and Divya off after an hour of catching up in my car in the parking lot the day before, and now here we were, discussing boys and chatting online. I was so glad to have them back . . . but still. I shot my computer a dirty look. How dare Neil not immediately be on my side with this whole thing?

He'd made me walk him through every one of my study dates with Jon, and he'd even admitted that Jon was pretty good at being charming. But he didn't seem to understand that I still had *time* to get Jon to accept me for who I was as a whole—I was doing this piecemeal. And Jon liked those pieces well enough, obviously.

As far as Philip was concerned—Neil kept saying he wasn't Team Philip—

I'm not!

I rolled my eyes at Phantom Neil.

Despite asserting that supposed fact, he kept asking me questions and poking at my feelings. I didn't like it. Next to me, an alert on my phone chimed. I glanced at the screen, and there was a notification that my math assignment had been accepted into the school system. Disappointed, and furious at being disappointed, I cleared out the notification with an aggressive swipe. I *hated* that every time my phone buzzed, my gut reaction was to expect a snarky text from Philip. We had gone from talking every day over the last month to complete radio silence.

That was your call.

I know!

I know.

But knowing and feeling were two different things. Knowing that this was my decision didn't mean I didn't miss him. It didn't mean I stopped expecting him to show up with a dry *Mehta*. Or that I'd reach for my phone to text him when something made me laugh, only to stop myself short. I could admit that much. Neil had walked me through what happened when Philip told him. Neil ghosting me had been more Neil's fault than Philip's, and there was a little pit of guilt inside of me that grew the more time I spent thinking about it.

"He got exactly three sentences out before I got mad and walked away and didn't give him the chance to explain," Neil had said. "I think it was like 'Mehta is trying to get Jon Slate to go out with her because she thinks it's the key to fixing him, or *her*, or something.' But I was still mad about what you said about Finn, and I never gave him the chance to explain further. To be honest, I really think he was trying to help you. He even tried calling me, but I wasn't having it." That confirmed that the day I'd overheard Neil in the halls he'd been talking to Philip.

I pushed up off the bed and walked downstairs to the kitchen. Food could distract me from thinking about this. I went for the cabinet with the snacks and pulled out some spicy channa along with a bag of Flamin' Hot Cheetos. Then I hightailed it back up to my room before my mom yelled at me for ruining my appetite before dinner.

I settled back on my bed and reopened my laptop, then navigated to Netflix to put on a show I'd already seen a hundred times so I could disassociate and eat enough Hot Cheetos to lose feeling in my tongue.

I popped one in my mouth, and the tangy, spicy flavor immediately had me sucking in air between my teeth. Inexplicably, I thought of Philip making fun of me for not wanting hot sauce on my fries when we went to the baseball game. *Ugh! Get out of my* head! Everything was so confusing! I liked being around Philip, and I liked when he kissed me. But . . . I also liked hanging out with Jon. And I hadn't even gotten to kiss him yet!

I pushed the food to the side of my bed and lay back, closing my eyes. Had it really only been a few months ago that I had been here for an entirely different Jon Slate–related reason?

"Payal?" A light knock sounded at my door. I shot up.

"Just a minute!" I cried. Panicked, I scrambled to shove the Cheetos and channa into my night table. "Come in!" I called out once they were safely tucked away. My mom's footsteps were light as she moved into the room.

"Payal, kya kar rahe ho? What is this smell?" She was looking around my room, frowning.

"Nothing," I replied, and then hoping to distract her from actually searching for the food, I added, "And I'm just thinking." I lay back against my headboard.

"About what?" she asked, taking a seat on the edge of my bed. Her loose track pants rose up a few inches, and I could see the tops of her faded house slippers in my peripheral vision.

"Stuff," I answered noncommittally. "Mom," I said, suddenly deciding to get some answers. "How come you guys don't get that I'm American, or if you do, it always feels like an insult?"

Her face took on an apologetic tone. "Bete, we know you're American."

"And Indian," I couldn't help but interject crankily.

"And Indian," she added, patting my leg in a soft rhythm. "But we are also learning, na? You're so different from us, and so much the same too." She said this quickly at the end, probably because my expression was morphing into a glower. "There are things we don't understand, and so we call them *American*. There are things we were never allowed to understand, and we call that *American*."

"But it *sucks*," I whined. I hated whining. But it was fair! It did

263

suck! "Sometimes you and Dad make me feel like I'm not allowed to be Indian, and the outside world is sitting there telling me I'm too brown to be American. And you do that too! *White* people are Americans to you, but I belong here too. There's nothing not American about *me*—what the heck?!"

She frowned, the corners of her mouth coming down and her chin dimpling. She looked at me thoughtfully.

"I didn't think about it that way, and you're right. It's not fair, and it does . . ." She hesitated. "It does . . . suck."

"Mom!" I'd *never* heard my mom say that before, and I was momentarily distracted from the fact that she'd agreed with me. "Wait, what?"

"Sahee keh rahi ho. It's true. We shouldn't say those things— but when we came here, a lot of people didn't think we could be American, and so we put that on you." She was still patting my leg in that rhythmic way that always made me sleepy. "I'll talk to your dad about it. We shouldn't say such things anymore. You're perfectly Indian and perfectly American, and you can be both. And don't let anyone tell you that you can't."

And it was like a light bulb went off in my head. My mom was *right*.

"Hey, Mom, is it okay if I go to a party on Friday?" I asked, partly because I was tired of lying to my parents and partly because she was likely feeling pretty guilty right now and would probably say yes[61].

"Will Divya and Neil be there?" she asked with a slight smile. Like she was looking for a way to say yes.

"Yep," I answered.

---

[61] Don't judge! This is how we survive!!!

"Then as long as you're home by . . ." She paused.

"Eleven?" I prompted, with some hope in my gut.

"Eleven," she agreed, giving me a soft pinch to my arm. "And not one minute later."

CHAPTER THIRTY-FOUR

It was *finally* the night of the party, and I was on my way to Jon's house. I was picking him up. As cool as my mom was being about letting me go to this thing, there was no way in hell I'd be able to go the party *with* Jon. At least not without my parents meeting his parents, and that was never going to happen.

Jon was waiting for me on the steps when I pulled up to the house. He started bounding down the stairs as soon as I rolled to a stop and parked. He yanked the door open and smiled wide, teeth white in the light from the streetlamps. His hair was falling forward, and his blue eyes were crinkling at the corners. He looked absurdly handsome in what was a simple outfit. Jeans and a plain black T-shirt, but the sleeves were *hugging* his biceps.

Payal! Relax!

"Hey, S. P.!" he said, gracefully falling into the passenger seat. Without asking, he paused my music and connected his. "You've *got* to hear this new song that John Thompson dropped two days ago."

"Hey," I said, nodding. "Sure."

A light guitar strummed a major chord through the speakers, and Jon hummed along to a tune I'd never heard before. I cringed a little at the music, wishing he'd put on something more interesting to hype us up for this party. I was *nervous*. Actually, I wished my music

266

were still playing. Something familiar to pull me back to reality.

"So," I said, trying to break through Jon's humming, "this is going to be interesting."

"Huh?" Jon replied, clearly distracted. "Oh! Oh. Right, no, what? It'll be fun! Don't worry, I already told everyone we're on our way."

I pretended to check the car to my right to hide the panic on my face. He did *what*? But I couldn't actually ask that. Instead, I gripped the steering wheel tighter and said, "Oh. Cool."

The signal ahead of us turned yellow and then red before we reached it. I slowed to a stop, staring resolutely ahead. I felt something tapping at my wrist, and then Jon fingers were gripping me, pulling one hand away from the wheel.

"S. P.," he said, and I looked at him. He had a soft smile warming his face, and he took my hand, fitting it against his. I hoped my palms weren't as sweaty as they felt. Oh god. "I think I've gotten to know you a bit, and I feel like you're probably stressed out about this for some reason." For some reason? *For some reason?* Did he really not know what the reason was? "But it's gonna be great. Everyone already likes you. They'll think you're hilarious."

If there was one thing I was not worried about, it was being funny. I was very confident in my ability to be funny. In my ability to present as someone who looked good, or even *normal*, next to Jon Slate? Questionable at best.

But I didn't know how to say that out loud; I didn't trust myself to be able to actually communicate it in a way Jon would understand.

I gave him a shaky grin. It was best I could do given the circumstances.

"And I promise you, your parents will never know a thing about where you are or what you're doing," he added in a joking tone that rankled. But then the light turned green, and I pulled my hand away to put it back on the wheel before pressing lightly on the accelerator. Jon went back to drumming against the dashboard along to his playlist, and I took a deep breath, trying to psych myself into getting ready to walk through Will's door.

When I turned the corner onto Will's street, it was quickly apparent which house was his. I think last year, Neil, Divya, and I must have gotten a ride with someone, because I couldn't remember trying to find parking in this mess. There were cars *everywhere*. I drove past the house, which looked deceptively quiet despite the four cars in the driveway and the several others spilling out behind those, and finally found a spot a few doors down.

I turned off the car, and Jon flung his door open with a whoop, stepping out onto someone's manicured lawn.

"Let's go!"

I was slower in my movement. I climbed out of the car and onto the street, slowly putting one foot in front of the other toward Will's long, one-story home. Through the huge windows of the Florida room built on one end of the house, I could see kids partying, their laughter and music carrying through the air. I stumbled a little on the dark concrete, and I cursed my shoe choice for the evening as I looked down at the offending pair.

Was I even dressed okay? Jon hadn't said anything about how I looked. Neil, disapproving as he was, still felt beholden to making sure I looked and felt great. At the end of a very long let's-go-through-Payal's-closet video chat session, he and Divya had both called out, "You look amazing," and "Good luck," and "We'll see you soon," before they'd sent me out the door with the new Stray Kids song playing loudly in the background. The dress we'd settled on was bright yellow and loose and short, hitting mid-thigh. The white chunky sneakers I'd paired it with felt cool an hour ago, but now I felt like an anime character with stick-thin legs and giant feet. I should have worn jeans and a T-shirt and flip-flops. *Argh.*

"You coming?" Jon said from a few feet ahead of me. He must have turned back to wait for me when I wasn't immediately next to him. I shot him a half smile and hoped it covered my nerves.

"Yeah, definitely, let's go," I said, speed-walking to find my place next to him. Jon interlaced his fingers with mine again, and I held in a flinch. I needed to get used to this! This was *fine*! I liked *the idea* of holding hands with Jon Slate a lot.

In practice, it was kind of different, I was finding out. He walked a little too fast for me and pulled me along, and then I had to shuffle quickly to keep pace. I nearly pulled my hand away before dismissing the thought and resolutely gripping his hand tighter. I needed to remember this was Jonathan Slate holding *my* hand. In the span of a few short months, *I* had gotten here. And it was because he liked me. Or most of me anyway. Some of me.

I shook my head, clearing out the thought. In my pocket, I felt my phone go off. It was probably Divya or Neil letting me know they were on their way. No way they'd get here *this* early. Finally, we'd reached the sidewalk. Jon squeezed my hand. His smile was loud.

"Ready?" he said, and I raised my eyebrows.

"As I'll ever be!" I said, lying. Together, we moved down the perfectly even sidewalk squares toward Will's front door. We passed some black-eyed Susans along the path, their bright yellow petals echoing the color of my dress in a way that brightened my spirits.

Jon opened the door for me when we got to it, not bothering with the doorbell or with knocking—it was not that kind of party. We walked in holding hands. I was ready to feel like the music stopped again, and like everyone was staring. But this time . . . no one batted an eye. People were caught up in their own moments. Mildly irritated at the lack of reception, I let Jon pull me through the throng of people.

I waved at Caitlin, who was standing near the wall, and her eyes went wide in response. I bit back a grin. That was more like it. I thought I saw a group of Philip's friends out of the corner of my eye, standing around one of Will's dad's sculptures. But we turned a corner, and I didn't get a chance to actually see who was in their crowd. I still strained my eyes for Philip's familiar bomber, unsure if I wanted him to be there or not.

Finally, we came up on a loud group of kids in the kitchen—Jon's group. A drop of sweat rolled down my back. I was immediately thrown. In our time together over the last few weeks, it had been me and Jon *on our own*. I never had to figure out how to be around him around *people*. Especially not like this—we were crowded into the small area near the stove, where the keg was situated. There were maybe ten people in there, and I was the only one who had any melanin whatsoever. I didn't even see Josh.

This was something I'd been through before, of course, being the only brown person in a room. You couldn't help but notice it when you were alone, and it always felt a little awkward or strange or uncomfortable.

"Hey, Payal!" A gigantic guy with a dark brown buzz cut said. I knew two things: His name was Corey and he'd never actually spoken to me directly before. I appreciated it, though, because Jon had let my hand loose and was heading toward the line at the keg.

"Hey, Corey," I answered with a practiced smile. Corey moved near me, and we stood leaning against the faux-marble counters, watching as the kids around us got rowdy.

"So how'd you get out the house?" he asked.

"Huh?"

"Jon said your parents are, like, super strict and they'd probably ship you out of here to India or something if they knew you were hanging out."

"*Huh?*"

I'd never said anything to like that *to Jon*. That was a joke with Philip because it was so ridiculous it would never be true. *What even?* "He—" I started, intending to tell Corey that no part of that was true and ask him when Jon had told him it was. But I was interrupted.

"Corey!" someone called to him. "It's your turn!" Corey gave me a snapping finger gun and said, "Later." And then walked away.

"Payal, here, I got you a soda!" Jon came back holding two cups in his hands. I took the cup from his hand, and I was reminded of what had started this whole thing. Our fingers grazed, and Jon bit his bottom lip and grinned before taking the space Corey had been occupying a few seconds earlier.

"Did you tell your friends that my parents were gonna send me to India if they found out about you?" I asked, refusing to get distracted.

He cocked an eyebrow and shot me a crooked grin. "Oh, I was messing with them. I know that's not true. I mean, you're, like, the most normal Indian kid I've ever met. But I know Josh has to lie to his parents *constantly*. I'm guessing yours think you're at Neil's or something?"

I took a step back, and something snapped inside me.

"Wha—I am—My mom knows I'm here, Jon!" And even if I did have to lie to them sometimes about where I was going, it didn't need to freakin' *define* me. Plenty of kids lied to their parents. It was—"People lied to their parents about going to parties in that movie we watched! Why is it an Indian thing?!" I said, not shouting but definitely *emphatic*. Jon put his cup on the counter and raised his hands palms outward in the universal gesture of *yo, relax, stop overreacting*.

"Whoa, where is this coming from? I was literally saying you're cool."

"No." I shook my head vehemently. "You said I was 'normal.' What does that even mean?"

A weird look came over his face. "Wait, did you not like the movie?" he asked, his brows furrowed in confusion.

"What? No, the movie was fine. I'm trying to point out that it is not *weird* if I have to pretend I'm going somewhere else so I don't get in trouble."

"But the dad is unhinged in that movie. Like, that's the point?"

"Oh my god. *OH MY GOD*," I exclaimed. How was this happening right now? This wasn't even a good conversation! He wasn't understanding anything! "I am trying to say that you keep making these weird comments implying things about me because I'm Indian, but you never bothered to ask me any questions or learn anything about it, it's—"

"What is happening right now?" he asked, echoing my own internal monologue. Narrowing his eyes, he frowned. He still looked hot as hell, only now he looked hot and upset.

"You texted my number to a bunch of random brown dudes," I sputtered, and that's when I realized that I was just throwing everything at him. Everything that had been festering in my stomach for weeks and weeks. Every time I'd stopped myself from speaking or ignored a comment. It was falling out of my mouth like, well, vomit.

"I—What? I didn't—How did you—I mean, I'm sorry about that?" he more asked than stated.

"You're sorry about *that*?!" I couldn't stop myself. I was so furious at him. And myself. And what was I doing here?

"Yes?" he asked. "S. P., should we, uh, take this somewhere else?" he said, reaching for my hand. Instead of taking his, I shoved mine into the pockets of my dress.

"No, no, I don't think so. I'm not—I don't know what I'm doing here. I *am* normal, Jon. And not because I can adapt to what you think is cool, or because I can 'hang' and turn off how brown I am, but because I exist. And, also, there's no such thing as normal! Everyone's weird. You're weird!" This was getting away from me. But Neil was right. Philip was right. *My mom was right.* "I have to go. This is . . ." I gestured between us. "This isn't working. I was tricking myself into thinking it was."

"What?" Jon asked again. I passed the drink in my hand back to him, and, dumbfounded, he took it from me. My stomach was doing jumping jacks. Jon should probably be thankful that I didn't *literally* throw up on him.

"I have to go!" I said again, already moving away from him. I pulled my phone out of my dress pocket, careful not to pull the entire bottom of the dress up, and there was a text from Neil.

NEIL PATEL

We'll be there in 10 min c u soonzzz

He'd sent it fifteen minutes ago, so he and Divya should be rolling up soon, but I had no idea where they could possibly be. I halted behind the couch in the living room and typed out a quick reply while Rachel and her friends shot a viral dance video on the side. I hoped I wasn't in it, but this was *urgent*.

PAYAL MEHTA

Where are you? I did something.

CHAPTER THIRTY-FIVE

YAARON SUN LO ZARA

NEIL PATEL

Ah, sorry we are not there yet! What happened, WHAT HAPPENED! Full disclosure: we haven't left Div's house

DIVYA BHATT

I have three letters 4 u

I

S

T [62]

PAYAL MEHTA

I freaked out on Jon and told him he was weird and that being brown was NOT weird also maybe confused the crap out of him bc idk if anything I said made sense to him n now I am at this party alone n he didn't even tell me I look cute what the helllll

---

[62] iykyk

275

DIVYA BHATT

U LOOK SO CUTE WHAT THE HELL

NEIL PATEL

Did you do this in front of everyone?!

PAYAL MEHTA

I mean for once I don't think anyone was paying attn but yes all of his friends were there except weirdly josh patel who was nowhere to be seen

DIVYA BHATT

O ya Josh is at his cousin Bhavik's house in Miami for the weekend for some sports thing

But also WHAT WHAT WHAT

NEIL PATEL

I AM SO PROUD

PAYAL MEHTA

I am freaking out freaking out what did I do!

NEIL PATEL

You told the truth!

👀 is Philip there?

PAYAL MEHTA

Omg idk idk!!! But I'm gonna see.

I gotta find him right?

I'm the worst.

NEIL PATEL

Not the worst, just distracted by distracting people. Man, I still can't believe it's Philip Kim

PAYAL MEHTA

Maybe, if he doesn't hate me by now

DIVYA BHATT

He doesn't hate u!! No one could hate u!

PAYAL MEHTA

I mean neil hated me for like five minutes

NEIL PATEL

Thats gonna get real old real fast

Go find PK

Omg omg omg chaar kadam[63] much, he's probably two seconds away

PAYAL MEHTA

Hey Philip are u at this thing

Read

I'm rly sorry

Read

I uh need to talk to u

Read

Payal Mehta REALLY Doesn't Know What She's Doing [Google Doc]

Read

---

[63] I can't believe I never put together Philip Kim and the movie *PK* until Neil just said that oh myyy god!

277

Payal Mehta REALLY Doesn't Know What She's Doing

- Needs to talk to someone who gets her
- ASAP
- Hopefully at this party
- Will hang for one (1) samosa?
- Is definitely not feeling weird about spending so much time typing into her phone while everyone at this party is debauching

CHAPTER THIRTY-SIX

I spent twenty more minutes walking around the party trying to see if Philip was there. I spied his friends again, playing some kind of drinking card game at a table in the basement, but no sign of Philip. I did two full rounds of the house and saw things I would *never* unsee. Did you know what color boxers Jeremy Owens had on? Because now I could say that *I did*. Unfortunately.

Finally, I had to admit it to myself: Philip wasn't at this party, and if he was, he clearly didn't want to talk to me. I dropped into an empty chair next to Caitlin, who was standing against a wall near the back door.

"Hey," she said, looking down at me, her brown hair curtaining her face. "Did I see you and Jon walk in here together *holding hands*?" She waggled her eyebrows at the end of her question.

I put my head in my hands. "No, definitely not. I came by myself because that is what smart Payal would have done and so that is what I did."

Caitlin raised one eyebrow and looked at me like I was speaking gibberish. Which, okay, fair.

"Uh . . . huh," she said, and turned back to her phone. But then, without looking up, she added, "You can tell me at school if you don't want to come clean here. We'll pause on calc studying."

I bumped her hip with my shoulder and found enough calm inside of me to smile. "Thanks, Cait."

Against my thigh, I felt my phone go off. I took it out to see what Divya and Neil had added to our thread. I'd already crossed the fingers on my other hand in hopes that it was an actual arrival time. Ahead of me, Janet Kwon was holding a joint and grinning. She had actually not dropped it in her beer this time!

"AY! JANET!" I shouted my encouragement at her before looking back down to see if my friends were on their way.

Then I dropped my phone on the ground and yelped.

"Oh my god, what?!" Caitlin said. I'd clearly scared her. She leaned down to grab my phone for me and looked at the screen. "Why did you make that sound, Payal? It's only a Google Doc notification. God, you scared the crap out of me, and now I have orange soda on my jeans." She straightened up, handing my phone back to me at the same time.

"So sorry," I stammered. There, on my screen, covering my friends' faces, was a notification for an email from Google telling me that the *Payal Mehta REALLY Doesn't Know What She's Doing* document had been edited by Philip.Kim@brighths.edu. I tapped at the screen and clicked the link.

Payal Mehta REALLY Doesn't Know What She's Doing
AND THAT'S OKAY

- Needs to talk to someone who gets her
  - Someone's waiting outside

- ASAP
  - **Srsly, Mehta, right outside**
- Hopefully at this party
  - **I'm telling you outside**
- Will hang for one (1) samosa?
  - **Let's be real, we'll need at least two**
- Is definitely not feeling weird about spending so much time typing into her phone while everyone is debauching
    - **first: gross and b: It's ok I probably should've texted but this felt more . . . what word would you use? cute.**

I jumped out of the chair as soon as I'd read the words Philip had added. He was *outside*. I hurried through Will's house, ducking through the crowd, and counted two near misses of entire drinks being dropped down my dress, but I made it to the entry hallway, a few feet back from the door. But then I stopped short. My whole body was vibrating with anticipation.

Was I ready for this? I wasn't even sure what "this" was. For some reason, I'd spent the last several weeks trying to convince myself that what would make me feel bigger again, like a human again, was validation from the person who'd made me feel small. And I'd ignored the people who loved me. Who in their own ways were trying to make me remember how great *I* was. And I'd ignored the unexpected way I'd felt around someone I'd never even seen before. Not *really*.

I opened my phone and typed a message out to my friends with shaking fingers.

PAYAL MEHTA

Philip's here. Gonna go talk 2 him.

NEIL PATEL

WE R 2 MIN AWAY HAD TO PICK UP
FINN BUT YOU GOT THIS WHATEVER
YOU WANT TO HAPPEN WILL HAPPEN

Div is parking but says quote Ahhhh text
us IMMEDIATELY AFTER PLZ & THX 🤏

I took a deep breath and a step forward.

"MOVE, I HAVE TO FIND THE BATHROOM!" And then some dick, with a hand covering his mouth, shoved me out of the way. I have never moved so fast in my life. My giant sneakers scuffed Will's floor in my attempt to get out of the line of fire that I *knew* was coming. *Not this time!* I didn't even wait to see it happen. I hopped to the right, sprinted forward, and flung myself out of the front door, letting it slam closed behind me.

Safe on the porch, I leaned down with my hands on my knees and tried to get my heart rate down. That was a lot of excitement, and I needed to be calm. After the energy of the party, it was jarringly quiet and still outside. I glanced to the side and saw that the Florida room was dark and empty.

"I can do this. I can do this. I can totally do this."

I was talking to myself. Cool, cool, cool. Totally normal, Payal. Not weird.

Looking around, I didn't see *anyone*, let alone Philip Kim. The same cars were in the driveway, and there were some low streetlamps giving spots of yellow light off in dots along the road.

But there was no movement, no silhouettes of lanky Korean American boys loping toward me.

"Where is he?" I brushed at the bottom of my dress to straighten the fabric and then tried to see between the dark of the cars parked on the street. "Well, this is pretty anticlimactic."

Suddenly, a voice cut in through the dark in front of me.

"I've been watching you stand there for five minutes. Are you going to stop talking to yourself and get over here?"

"AH!" I let out a short screech before I peered into the lawn. "Philip, what the hell? Where are you even creeping around? I can't see you, you weirdo!"

Then he was there, stepping into the light from the porch. My eyes adjusted, and I could see he'd been standing on the other side of the same Nissan I'd seen in front of my house two weeks ago. He had on that jacket again, even though it was warm out, and I liked it. It was familiar. The pins glinted, and he looked sparkly. He was grinning at me, wide and honest, showing a full row of teeth. His sideswept bangs had gotten longer, nearly down to his eyes. He looked so good.

"The reflections in your pins make you look like you're in a Stray Kids music video."

"Is that a baby racism, you giant samosa?"

I stepped down to meet him on the sidewalk. We were facing each other, maybe an arm's length of distance between us. Philip's eyes were shining, and now that I was closer, I could that his hands were shaking slightly. I bit my bottom lip to keep from smiling.

"No, it was the last hype-as-hell video I saw. The Korean connection is happenstance. Unlike *giant samosa,* which is deliberate."

He laughed softly. But then he immediately frowned.

"So, what . . . What happened with, uh . . ." He jutted his chin toward the door. "The big date?"

I sighed and tucked a piece of hair behind my ear, turning back to look at the house, scowling.

"He kept calling me *normal*." I looked back toward Philip.

"*Normal* is an insidious word," he scoffed. I threw my hands up and out in agreement.

"Right! And apparently he joked about how intense my family is with his friends even though he's never met them. So I had a little bit of a meltdown and called him weird and then I ran away."

Philip let out a loud bark of laughter, throwing his head back with the force of it and letting it out into the night air.

"Oh man, I *really* wish I'd seen that. The look on his face when this mostly perfect girl freaks out on him. I would have paid actual money."

I leaned forward and gave Philip an appraising look.

"Did you say, 'perfect girl'?" I teased. But Philip's face went serious, and he bowed his head, the shadows obscuring his expression.

"I . . ." He stopped. "I'm really sorry, Payal. Seriously. I shouldn't have—"

"Wait, no. No," I interrupted, ducking down and trying to see his face. "It's—I talked to Neil. You were trying to—"

"You deserve so much better than him, even if it's not me!" Philip burst out, eyes snapping back up to hold mine.

"You're right!"

"I know!"

"Okay! Why are we yelling?!" I yelled.

"I don't know!" Philip yelled back, but he was laughing too. And so was I. How had I missed seeing what this was? How much fun I had with him?

"So I do deserve someone better?" I finally asked, more quietly.

"Yeah," he said. "You do."

"Even if it's not you?" I said his words back to him. He shrugged, and I was close enough to hear the tiny scraping of his pins hitting each other with his movement.

"Yeah, though that would be embarrassing and I guess a fitting bump in our weird-ass friendship."

"Okay, but what if . . . " I said, unnecessary anxiety creeping into my belly and my voice shaky. "What if it is you?" I already knew he liked me. Why was I so scared of saying something?

Philip's dark eyes opened wide, and his mouth dropped open. I had to stop myself from mirroring him. I'd struck Philip Kim *speechless*. Again. I stepped forward and put a finger against his chin, pressing upward to close his mouth, and then I moved my hand to his cheek. His skin was soft.

"Philip, you're going to have say something or this is going to be very weird, very soon," I joked weakly. But he didn't say anything at all. Instead, he leaned down and met me halfway, pressing his lips against mine. After a few minutes, he pulled back the tiniest bit. I should have felt awkward, someone's face so near mine and our eyes staring right into each other's. But I didn't. I moved my arms around his neck, and his hands were circling my waist.

"I think we both win this one, Mehta," he said softly.

"No one threw up on anyone or anything," I whispered back.

Philip closed his eyes and groaned. "I guess I should prepare for a long relationship of you cutting our tension with terrible jokes?"

I reached up and kissed him again. "And I'll get used to your fake holier-than-thou attitude because I know it means you really, really, really like me. And you think I'm perfect."

Philip tightened his arms around me so he was hugging me. "Listen, you're mostly perfect, but I'll take every piece of you, Mehta," he whispered into my ear.

"AY BALLE BALLE!!!" Neil's loud voice broke into our tiny bubble, and I was pleasantly surprised to find Philip's arms tightening around me instead of dropping to his sides.

"Hey, Patel," he called out. I pressed my forehead into Philip's shoulder before pulling away with a smile tugging at my lips. My friends were coming up the sidewalk, Divya with her big and welcoming grin like she was about to invite Philip to her house for dinner, and Finn with one arm around Neil's waist, the other reaching out to wave our way. Neil, for his part, was singing at the top of his lungs,

"Jee lo jaise mast kalandar! Yaaron sun lo zara haan apna yeh kehna." He pulled away from Finn and grabbed my hands with his.

"Jeena ho toh apan ke, jaise hi jeena!"

"Jee lo jaise mast kalandar," I sang along off-key, jumping into a move with Neil while Finn, Divya, and Philip looked on in amusement.

"So, is there a group chat or something I can join to get in on these sing-alongs, or . . ." I heard him ask Divya.

"You're gonna regret that," I called to him, mid-twirl.

"Nah, I can hack it," he called back. "Every piece means *every piece*, Mehta."

One Month Later

BUT THEY'RE YOUR BEST FRIENDS YAAR

PHILIP KIM

http:///www.brightonhs.edu/PKIM19/
dskna;sdf.jpg

NEIL PATEL

if u send one more picture of your psych
project results i am kicking u out of this
thread pk

FINN JACOBS

PAYAL MEHTA

SEND 1000 MORE, PHILIP, I WILL LIKE
EVERY SINGLE ONE OF THEM even if it
was the most boring and basic experiment
that could have possibly been conceived

PHILIP KIM

did we or did we not get 💯

DIVYA BHATT

Vikash said to tell you this is why he left the group chat last week

NEIL PATEL

if i can't send finn romantic song lyrics in the group chat you guys are def not allowed to nerd flirt in here

PHILIP KIM 😒💜

did u watch the movie?

PAYAL MEHTA

yeah dude, watched it with my parents last night. my dad loooooooooooooved it u were right

WAIT DO NOT TAKE A SCREENSHOT OF ME SAYING U WERE RIGHT I S2G

if i get a notification that you tagged me in something on hotgoss i'm gna ruin ur life

PHILIP KIM 😒💜

couldn't ruin it if you tried, Mehta

PAYAL MEHTA

why? bc you like me??????????? 😂😂😂😂 😂😂😂😂😂😂😂😂😂😂😂😂😂😂😂

PHILIP KIM 😒💜

obvio

ACKNOWLEDGMENTS

In 2019, I quit my full-time position to write a funny book about love and identity and racism and diaspora. To write *this* book. Technically, I'd already been writing it for a few years by the time I quit, but I didn't know how I'd finish it if I didn't make a serious life change. So I quit my job, and now, five years later, this book is out in the world thanks to the support of a *lot* of people. I have to first thank my agent, Michael Bourret, who (sort of) instigated this publishing journey by listening to me awkwardly pitch what I told him was a romantic comedy told through the lens of microaggressions and then immediately saying, "Send this to me as soon as it's ready." I couldn't have done it without his belief in Payal and her story.

To the team at Kokila, Sydnee Monday, Asiya Ahmed, and Jenny Ly, I love that all of you touched this novel and had a hand in getting it out into the world. To Rakesh Satyal for your thoughtful notes and kind words. To Hanifa Abdul Hameen for that beautiful illustration of Payal, so unapologetically Indian in her look and feel and dress. To Kelley Brady for the cover's thoughtful design and for working to bring culture and specificity to it. My marketing and publicity team, Christine Colangelo and Felicity Vallence (and Trevor, but more to you later, ha!), without whom no one would know this book exists! And to my editors, Nami and Zareen, the comfort and privilege it's been getting to work with people who already speak the language, who understand without explanations, who don't require a code switch . . . there are, hilariously, no words for what that did for me and my confidence in telling this story. It was everything.

My incredible friends who read and read and read and talked to me endlessly about how to write about anxiety! And romance! But also racism! I love you all. Jenn, for reading and cheerleading more than anyone I know. Celia, for squeeing and comforting and answering panicked texts. To Eric and Swapna for Petty Group Chat, and for validating and lifting me up on days when all I could do was lie on the ground and wonder if I could even write another word. Trevor Ingerson! My publishing BFF, who has all-caps all-exclammed about this book since the day I told you about it. To Ann Marie, I'm sorry I had to quit for this book, and I miss coming to work and getting to hang out with you all day! But I wouldn't be here without you and the life *and* professional advice you gave me. To Zack and Rafi, my fellow a*fiction*ados, for days of going over the same summary seventeen times before I even had the beginnings of a query letter. To Mark Oshiro and Julian Winters for welcoming me into the Atlanta writers' club and being around for writing dates and Costco runs and always answering "Is this funny or . . . not good?"

I wrote this book not just for me, but for all the South Asian women in the diaspora who will see parts of themselves in Payal—in the ways we changed ourselves or cut pieces away to be more palatable in a world that was going to try and spit us out anyway. And I wrote it under the eyes and words of my fellow SA writers who *have* been writing our stories: Sona Charaipotra, Nisha Sharma, Samira Ahmed, Roshani Chokshi, Sayantani DasGupta . . . the list goes on and on, and it makes my heart full to see how many of us there are, and how many of us there will continue to be. To Sona and Nisha especially, for always being around to answer questions and give me guidance, and for sending that elevator back down from where you are.

My family—my mother for being strong and smart and teaching me to *think*. And (though she had a brief moment of regretting it) for making me read books as a kid. I'm not sorry I never went to med school, but that's all on you. And I'm so glad it never happened. Papa for giving me the space to write when I left New York. My brother and sister, Vinny and Heeral. Oh, my incredible and talented Chhibblings—knowing I can talk to you as fellow creatives, that you will understand and respect the work that goes into Making Things, means so much to me. Thank you for always being around to talk and for the help you give me, whether it's Heeral designing stickers and websites and promotional images, or Vinny talking through plot points or plans on *how* to get people to read it, or just both of you getting the word about my book out to everyone you know . . . I see and appreciate every single thing. I can't believe I got to grow up with you in a family of artists who value creativity.

Lastly, to the kid who spent two hours talking to me at a party in 2003 only to end the night by offering me up to his Indian friend, whom he had not mentioned and who was not at the party . . . thanks for filling me with enough spite to write a book. I'll never forget you. #AriesEnergy.